What people are saying about

In the Shadow of Lions

"Ginger Garrett has brilliantly blended fact and fiction, faith, and fallacy to create a saga so real that I hung on every word. I will never again open my Bible without gratitude for the women of faith who dared to defy the deceived that God's Word might be read by all. *In the Shadow of Lions* is truly a masterpiece!"

Kathy Herman, author of the Phantom
Hollow series and Sophie Trace Trilogy

"Garrett unveils history's secrets to tell you the tale you've never heard about the greatest story ever told. Exceptional in every way, with characters that will haunt your dreams long after you've turned the last page. Don't miss it!"

Siri Mitchell, author of *A Constant Heart*

"Angels, demons, life and death, a religion gone mad, love, murder, the power of a crazed king, and three women's lives, two in the past and one in the present, all consumed by one mighty book that set the world aflame, sparking the Reformation. This is one of those stories that will keep you captivated to the very last page and one you'll be thinking about long after you're done reading it."

M. L. Tyndall, author of the award-winning
Legacy of the King's Pirates series

"Far more than just a beautiful cover, *In the Shadow of Lions* drew me into the life of Anne Boleyn and presented a side to this tragic historical figure I had never considered. Elegantly, and with no small amount of intrigue, Ginger Garrett posits that history may have cast Anne into an undeserved light, which reminds the reader that it is not for us to judge others and their motivations. Enthusiastically recommended!"

Tamara Leigh, best-selling author of *Splitting Harriet* and *Faking Grace*

"An imaginative and evocative tale of Anne Boleyn's battle for a king's heart and her soul's salvation, *In the Shadow of Lions* etches the eternal struggle between church and state in swift, vivid prose."

India Edghill, author of *Queenmaker* and *Wisdom's Daughter*

"In this beautifully written novel, Ginger Garrett honors the strength and insight of two English women willing to die for their faith. *In the Shadow of Lions* takes readers on a remarkable journey back to the sixteenth century and shows the incredible power of a book shared in secret by women across London."

Melanie Dobson, author of *The Black Cloister* and *Going for Broke*

IN THE SHADOW OF LIONS

GINGER GARRETT

David C Cook®

transforming lives together

IN THE SHADOW OF LIONS
Published by David C. Cook
4050 Lee Vance View
Colorado Springs, CO 80918 U.S.A.

David C. Cook Distribution Canada
55 Woodslee Avenue, Paris, Ontario, Canada N3L 3E5

David C. Cook U.K., Kingsway Communications
Eastbourne, East Sussex BN23 6NT, England

David C. Cook and the graphic circle C logo
are registered trademarks of Cook Communications Ministries.

This story is a work of fiction. All characters and events are the product of the author's
imagination, although some are based on real-life events and people.

With the exception of Job 42 and Job 31, Scripture quotations are taken from
Tyndale's New Testament, translated by William Tyndale, a modern-spelling
edition of the 1534 translation by David Daniell © 1989, Yale University.

Job 42 Scripture quotation is taken from *THE MESSAGE*. Copyright
© Eugene H. Peterson 1993, 1994, 1995, 1996, 2000, 2001,
2002. Used by permission of NavPress Publishing Group.

Job 31 Scripture quotation is taken from King James
Version of the Bible. (Public domain.)

LCCN 2008928480
Mass Market ISBN 978-1-4347-6444-7

Ginger Garrett is represented by MacGregor Literary.
Visit Ginger at her Web site: www.GingerGarrett.com
Author photo © Don Sparks Photography

The Team: Andrea Christian, Ramona Tucker, Amy Kiechlin,
Sarah Schultz, Jaci Schneider, and Karen Athen
Cover Design: John Hamilton Design
Cover Photo: © HarperPoint
Interior Design: The Visual Republic, Alexis Goodman

Printed in the United States of America
First Edition 2008

1 2 3 4 5 6 7 8 9 10

052008

For my dad

And Job answered God …
"I admit I once lived by rumors of you;
now I have it all firsthand …
I'll never again live
on crusts of hearsay, crumbs of rumor."
Job 42 MSG

ACKNOWLEDGMENTS

For the Scribe: When we meet someday, and you finish your book on my life, please be gentle. I tried to make you quite dashing. If you want to do the same for me, that would be appreciated.

For my friends at Cook, including Andrea Christian, Terry Behimer, Dan Rich, Don Pape, Jaci Schneider, Ingrid Beck, and Melanie Larson: Thank you for believing in me. Working with you is such an honor and I look forward to many years together. And for John and Nannette Hamilton, who designed the cover, thank you for your incredible artistry!

Chip MacGregor, my fearless literary agent: Thank you a million times over for your wise advice and reality checks. I've seen incredible growth in my career since you began to shape my decisions. I am really thankful God connected us ... and I hope Patti likes this one!

Don Maass, Lisa Rector-Maass, and the team at Free Expressions: Lorin, Jason, and Brenda. I am forever indebted to each of you. Thank you for your passion for words and your willingness to walk authors through lonely passages. If any author is looking for a way to invest in their gifts, I would highly recommend a workshop offered through Free Expressions, as well as any of Don Maass's books.

My editor, Ramona Tucker, gently held my hand and helped me see the weaknesses in the manuscript. Working with you, Ramona, was a gift!

My friends, both in the writing community and in my everyday life: Thanks for always asking about the book, even if you couldn't remember which one I was working on. (I rarely could either.) For Siri, who makes trade shows memorable and shares my oddball sense of humor, thanks for praying me through another one and sharing your research. For the "Cat Pack" of women in publishing that meets for girls' night out once a year, and keeps my secrets. For Courtney, Riki, Stephanie, Alecia, Dani, Niki, Kris, Louise, Carolynn, Tina, DeDe, Karetha, Allison, Amy, Shannon, Tinsley, Laura, Sherrill, Jennifer and Judy: One of my life goals is to love my friends well. You make it easy.

Finally, my husband and family sacrificed more for this book than for any other. Whether I needed to travel to London to walk through the events in the novel or go away for a long week to write, they supported me, keeping the family running smoothly. Mitch, your quiet strength gave me courage. My parents did without sleep to watch the kids and made endless stacks of Saturday-morning pancakes. My in-laws, Andi and Chris, made their house available for ransacking too. My daughters drew me pictures and insisted that I take breaks to snuggle on the couch. They have an uncanny sense of when my writing day should end, which often corresponds to their hunger level. My son, the coolest defensive tackle football has ever known, is always fighting to knock players on their rears. He told me to work hard so I could knock readers on their rears too. I tried, baby.

Chapter One

Tomorrow, someone else will die in my bed.

Someone died in it last month, which is how it came to be called mine.

The infernal clock moved confidently toward 1 a.m., and I turned my head to look at the window. The window of this room is a miserly gesture from the contractors, producing more fog than visage. I watched the gold orbs—the lamps on the lawn of the hospice sputtering off and on in the darkness—that dotted the fogged glass.

That was the last moment I lived as an *iver*, one whose eyes are veiled.

One orb did not sputter but moved, gliding between the others, moving closer to the window, growing larger and brighter until the light consumed the entire view. I winced from the searing glare and tried to shield my eyes, but the IV line pulled taut. Wrestling with the line to get some slack, I saw the next movement out of the

corner of my eye. I bit down hard on my tongue, my
body jerking in reflex, and felt the warm blood run back
to my throat.

Outside, a hand wiped the fog away from the glass,
and I watched the water beads running down the inside
of my window. There was no searing light, only this
mammoth hand with deep creases in the palms wiping
down the window until we both could see each other.
A man's face was against the glass, but no breath fogged
his vision. He was a giant, grim man, with a ring in
one ear and dark glasses, and he was staring in at me.
Even through the morphine, fear snaked along my arms,
biting into my stomach, constricting around my throat.
I tried to scream, but I could only gulp air and heave
little gasps. His expression did not change as he lifted
his hands, curling them into fists. I flinched at the last
moment, thinking him to be Death, expecting to receive
the blow and die.

Then I grew suddenly warm, like the feeling you
get stepping from an old, dark city library into the busy
street and a warm spring sun.

Death didn't even hurt, I rejoiced. I could slip into it
like I slipped onto that street, eyes down, my thoughts
my own, and simply turn a corner and be gone. I lifted
my fingers to beckon him. *Yes,* I thought. I saw the
beautiful Rolex on my birdlike wrist and saw that it had
stopped. *It is time.*

When I looked back up, he was beside me, staring
down, not speaking. I wasn't dead. His frame was mon-
strously large, hitting what must be seven feet tall, with a
width of muscle strapped across him that was inhuman.
As he watched me, his chest didn't move, and his nostrils

didn't flare, but heat and warm breath radiated from him. When he laid his hands across my eyes, I was too scared to move my head away. His palms covered most of my face, and a sharp buzzing drilled into every pore. He began to move his hands elsewhere, touching and bringing to life every splintered inch of my body. When he got to the cancer, with one swollen lymph node visible even through my stained blue gown, he rested his hands there until the swelling sighed, and he swept it away with his hand.

"Wait!" I screamed.

I didn't want to live. I hadn't known that was going to be an option. I deserved to be damned. To return to my life was too much to ask of me. I was finished.

"You'll still be dead by morning," he reassured me. His voice was deep and clean, no telltale dialect or inflection. Taking off his glasses, I saw he had enormous gold eyes, with a black pinhole in the center that stayed round and cold. There was no white in them at all, and they were rimmed all the way around the outside with black. I stared at them, trying to remember where I had seen eyes like this. It had been years ago, this much I remembered.

I had to shake myself back to the present moment. Clearly, morphine was not setting well with me tonight. I wanted to die in peace. That's what I paid these extravagant sums for. My hand moved to the nurses' call button. Mariskka was just down the hall, waiting for her moment to steal my watch. I knew she'd come running.

He grabbed my hand, and the shock seared like a hot iron. Crying out, I shook him off and clutched my hand between my breasts, doing my best to sit up with my atrophied stomach muscles and tangled IV.

He leaned in. "I have something for you."

"What?"

He leaned in closer. "A second chance."

Second chances were not my forte. As the most celebrated editor in New York City, I had made a killing. I loved the words that trembling writers slid across my desk, those little black flecks that could destroy their life's dream or launch a career. I bled red ink over every page, slashing words, cutting lines. No one understood how beautiful words were to me, why I tormented the best writers, always pushing them to bring me more. The crueler I was to the best of them, the more they loved me, like flagellants worshipping me as the master of their order. Only at the end, lying here facing my own death, did I understand why. They embraced the pain, thinking it birthed something greater than themselves. I saw how pitifully wrong they were. There was only pain. This is why I was ready to die. When you finish the last chapter and close the book, there is nothing but pain. It would have been better never to have written. Words betrayed me. And for that, I betrayed the best writer of them all.

"Burn any manuscripts that arrive for me," I had ordered my nurse, Marisska. "Tell them I'm already dead. Tell them anything."

"I'll let you write the truth," the man whispered. I focused on him again.

"I'm not a writer," I replied. My fear tumbled down into the dark place of my secrets.

"No, you're not," he answered. "But you coveted

those best sellers, didn't you? You knew you could do better. This is your second chance."

It caught my attention. "How?"

"I will dictate my story to you," he said. "Then you'll die."

Taking dictation? My mouth fell open. "I'm in hell, aren't I?"

He tilted his head. "Not yet."

I pushed away from the pillows and grabbed him. Blisters sprang up on my palms and in between my fingers, but I gritted my teeth and spat out my words. "Who are you?"

"The first writer, the Scribe. My books lie open before the Throne and someday will be the only witness of your people and their time in this world. The stories are forgotten here, and the Day draws close. I will tell you one of my stories. You will record it."

"Why me?"

"I like your work."

I started laughing, the first time I had laughed since I had been brought to this wing of the hospice, where the dying are readied for death, their papers ordered and discreet pamphlets on "end-of-life options" left by quiet-soled salesmen. I laughed until I was winded. He rested his hand on my chest, and I caught my breath as he spoke.

"Let's go find Marisska."

Chapter Two

I grabbed the IV pole and stood, careful to conceal that awful opening in the back of my gown. I expected to find my leg muscles as sturdy as pudding, but his life had found its way into them, too.

He saw my undignified writhing to get the gown's gaps in order but made no move to assist. "A desk job hasn't been kind to you, has it?"

I followed him down the hall, glaring at his back, the size of a billboard, and shaking my wrist. The Rolex still stayed frozen at a few minutes before 1 a.m.

A nurse pushing a half-awake Crazy Betty wheeled past us. I flattened myself to the wall, bracing for the screams when the two women saw this man.

The nurse didn't see us.

Crazy Betty did. She began yelling at him, shaking her fingers in fury. "Go back where you belong and leave us alone! Always sneaking around, in and out of rooms whenever you like, always scribbling in your little book!"

I froze.

The Scribe kept walking, pressing a finger to his lips to urge her to be quiet.

The nurse rolled her eyes and shushed Betty. "We'll get you some tea and get you back in bed," she comforted her.

Betty was hearing none of it. As she was wheeled away, she turned and screamed at him, "What are you writing, anyway?"

The Scribe kept walking.

"What was all that?" I asked.

He shrugged and kept walking. "Not everyone is happy to see us."

"She could see you? She's not crazy?"

"She's crazy. But she can see us."

He arrived at the nurses' station.

Mariskka was there, her tone sharp as she argued with someone on the phone. "I said no. It's against our policy here, David. I refuse to give her hope when we both know she's going to die."

Mariskka didn't miss anything, especially when wealthy patients were nearing death but still lucid enough to update their wills. When she finally whirled around in her chair, she would faint from shock to see me up and walking, never mind with a Jolly Black Giant.

He leaned down behind Marisska. I covered my mouth with my hands and held my breath.

Resting his hands on her shoulders, he whispered into her ear, "You need chocolate. Right now. There's some in the kitchen."

"If you show up here, I'll call the cops," Mariskka spat as she slammed down the phone. "I think there's some chocolate calling me." She kicked back her chair and stomped off, in the direction of the kitchen.

"What are you doing?" I hissed at him, watching him remove her Mac and tuck it under his beefy arm. It was barely visibly in between folds of bicep and elbow.

"Borrowing her laptop. You need it."

There were so many reasons this night was all wrong. I could only come up with one to say. "That's a Mac. I don't use Macs."

"Macs don't need as many miracles," he said. "I'm an angel, not a genie."

I stood there, my mouth opening and closing again, trying to say something cruel or anything at all. The jolly freakish giant took off, with strides that out-reached mine three to one, heading back to my room.

I should have been out of breath by the time we reached my room, but I was feeling stronger. I was stronger when he was near. When he exhaled it entered my body as a second wind. I edged closer and inhaled as we crossed through the threshold to my room. He turned and smiled, the first smile I had seen. I had almost rather he not do it again. His face was so big that even a smile made me edgy. I'd prefer for a man of this size to have as few emotions as possible.

He went to work plugging the Mac in, moving my bed to find the closest outlet. When it was plugged in, he set it on the edge of the bed and turned to me. My body went bloodless, like fish diving to the deepest refuge, all of my extremities going pale and limp, abandoned. He walked toward me, and my mouth stayed open, with not even the strength to close it. He reached out and took my arm. His warming touch did not hurt, though if I had tried to resist him he could have snapped my arm like a twig. He ran his finger down my arm, resting it on the IV line. Closing his eyes, he opened his hand and gently wiped my arm. The IV line fell to the floor, my arm whole and without a mark.

"It will be easier to work without that," he said.

Blood began to flow back into my arms and legs, and I made my way to the bed as he propped up a few pillows for me. I climbed in, and he handed me the laptop. I began to type, just to feel the keys under my fingertips. It was like coming home.

I'm dying in the middle of the wildest dream! I typed.

He crossed his arms. I could see his jaw shift and set.

Another voice growled. "You wanted the heir."

"She's difficult," the Scribe replied. He didn't turn his head to any direction, and I couldn't tell where the voice came from. "Writing her story for years was easier than living with her for a few minutes."

"She is the heir," the voice replied.

"I'm the heir of what?" I asked. There was a sound like wind, but nothing moved in the room. The Scribe shook his head and looked for a place to sit. The steel-armed chair wasn't large enough. He ran his hands along its frame and it groaned, stretching in all directions until he could comfortably sit. He opened his palms and a book appeared in them, a book bound in black frayed leather, with gold dust along the edges and thick iron locks keeping the pages sealed tight.

"The Tablets of Destiny," he said. "It was last seen in the days of ancient Mesopotamia. It is referenced in the Bible, though never by its name."

My fingers were raised above the keypad but didn't move.

"Names have power," he said. "The past has power. The two meet in this book. No one among you will be allowed to know its full contents until the Day."

My fingers were still immobile.

"Two thousand years ago, on an island infested with fleas and thieves and the condemned," he said, "a dying man was allowed to see the invisible world. He recorded this vision in the book that came to be called The Revelation. He saw that every church has an angel, every nation has an angel, and every child has an angel."

My fingers had begun to move.

"But there was one class of angels he could not see. There are archangels, the strangest and fiercest of us who remain always near the women. Every bloodline of women has been followed by the same archangel since the beginning of the line. The angel of your line has watched you grow from a child into a woman, and he knows your past far beyond what is told to you by your mother and aunts. He knows who your women were, and who you can become."

He stroked the book lovingly and its hinges sprang open, the pages fluttering and turning, settling at last on a dark page. It looked brown from age or heat, its edges crumbling and flaking onto his leg. The ink was faded, almost to the color of the page, and I couldn't make out the words or language, though it was ornately drawn.

He sighed and touched the page. "These words die. They have not been spoken for so long."

"Long ago, in the kingdom you call England, under the reign of King Henry VIII, there lived two women. One loved God, one hated Him, and neither knew Him. Both women, however, heard tell of a book, a dangerous book. When it touched the world around them, it burned all to the ground. When it touched the women, it consumed everything they had built their lives around, until all that is left of them today is rumor and innuendo. For this reason you are brought to this story, for the women of your past have seen this book and its great power. They bought it for you with their lives and know that it is watching you, listening, waiting...."

The ink of the words grew darker, and the page began to turn brighter. He smiled and stroked the words.

I continued to type as he closed his eyes and began. His voice moved all around me and multiplied, changing. I began to see as he saw, the people and voices coming together as my fingers stayed on the keyboard, flying to keep up with the vision as it unfolded....

Chapter Three

The rain made the April air cold. Water ran in ripples down the path that led to the church with a crucifix hoisted above the door, Christ's bleeding arms outstretched as thunder punctuated the voices of men digging with shovels. The despised Grimbald stood to their right, his candlebox giving them a palsied light as they worked. The rain had let up enough that the flame was in no danger.

She saw they had kicked over the headstone, dragging it away and throwing the dirt over it as they worked. She heard the shovel strike wood and the men growl with pleasure. They dropped ropes to a boy, who shimmied through the mud to the coffin and worked to secure the ropes around each end.

She crept closer to watch, careful to let the trees shield her in her shame. Blood had clotted on the underside of her dress, soaking through to the final outer layer of the skirt. The rain had dispensed with it well enough, but he would get no further remembrance of her body. She cursed her body, and the rain, for soiling the last thing on earth she had. The dress was blue silk, an illicit treasure she had found in an untended parcel outside a gentleman's house. Silk was forbidden for her class to wear, so she found the courage to wear it only on her worst days. Some woman had a beautiful life; this dress was its proof. As she slid into a stranger's dress, she willed that woman's good fortune to befall her.

One man wore the robes of a statesman: golden damask and linen, with an ermine collar around his cloak that she could smell from where she was. The rain was unkind to the rich and poor alike, for it made the poor cold and the rich stink.

Another man wore scarlet robes of a thickly done fabric, with a gold chain looping at his neck and a cross swinging from his breast—a cardinal from the church. She recognized him, her knees going soft, sinking her into the buried memories. She remembered the last time she saw him as he proceeded down the London streets, boys carrying gilded silver crosses running ahead and children begging alms running behind. He would always stare straight ahead, oblivious to both cross and hunger. But she knew his secret.

He commanded the men at their work, simple men from nearby, probably Southwark, who had no qualms about raising a man if it meant they drank well later. One man jammed an iron into the casket, prying it open. The cardinal peered into it, shoulder to shoulder with the statesman. They looked at each other and conversed.

"Set a stake."

The boy ran to fetch the stake as the diggers pierced

the earth, rending a deep hole to set the stake in, filling
it back with dirt and rocks, testing the stake to see if it
would hold the body. Grimbald hauled chains to the
foot of the stake and waited while the men lifted the man
from the coffin. She watched in horror as a priest, dead
and limp, rose in front of her from the dark pit where
death's seal had been broken. His priestly robes were
rotted, hanging in loose shreds, some staining making
the holy inscriptions unreadable. His eye sockets were
sunken and black, and his mouth hung open stiffly, as if
he had one last word to preach.

The statesman and cardinal motioned for them to
stop, and approached.

"The knife," the statesman said, his palm extended to
the cardinal.

The cardinal hesitated, then produced a knife from
his cloak and laid it across the open palm. "Sir Thomas,"
he replied, looking as if the knife was as foul as the
corpse.

He obviously had no appetite for this work. But
Sir Thomas did. He licked his lips and breathed on the
knife, rubbing it on his robes so it flashed like lightning
before it struck.

"*Ecclesia non novit sanguinem,*" More said. He
walked to the body, kneeling before it, stroking the
face with the blade. "'Now also is the axe laid unto
the root of the trees: so that every tree which bringeth
forth not good fruit, shall be hewn down, and cast into
the fire.'"

He plunged the knife parallel to the body and up,
slicing the holy robes off, tossing them into a pile behind
him. He grabbed the hat that had identified the man as a

priest of God and jerked it away with such force that the head turned almost backward.

The corpse's open mouth faced her, as if his last words were for her. She narrowed her eyes and felt hate. She would not forgive a priest.

He took the knife and lifted the head closer. Cradling the head in one of his arms as if the man were a fallen friend, he dragged the knife across the rotting flesh of the skull, scraping clean hair and bits of skin. He dropped the head, and it made a sucking thud as it hit the wet earth. Next he lifted the dead man's fingers, scraping the knife against each one.

"You have betrayed the anointing of your office, and it is removed." Sir Thomas stood.

She bowed her head. God's punishment had found this man only in death. She feared her own would be slow in coming too. She wanted it now.

"Come brothers, good men of God, and curse this heretic! Send him to hell that he may trouble us no more!"

The men came round and mumbled uncertain words, until More shouted above them: "*Poena Damni.* You are sentenced to the eternal night, where their worm does not die and the fire does not go out."

All spit on the dead man, and the boy darted in to secure the body to the stake with the irons. They stacked bundles of wood and kindling against the base, building up until the wood touched the man's breast.

"The rain has stopped that we may finish the work," More said. "God be praised."

Grimbald, the parish priest who had betrayed her, took the sinking candle from its box and set the wood on fire. It snapped from branch to branch, consuming the body with great speed, death having drained it of much fluid by this night.

No one spoke as they watched the body sag into the flames and disappear.

When the flames began to concentrate their efforts at the base of the stake, they knew the body was no more. More grabbed the iron and ran it into the fire, over and over, until it hit upon what he wanted. He withdrew it, the skull sticking to one end. He crushed it under his boot with a fierce strike, grinding it down, grunting as it resisted in places.

"Boy."

The boy ran to him.

"Scrape the shards into a bucket and dump them into the river. Do not wait for morning. The rain may grow heavy again."

"Sir Thomas?" the boy asked.

More beckoned him closer and knelt to hear him. "You have done well tonight, my friend." He touched the boy's cheek. "You will make your father proud." He slipped the boy a thick silver groat as payment.

"But Sir Thomas," the boy asked, "what was his crime?"

More smiled. "Throwing pearls to pigs."

The boy ran off to complete his work. While the men moved to gather their supplies and disperse, the cardinal and More began discussing something quietly between them that she couldn't hear from her hiding place. They were walking to their horses and mounting as a new slate of rain broke above them.

His words displaced her cold repulsion with another

grief, a slow, sinking guilt. His words forced themselves down her throat so that she gagged, grasped her neck, and fell to her knees. Guilt swarmed in her roiling stomach as a thousand accusations worked their way into her blood. She retched as she forced herself to her knees and to stand.

She timed it just right, staggering onto the path in front of the men on horseback, who with a smart spur had forced the horses into a dead run to beat the returning rain. She wore her best gown for this moment. Bloodstained and broken, she lurched onto the path, lifting her arms to embrace the relief of her death, lifting her angry face to heaven as the horses bore down, their hooves lifting to strike the beautiful blow. She wanted to die here, where the bleeding Christ and His cardinal would both be witnesses, and see what their work had accomplished.

Swift arms encircled her, lowering her to the ground as the hooves thundered all around her head. He lay upon her, absorbing the strikes on his back, his tears washing hers away....

When she awoke she tasted her lips. They had the taste of another's tears, and she could smell her son again.

❊ ❊ ❊ ❊ ❊

I stopped him there. He was ready to turn the page.

"Wait!"

He raised his metallic eyes and looked at me.

"Whose arms? Did he die when the horses hit him? Why could she smell her son? Why did they burn a dead priest?"

He began to turn the page again. "I tell this story as I choose."

"I'll write it as I please! Haven't you ever heard the law of Chekov's Gun? 'If you plant a gun in the first act, it better go off in the third.' I'm telling you, readers will spend the rest of the story wondering who those arms were attached to, so you better tell them, or just leave that part out. I'm not going to write a sloppy book."

"You're going to write the truth," he replied. "Do you like fish?"

Chapter Four

At the next moment we were in the lobby, staring at an aquarium of gorgeous blue and yellow cichlids, devilishly fat fish that would eat us if they were any bigger. They zipped around the tank and darted away when we pressed our faces near.

"What do they see?" he asked me.

"A distortion," I replied. "A distortion of the world beyond them."

He smiled, and the blood drained from my legs again. I wished he wouldn't do that.

"What do we see?" he asked.

"We see everything. And we control the lighting, the food, the temperature, their tankmates. We scare them when they see us, but they don't see us clearly. They don't understand who we are."

"So they don't know the truth?" he asked.

"*Their* truth is not *the* truth," I said.

We walked back to my room, though how I had arrived at the tank I couldn't remember. We passed Crazy Betty's room, and he walked in as I grimaced. Mercifully, Betty was sleeping deeply, a marvel of pharmaceutical intervention. Mariskka told me that Betty's blood type was B positive, because she usually came in positive for barbiturates. She had been scheduled for surgery last May and was put on a diet of nothing but clear liquids the day before as they prepped her. Mariskka found her in the courtyard drinking pilfered vodka a few hours later. She had protested that it was clear.

He adjusted her covers that had begun to slip down and looked around the room. Seeing the blanket across the chair, he motioned for me to grab it. I handed it to him, and he draped it over her.

"It's too cold in here," he said. "She has bad dreams when she's cold. Mariskka blames the drugs and never checks the thermostat."

We walked back to my room, where he continued the story.

"The one on the path with her was Aryeh, the guardian of her line. He is more lion than angel, but these things are hard to explain in your words. She smelled her son because Aryeh had held him."

"An angel held her son? So is he dead?"

"Let the story continue," he replied.

"How can I be her heir if her son died?"

The words glowed like burning coals, and I heard a noise like a broken bow being dragged across violin strings. The words strained against the page. I could see them rising up. I swallowed and sat back, my fingers returning to the keyboard.

❀ ❀ ❀ ❀ ❀

She came to in a large bed with an embroidered coverlet, in a room of tapestries and tables laid with pitchers of wine and a bowl of dried apple rings. She could hear the soft warblings of a lute being strangled, its player having not much skill, and children's laughter.

An elderly man, possibly a doctor because of his thick spectacles and a faint odour of vinegar, pulled the coverlet up around her shoulders and patted her cheek, having a few whispered words at the door with a younger man. She could remember nothing but images: her son, a great horse bearing down on her, his cold snorting breath clouding her vision of his rider, and … something else. A warmth, a cocooning sleep in which she felt nothing but peace.

The younger man approached her, his hands behind his back, his face fleshy and soft, with rough whiskers all around his cheeks. He had a peasant's broad nose and whip-thin lips. His eyes were wide and brown, much like the eyes of a boy, with thick lashes … eyes that lingered innocently, revealing no fear or desire.

"What is your name?" he asked.

"Rose."

"Rose, I am Sir Thomas More, and this is my home. Do you know how you arrived here?"

The name disturbed her, but she could not think why. She could only remember those last moments. "I threw myself in front of your horse, and you saved me."

"No," he said, frowning. "I quite trampled you. In my horror, I could not turn the horse fast enough, my reflexes being frozen. But you survived, though you have lost much blood. To my poor mind, it is a miracle, God's work."

Rose turned her face to the wall. Little images strung themselves together—beads of thought and memory making an unbroken line at last, and she groaned. The blood was not from the horse.

"Why did you want to die?" he asked.

"Because I could not afford a pilgrimage," she replied, thankful to be facing the wall so the sarcasm would show itself only in the turn of her mouth. "And I was wearied of my sin."

"My child."

The words carried such tenderness that she turned to him. He was so kind. Had she witnessed the burning, or was that a dream? The man she saw was too tender and soft to commit such strange violence.

"Do you have a home?" he asked.

"I am an orphan."

"You are not married or betrothed?"

"No. I have never known a man's love," Rose lied. It was true.

He was silent for a moment. "You will stay on with us as a house servant. If your great passion for God is matched in obedience to men, you will find this day to be the happiest moment of fortune to befall you." He smiled at her. "I am a gentle master. You will have no harsh treatment and the best of provision. This is a home of great peace."

She hardened her eyes and watched him. He was a man, despite all his words. And men didn't keep promises to helpless women. Not without some enticement. She waited for the flicker of his eyes as she lay there, the upturning of a corner of his mouth.

She could see nothing, and it made her want to vomit. He was treating her as he would a proper woman, a clean one.

"I cannot accept this grace," she whispered. "You must send me from here."

He moved as if to touch and reassure her, but she saw his muscles twitch and reverse, a set coming to his mouth as his hands returned behind his back. "You must rest."

He left and she turned back to the wall. These waking moments were as strange and terrible to her as the dreamed ones. The memory of something pressed against her as the horses thundering overhead returned.

"Let me die," she whispered. No one answered.

With her eyes closing, stray golden hairs on her gown caught her attention but did not hold it as she sank into her dreams. Once in the night she awoke and sat up. She sensed someone's eyes upon her, but the room was dark and the candle extinguished. She was not afraid.

❈ ❈ ❈ ❈ ❈

"You're showing this story to me because I want to die too?" I yelled at him. "You think I'll root for her to live, and remember everything good I have left to live for, that I'll skip out of here and head straight to some *It's a Wonderful Life* matinee?"

"You don't want to die," he said, still sitting in his chair. His shadow rose above him on the wall, growing larger, with wings spreading out, touching each of the walls surrounding me. "You want to run away. The afterlife is not a place for cowards."

Fear dripped from my heart to my stomach. "I don't want to do this anymore. I just want to die."

"You don't want to live," he said. "They are not the same. Death is no escape."

"Let me die!" I screamed, throwing the computer on the floor. The screen went black. "What's the use of writing a book if I'm going to die?"

"Perhaps you never really loved words," he replied.

He waved his hands over the Tablets of Destiny and another story sprang to life. I got a flash of my book, sitting on top of a best-sellers list with people lined up to buy it. One face in the crowd saw me, too. I reached out to him, but the vision fled back into the pages, and the other story leapt into action again.

"Wait! Fix it!" I screamed, pointing to the computer.

He shrugged. "Call customer support."

I scrambled for the bedside table, finding a pen but no paper. I wrote what I saw next on my bedsheet. I would have to move on to the walls before he paused again.

❀ ❀ ❀ ❀ ❀

Within weeks Rose had established herself among the servants as a relentless worker, a woman who accepted work from the hand of her master without complaint. It saved her the grief of talking to anyone. She rose first in the servants' quarters, washing her neck and face, pinning up her hair, and being away before the others woke.

Sir Thomas moved her from laundry and feeding the

animals to tending his children. It horrified her. Their high voices and quick little movements, like a pack of young rabbits who knew nothing of the world of blood and terror just beyond their door. Their innocence made her worry that at any moment she would be discovered and turned out. She wondered that they could not smell the past as she could, her sins that had decayed and piled up. She could no more be free of them than these children could perceive such a woman existed.

Sir Thomas had built a world for them where suffering was light and food was fresh and no one was damned at birth. Children all over London were whipped for disobediences. Sir Thomas believed in whipping, he said, and produced a peacock's feather to punish the children with. He was too casual about their innocence, and it made her nervous. He did not know how it could be shattered.

Being utterly unnerved by the children, she unwittingly became a good mistress to them, watching them constantly so they would not stumble and touch her. She resolved their squabbles so there would be no need for tears and the hugs those required.

Sir Thomas bragged about her often to those who came to the home. "This is Mistress Rose, a poor child plucked from the streets of London, fatherless, motherless, but with a heart of devotion to Christ. I have seen no other maid give such love and care to my children."

Sometimes his eyes rested not so much on the children but on Rose. She always averted her face. His gaze made her stomach leap. Sometimes she thought he would speak something more, something just for her, but he moved on each time, with his hands behind his back, returning with his guests to the parlor. It was a stupid thing, she knew, to have desire for a man, but she had not known her heart was still alive. She had forgotten its language.

The gentlemen would nod and move on with him, and the muscles in her back would release, so that she slumped down and caught a full breath. He would never suspect he had left a fool in charge of his children. There could be nothing to fear from her past, either. Sir Thomas never brought men from filthy Southwark into his home. No one who knew her could ever cross that threshold, save for one, and his name had never been mentioned. Still, at the first blooming of the hawthorn in a few weeks, she would tie a bundle above the door to keep that evil out.

She stiffened as one of the children grabbed her hand, leading her into the garden after breakfast. There were rows of fruit trees, entire plots of herbs and vegetables for the kitchen, ornaments and flowering bushes, whose blossoms the gardener clipped often to fill the house until it smelled of nothing but roses and kitchen stews, children and drying apples. The sun was not unkind as it burned, making the garden stretch and grow. There were grand trees, yew and beech, with drooping leaves that the children sought refuge under before dinner. She listened to them recite their psalters and poetry as the squirrels dashed past them, maniacally stripping the bark from the yew trees.

"Aye, your father is a great believer in God," she commented.

Margaret piped up first, her earnest face already

showing a woman's frown lines above her brow. "God is everything to Father. There is nothing besides God, is there?"

Rose swallowed so she could lie with a distracting smile. "No, indeed. You must always remember that. There is nothing besides God, and God is within these gates."

Gardeners worked around them, and she watched them saw and clip the errant branches, burning the refuse. She had never seen a garden, never watched as it was tended. She marveled that their violence produced such beauty, how order was established with the sweep of a blade, making all things more perfect. She had developed an eye for their work, seeing the stray branch that searched for its own light as a nuisance, marking it in her head to point out to the gardeners.

Margaret came and sat beside her. "Father was going to be a priest."

Rose scooted away.

"He was going to be a priest, but he fell in love with a beautiful girl. She was our mother. She died."

Rose stopped herself from the quick reply on her tongue. Perhaps the children knew a blush of life's secrets, of the suffering that found them all. "I am sorry," she said.

Margaret moved closer. "Father remarried. A nasty woman named Dame Alice. You probably won't meet her for ages. She's always away, spending money. She has furious fits, saying she must escape this prison and go into the city for some shopping. She comes home with enormous packages and shrieks about cheating merchants and scandalous prices."

It made Rose laugh.

Margaret looked up and laughed too. "Father says money never makes anyone happy." She stood and ran back off to play.

That surprised Rose. The chasm between the two worlds of London shrank.

Her monthly bleeding had begun again, and she felt her past fading. The other servants treated her as an equal, and the children made no distinction between her and the others, except that they loved her more because she never spat on her sleeves to tend to their faces. Perhaps the past could be forgotten, she thought, like a dream that terrorizes but is swept away by light and time ... so one only remembers the dread of it, and later, not even that. At night she listened as the other servants dreamed. There was Manny, the pastry cook, a fluffy little woman with doughy cheeks and long white hair that she swirled on top of her head like a meringue, who dreamed aloud of missing ingredients and mice in the larder. And Candice, the tutor, who had nightmares of wrestling with letters that would not stand straight, her vowels running away on the page into a wild life of their own.

It was these murmurings, their nightmares, that finally broke open her heart to this place. If its terrors were no more than mice and ruined parchments, Rose would live here forever. She did not believe in God, or grace, but they were here, and she agreed to live among them. Rose knew pleasure for the first time, and the absence of shame. It was a wine that made her heart light, and it did not turn sour in the dark hours of the morning. With her baby saved, and her safely in Sir Thomas's house, the past was a washed, clean thing that could trouble her no more.

Margaret, the oldest child, was stealing glances at Rose while they ate. Rose tried to ignore it. Margaret whispered something to the server, who set an extra bowl of porridge before Rose.

"Why do you give me this?"

"Margaret seeks to elevate your status in the house."

"With porridge?"

"By law, you may not eat as many courses as the children, for they are children of Sir Thomas, a member of the king's court," he whispered, pushing to her the crockery filled with the porridge of oatmeal, beef, and thyme.

They saw Margaret watching them intensely, and Rose shook her head, pointing to her full bowl of pottage as evidence of the girl's machinations.

Margaret giggled and went back to her own pottage.

"It's useless," the server told her. "She's a wild one. Besides, you look very much like Sir Thomas's first wife, when she was in the bloom of health. Goodness mercy, but he loved her."

Just then the server's face went white, and he hurried away from the table. Rose turned and saw that Sir Thomas was in the room. He cleared his throat, beginning to recite the morning psalters, but Margaret raised her hand.

"Yes?"

"Father, Rose needs a hornbook."

Sir Thomas did not reply.

"She must learn her letters so she can read to us in the garden," Margaret said, her voice getting higher. "She desires this greatly."

"Margaret!" Rose's voice was too sharp. Everyone was staring at her, and she had to say more. "It is time to devote ourselves to prayer, not speak of earthly desires."

Sir Thomas stroked his chin and did not draw his customary deep breath before beginning the prayers. "Margaret, I have stirred many nests by daring to educate my girls. I see you have inherited my bent for revolution." Margaret grinned at him. "Rose will have a hornbook, and you yourself may tutor her."

Rose tapped her foot and stuffed a spoonful of porridge into her mouth. She had never seen a real book until coming here and regarded them with a bit of suspicion. Only the wealthiest knew how to read, and their books were done in Latin. One book could cost four year's wages for a common man, and there were no common men who could read.

Christ had held a book too. It beckoned them all to a cross. Why Sir Thomas brought books to his children she did not know. They smelled of leather cords binding down the washed linen, stretched tight across a wood frame to receive the dark ink. To her, it was the stench of death.

"Rose, you may kiss me in gratitude, but only once."

Margaret beamed at her, a flicker of mischief in her eyes. Rose looked around the room, and everyone was staring at her.

"Come, hurry, let's not miss our psalters," Margaret said.

Rose pushed back from the table, feeling the air tingling on her arms, goosebumps rising on her skin. She walked between the tables of servants and children, and leaning down to Margaret, kissed her on the cheek. She clenched her jaw and returned to her seat.

Sir Thomas, pleased, was already beginning the psalters. Rose was too angry to listen, though she loved the way Latin sounded even if she couldn't understand a word of it. She decided to give Margaret her most punishing of looks, a promise of a bitter scolding to come. Then she saw Margaret wipe a tear from her cheek and, embarrassed, stuff her hands back into her skirts. Rose shot the scowl down to her own shoes instead. She would not cause more tears. Children were indeed a mystery, she thought, but those maturing into adults were simply unfathomable.

So it was that Rose began to love, growing less afraid of them all. They cared nothing of her past; they were too busy weaving her into their futures. The affection she gave them meant nothing to her, though its magic worked within her. Her heart softened and coaxed her arms to hang more loosely at her sides, instead of folded at her chest, so she would receive a hug without bristling. She learned how to give one, too: The proper technique for hugging a child involved sitting on her haunches as the children wrapped thin, tender arms around her neck, pressing their soft cheeks against hers. She learned to wrap her arms around their waists and give a little squeeze back. It was almost always over in a moment, which helped.

One afternoon she settled the children around the table at dinner and retreated to another table at the end of the room to eat her own meal. She lowered herself into the chair, its wood creaking a bit. She had filled out since coming here, discovering little rolls of fat around her waist. Her thighs had lost their harsh definition. She loved the changes, believing them to be proof that she could become a different woman with the regularity of honest work and frequent meals, two things she had never known. Leaning over the children's books, seeing sketches by the artists of Europe, the fine ladies they drew with round faces and generous bodies, Rose began to believe that she would become one someday herself.

Her face was still warm from the sun, and she was glad to have a moment's rest. She tucked her hornbook into her skirts, and Margaret made eyes at her. Rose sighed and took it out, setting it beside her bowl. Though she had worked all morning and could read simple sentences, Margaret was not satisfied.

Sir Thomas entered the room and everyone cried out for his attention. The youngest ones giggled and sprang from their chair, forgetting all the lessons of decorum. Their hungry affection for him left no room for pride, and he scolded them only gently as he scooted them back to their chairs. Rose noticed he did not embrace them or return their hugs.

"Come to my study, Rose. I have a special guest who would ask a question of you."

She swallowed her soup and followed, her thoughts swirling through muddy fear. Sir Thomas opened the door to his study, and she knew. Her stain was discovered.

❀ ❀ ❀ ❀ ❀

I was aggravated as I waited for the Scribe to turn the page. It did not turn as a normal book would but had to be coaxed. He spoke a language not of words, but of notes, I suppose, and the pages began to slowly curl, revealing the story word by word.

I was aware of nothing but my breathing. My fingers crushed around a pen, ready to drill out the next chapter. Thomas More, of course, was one of history's darlings, and every teenager in America was still forced to read his *Utopia* in English class. At least this story had appeal to history buffs, so I would die writing something that might even turn a profit. My executor would be thrilled.

"He's a hero everyone loves," I said, waiting for the stubborn page to unveil the next chapter. It snapped closed over the words like a blanket yanked up in a cold room in winter.

"I just meant that your readers will know who he is, if they stayed awake in English class." The Scribe glared at me, his immobile face making me feel like a child, or an idiot, or both.

"What *you* call history is written by another scribe, one who sets each generation upon the next, like dominoes."

He shook his head. "Real history is a dangerous, unfinished story." He heard something and his face turned to the door. I jerked and looked, but there was nothing.

He stared at the door, his eyes narrowing, one hand lifting, pointing to it. He spoke to me, still watching the door, as he nodded and began to lower his arm. "A *selasal*, a roach, is at the door. He desired entrance, but your guardian has removed him. Hurry. They know the Tablets of Destiny has been opened. You are not safe."

The irony was not lost on me.

"You've got to keep me safe until I die?" I asked.

He turned to me. "No one dies alone. Before the night is done, you must choose who will carry you over that threshold." He spoke to the book and its page turned. "Though Rose is in trouble, I must begin a new story."

Chapter Five

The pages of the book fluttered in the midnight breeze. The noise, like the snapping of a flag in the wind, startled her from her dreams of her wedding night soon to come, imagining Percy's face as her shift fell away from her shoulders, imagining his child growing within her and the pleased expression Percy would wear every day among the men of law. Never again would she spend her days flattering strangers; she would at last have an honest life. It would be the end of her secrets.

The other ladies-in-waiting were sleeping heavily in the dark room. Some of them snored, and Anne often wished for a light to know who it was. But this was not what had awakened her. From her dream, she had heard the words spoken.

Sitting up, she saw the book was open and near her feet on the bed. She reached down and shut it but heard them whispered again. It was a language she had never known, except perhaps in childhood, when she could read the moods of the sun and hear the dialect of rain. Those were the days she could laugh with George and play wicked pranks on their father, and they had nothing to fear in the world but scoldings and early bedtimes.

She remembered nothing of the whispered words, but their effect remained. Her heart pounded with an urgency that made her thoughts race. Anne fled from the chamber, something drawing her away from the sleeping court into the gardens below.

The garden was alive and rejoicing in its dark seclusion. Dew fed the roses and hawthorn, each with great tight buds ready to burst open. Crickets sang the same note, over and over, like a needle and thread bobbing in and out of the dark blanket of the night sky. She had worn no wooden pattens on her soft shoes, which she regretted immediately once her feet set upon the garden path. Thousands of small stones were unkind to her soles. She walked down the path, weaving between clusters of sleeping buds and cool vines, moving farther and farther from the palace, watching her linen shift float about her, lit only by stars. Something was drawing her.

Anne saw there was a small chapel at the end of the path she had followed. Despite the hour, a lamp burned within. The chapel was made of stone, with plain windows instead of elaborate scenes of glass. There would be only enough room in such a place for a handful of people and its altar. This chapel was for earnest prayer, surely, and not ceremony. This thought comforted her and pulled her farther in, until she was about to step out from the path and open the door. She would wait here for the voice to return.

She heard a noise that made her throat seize even as her arms jerked. It was a scraping, a thick scraping of stone against something soft, with a gutted moan upon that.

"Deus meus, ex toto corde pænitet me ómnium meórum peccatórum, éaque detéstor, quia peccándo, non solum pœnas a te iuste statútas proméritus sum, sed præsértim quia offéndi te, summum bonum, ac dignum qui super ómnia diligáris!"

She was too frightened to peer out from behind the plantings. The dragging continued, and the moans changed to weeping. Something heavy dragged itself along the path, or was being dragged. She strained to hear if there were any more words, until in a wail she understood its pain, ground up and spat out in one word.

"Why?"

When it became visible to her, her fear changed to wrenching pity. A man, clothed in a rough brown cloak, edged his way along to the chapel on bare knees. The stones had bit and cut into his flesh, and she could see he left a glistening black trail behind him.

He collapsed on the steps, crying out. "I have repented, my Lord! God, in Your mercy, give me a way to repair my great sin, so that no more may die!"

His face sank into his arms, and he did not move again. Anne stood in her dark shelter, unsure what she should do. Christian charity would have her comfort him and see to his wounds, but she was alone and unprotected. She looked at the fallen man and feared him for his size and great distress; he might do anything to her if he caught her witnessing this.

She saw the glistening stain spreading out from under his cloak, and the way the cloak moved with his breath. She couldn't be sure if he was conscious. She bit her lip and looked around, but there was no one in the garden or approaching the chapel. Exhaling hard, she pulled her shift tightly about her and went to him. Kneeling, she stroked his back and whispered what words of comfort she knew.

"*Et lux perpétua lúceat eis*. Amen."

His back tensed under her first touch, then softened and his breathing grew strong. He began to sit up, his cloak falling over his face, and she lifted the wet cloth away from his bloodied knees. He wanted to cry out— she could tell by the way a breath was forced back down when she touched his leg—but he did not.

His knees were desperately in need of tending. They were cut at all angles, deep slices shooting out from the center like starbursts, the tiniest stones still embedded. Indeed, these stones were all that was stopping the bleeding in places. Anne looked around for anything she could use and saw a fountain not far from them. She ran and dipped the edges of her shift in it, running back and carefully dabbing at the wounds, hoping to expel the dirt and stones that polluted it. She made several trips, neither of them speaking as she worked, cleaning the wounds and tearing the hem away from her sleeping gown to bandage them.

His hand caught hers as she began to tear.

"You mustn't do that," he whispered. His voice was dead, numb from exhaustion. His touch was weak. It made Anne pity him even more and fear him even less. It opened up her heart as nothing else had in this palace of pageant and pretense. She would be glad when her service here was done.

She pressed her hand over his for a moment, then removed it and continued to tear.

"No one here will ever see it," she whispered and thought of the voice she had heard from her bed. "I think I was sent to you." She stood, pulling her torn shift close. "I am grieved for you, my friend. May God answer your prayers with swift mercy."

"Wait!" He fumbled at his neck, removing a gold crucifix. "Wear this, for me."

"I do not require payment."

"It is not payment. It will keep you safe."

She held out her hand to him, uncertain, and he poured the cold chain and cross into her palm. The moonlight made it flash, and she was afraid.

A cock crowed and they both started. He tried to stand, but the pain drove him back to sitting.

"You must return," he urged. "The others will be waking."

She ran towards the palace, her feet finding their way through the plots and gathered bushes, straining to find the certain path back to the entrance she had used. But in the growing light the garden's paths made no sense. When she reached the doorway, she rested her head against the cold stone of the arched frame.

"Lord, I am a foolish woman to go wandering about at night. I should have obeyed the priests; I should not have brought that book with me. Please forgive me, and take me from this place."

A guard met her there with a professional disinterest, which she knew would be responsible for a thousand rumours by dinner.

Chapter Six

She was right.

At dinner every woman at the court paid great attention to Anne without speaking to her. She felt their eyes on her, and they were cold. She was not used to being so scorned. Steadying her fork as she raised it to her mouth, she swallowed only once when she raised her cup. She missed her friends at the French court, she missed her brother, she missed being liked. She had not even been allowed to see her betrothed, Lord Percy, since her return.

It was a cold rain the day she got off the ship and it rained still—at least in her soul—a sour rain that could cause nothing to grow. Perhaps soon she would be finished here, the family's name restored, and she would sleep beside Percy every night. Her small act of rebellion, bringing a forbidden book into the country, had gone unnoticed. Indeed, some of the nobles here already had it.

The servants set before her a bowl of steaming pottage and a plate of roasted venison. She sat at an enormous table with courtiers lined up according to rank and usefulness to the crown, servants and pages darting in among the diners to deliver food and messages. The cook's politics involved the belly only, not books, so the servers spoke freely with Anne. She silently blessed them for it.

"How do you like the venison, my lady?"

"It is wonderful," Anne said, throwing a bone on the floor, as was the custom. "Though I feel sympathy for it, having been hunted by this court. Everyone here relishes the suffering of the weak."

The server, a boy of about thirteen, noted the women staring at Anne. He winked at her and set a plate of fine bread on the table.

"Anyone hunting in here would need mighty sharp arrows to pierce those old hides," he remarked, and Anne laughed out loud.

Everyone stopped.

"Anne?" Queen Catherine spoke from the head of the table. King Henry was not beside her. He had not joined her at dinner since Anne had come to court. "What remark has pleased you?"

Anne wiped her fingers on her bread and rested her hands in her lap. "I meant no disrespect. I was enjoying the dinner."

Catherine stared at her, but Anne could not see what the queen weighed in her mind. Catherine brushed her hand across her face and returned to eating in silence, her cold face intent on Anne's. If Queen Catherine blamed her for her sister, Anne did not know. Anne's sister was carrying Henry's baby, and the family's shameful secret was everyone's favourite course at this table. Anne had been retrieved from the French queen's court to serve Catherine in humble apologetic submission, and her father hoped she would redeem the family's name. Anne wanted only to marry Percy and be free of them all. This was what pleased God, the priests said: Women living in obedient service, tending hearth and children. Anne had learned in France that she could never please both a royal court and God, and she had seen too many broken lives at court to set her heart there. She would marry and be free at last to live by the church's rules instead of men's.

With the next round of courses, the court returned their attention to Catherine, and Anne was relieved to be ignored again.

After dinner, the noon sun was burning the last of the morning clouds away, and Anne requested permission to rest in the quiet of her bedchamber rather than accompany the women to the garden for music. It was not a thing that would be done by another lady of the court, but Catherine walked as if in a dream and gave her leave with no further thought. Catherine did not have the energy to sustain a hatred for her. Anne noticed that Dr. Butts, the court physician, hovered around Catherine, testing her brow with his wrist and urging her to sit.

Anne gave it no more consideration and fled to her chamber, the delight of having it alone making it the sweetest place on earth. Ten empty beds greeted her and the drapes were drawn against the window so that it was shadowed, the still air sweet and heavy inside the thick castle walls, making exquisite conditions for a nap. She had slept, but not truly rested, in the weeks since she had been here, always awaking to the feeling that something had been near. The book was still on the foot of the bed, and she glared at it, moving it to a night table where it would not be disturbed by a breeze.

Taking off her farthingale and laying it over the foot of the bed, she pulled back her coverlets and saw it.

A new sleeping gown, soft white linen with ribbons gathering the neck and sleeves and painstaking lavender embroidery spiraling the sleeves and down the front of the gown, with a gold weave of the great Tudor rose. It had been folded and placed under her coverlet, and a note fell away as she lifted it up for inspection.

Because you did not despise the sorrow of a broken man.

There was no signature.

There was a stirring of air around her, and Anne covered her mouth with her hands. She could not tell where the stirring came from … if something was sweeping in or departing. Either way, she sensed the breaking fissure beneath her and prayed.

"Anne, Anne."

She opened her eyes and winced. Someone had pulled back the drapes and the sun was at its peak. It must have been nearly four in the afternoon, and the youngest of the ladies-in-waiting, a girl named Jane, was still shaking her.

"Anne, you must dress. The masquerade is starting!"

Anne sat up. She held the sleeping gown in her hands like a blanket and slid it out of view under the coverlet, frowning. Jane did not notice but grabbed Anne's hands and helped her dress. Anne studied the girl when she could, wondering why this lady-in-waiting had warmed to her.

"They made fun of me at music today. I have no ear for singing, yet they forced me to sing alone, just to make the queen laugh."

"I am sorry, Jane."

Anne was shivering in her chemise, though the sun was warm. She could see the dust floating through the air, kicked up when Jane helped her step into her petticoat, the farthingale going over this. The corset went over her head, and Anne began to feel like herself again after her nap, the layers of clothes bolstering her to face the women. Jane fastened the bumroll and parlet on next, and whipped around to grab the kirtle that went on top of the underskirts. The gown itself was the last piece, split open down the skirt so that the kirtle could be seen.

Anne favoured a headpiece she had brought from France, but Jane had trouble securing it.

"I am sorry, Anne! I can't set it right. Why don't you wear one of mine?"

"No, let me show you how," Anne offered, guiding her hand, holding the headpiece down so Jane could secure it.

"You shouldn't wear it. The queen does not like the ways of the French court."

"The queen will sooner send me away." She caught

Jane's hand after the piece was secured. "I am not like my sister, Jane."

"You shouldn't draw attention to yourself," Jane replied. "We are here to serve the court, not command it."

"Let it remind them that I am different," Anne said. "I will not make the mistakes of my sister, but neither will I atone for her. I want no part of this court."

"Aren't you afraid?" Jane asked.

Anne started to ask why just as a cannon went off from the palace wall. They both screamed from fright. Seeing each other's hysterical faces, they fled, laughing, down the hall to join the others.

Inside the gilded gold of the banquet hall, a towering white wall had been set in place, with windows and doors painted on it. Ladders leaned against the wall in several places, some connected with a plank across the top to make a scaffold. Workers tested the ladders as others brought in baskets of oranges, setting them beneath the ladders. Anne and Jane joined the other ladies attending Queen Catherine. Catherine sat on a carved dark wood chair, her skirts spreading wide so no one could stand less than five feet from her. Ladies had to shout to be heard over the noise of the work. Catherine's face was pinched and red, as if she had been weeping, and the women struggled to say merry things to her. Anne tried to smile with detached encouragement whenever Catherine's face turned in her direction. Catherine saw her headpiece and scowled.

The workers finished their efforts and ran from the room, closing all the doors behind them.

Catherine rose and pressed her palms against her cheeks, inhaling a ragged, determined breath. "Bolt the doors!" she commanded.

Her ladies squealed and ran for the doors, bolting them by pushing a brace against the handles. Anne stood stupidly at Catherine's side, having no idea what to do. In the time it took her to understand the queen's command, it was already done—the ladies, laughing, had rushed about, checking the windows, and had flown back to Catherine's side.

"They approach!" Jane cried out from her perch at a window.

Catherine stood. "When they breach the door, climb to the fortress and defend it! I will reward the maid who acts with courage—and an extra reward for the one with the best aim!"

Every woman stopped where she was and watched the doors, some women turning slow circles to see each one at either end of the room. Anne's heart pounded. When the first door received a thunderous blow, the spell was broken. Ladies ran screaming for the fortress, grabbing as many oranges as they could stuff into their bosoms and skirts and still navigate the ladders. They began to hand oranges up to the women on the scaffolds, working with speed to empty the baskets as the doors blasted open.

Jane grabbed Anne's hand and pulled her to the fortress as Catherine returned to sitting and watched with a vague smile. They climbed higher and higher up a ladder, struggling to balance their weight on the crude rungs, laughing when the fortress shook.

The doors slammed back with such force that the tapestries fluttered against the walls. Masked men poured into the room and ran for the fortress as the ladies pelted them with oranges, some hurling them with enough force to knock a man off his feet. Anne laughed, and no one turned to stare at her. In the chaos of flying oranges, frivolous taunts, and men smeared with pith and juice, Anne laughed as loudly as she wanted and no one scolded. She only wished she had taken more oranges.

A few of the men had maneuvered under a ladder, safely away from the stinging orange missiles, and used their swords to hack at the ladder's joints. A pair of ladies crashed to the floor in a collapse of wood and laughter, and the men turned their attention to another ladder and another pair of armed women.

One man was dressed like all the others but stood so tall that he caught her eye. He had to be at least six foot six, a monster compared to the smaller men in court, and he was well built too. He stood still, surveying the madness and marking each woman on the fortress. Anne noticed Catherine's sad, eager smile focused on him and his utter indifference to her. It infuriated Anne. Every court was the same: Pressed, thin lips and cold stillness polluting the room when words and action could clear the air.

Anne grabbed an orange and struck the man as hard as she could, hoping Catherine would see. It caught him on the back of the head, and he turned and smiled up at her as Catherine's mouth dropped open. His amusement did not please Catherine, whose pinched face grew redder as she spat out a word to Dr. Butts, who was checking her brow. Court politics, Anne decided, was perhaps not her own best talent.

The man walked straight towards Anne, evidently not minding where oranges flew or paying any attention to the cries of the captive maids who called down increasingly ridiculous insults on the victors.

Her knees jellied, and she held tight to the ladder as he climbed it.

He stood beneath her. She noted his sword and the men gathered at his feet, their women surrendered. She was the last woman on her ladder.

"How will you go?" he asked.

He took another step up and extended his arm. Beneath him were more men, their swords ready to bring down the ladder if she refused him. Everyone was silent, watching. Anne could feel their eyes on her, like the heat from a close fire that drew the blood to her cheeks. How did she always manage to shame herself? She bit her cheek to keep a tear from spilling out and lowered herself into his arms.

Her face was inches from his, his red whiskers scratching her cheek as she bumped against him. He smelled of smoky embers and honey, the yeast of English ale and salt of the sea. He was a foreign taste to her French palate of perfumes and gardens, and his mystery made her breath deeply, learning the scent of a man.

He pressed her into his muscular body to lower her down, and his warmth was a childish comfort to her. The confusions in her spirit calmed for a fleeting second.

His hands dug under her ribs as he lowered her, and

she tried to readjust her weight. He winced as her legs brushed his.

"Mind the knees," he whispered.

In the deepest hours of night, when everyone else staggered to their beds for sleep, the women returned from Catherine's chambers bursting with activity. Anne did not know why they refused sleep before the moon disappeared and breakfast was served. Now their faces appeared grim and determined as they forced their way out of the tight, boned bodices that had been known to crack ribs, and above yards and yards of fabric that announced station and wealth. Everyone was changing into simpler gowns, whispering little instructions to each other.

Jane spoke softly to her as Anne expelled a hard breath and pushed herself out of the bodice. "We must go into the countryside tonight, before the sun rises on the May Day festivities. We go to collect branches of mountain ash."

"Why?" Anne whispered back.

"A witch has been discovered in the castle. The branches will protect the queen."

"What evidence of a witch?" Anne asked, straining to turn and see Jane's face. Jane pressed her face nearer as she did up the laces of the new skirt and bodice. Her voice dropped lower again.

"Catherine miscarried a boy two nights ago, another boy. She always conceives but miscarries, except for Princess Mary. Henry has turned cold towards her and offers her no comfort. Catherine knows he has been seduced again. Tomorrow at dawn is the only moment of the year we may cast a witch out."

In silence they walked down to the garden and waited for the carriages to be brought round. Anne wondered if they would wait for an hour or more still. Catherine was old, Anne knew, at least forty, and always sleepy after banquets.

But not today. Catherine came to the garden straightaway and was first in a carriage. Anne strained to see if she was frightened, but her closest ladies-in-waiting kept her shrouded from view.

The horses took off with a great lurch and the ladies ran to clamber into their own carriages and follow. They went a short distance, about five or six miles, until the road became clogged with wet leaves and the trees were thick all around.

Catherine alighted first and urged the women to work. The branches had to be gathered while still wet with dew, or they would not work. Anne had no idea what she was to look for and tried to watch the other girls as they worked, but each girl would spy a small tree and remove the choice branches, tucking them into her skirts and dashing to deliver them to Catherine. The creeping fog made it all worse, and the servants held the torches too far away to help Anne see clearly. She arrived at each tree late and gathered nothing. She began to panic, her inexperience marking her out again for ridicule. She wanted to be sent away with honour, Catherine spying some greater piety in her that her sister did not possess. She had never been thought of as the fool, and she panicked to see her plan sliding into some unforeseen pit.

"Anne, quit thinking of yourself and help us!" one scolded her. "We won't do your work for you!"

But the only flowers she knew by sight here were the hawthorn, and they were not yet in bloom. Even then, she had brought nothing to offer the fairies, so it would not be wise to clip one.

The sun was rising. Catherine called the women back to their carriages, fleeing back to the castle with the witch's bane as the sun rose. The horses ran with great strength, but the roads were wet and rough, and Anne clung to the side of the carriage. She did not speak. All the words she could say were pooling in her eyes. It did not take the girls long to check and see that Anne had gathered nothing. She tried not to notice their stinging glee.

God, she prayed silently, *I thought I could serve You here, but I was wrong. I dishonour us both. Send me away!*

The horses were covered in sweat when they arrived, their earnest run under the drivers' whips having exhausted them. The ladies stepped out of their carriages and ran to attend to Catherine as she stepped down. Every girl except Anne carried her branches like a baby in her arms. Witches frightened them as much as the plague; both could steal in, unseen. Witches could make a man fantasize about another woman until he was driven mad with desire and forced to break the bonds of matrimony. Witches lured women to commit foul acts of desire, which led to the birth of misshapen babies and barren wombs. A single witch could undo the work of a hundred saints. Witches were birthed in hell, and every good Christian prayed to send them back there as well.

The morning sun was appearing over the white palace walls.

"Ladies!" the queen shouted. "Cast them across every threshold, secure them above the doorposts! And pray the Lord to cast the witch out!"

A page ran into the courtyard. "Anne Boleyn?" he called.

Everyone froze, looking at her, their mouths upturned with a hunger for more gossip.

The page followed their gaze and spoke to her directly. "Do not return to your quarters. You are commanded to submit yourself to Cardinal Wolsey. Forgive me, my queen, but she will not return."

"That's why she didn't collect any mountain ash," a girl told another as Anne walked past. "She's the witch."

"I belong to God!" Anne cried. With this, she touched the cross at her neck, still buried in the peeping layers of her bodice.

Catherine walked to her, an eyebrow raised, and jerked the necklace off Anne's neck. She lifted it so all the girls could see. "It is Henry's!" she cried out, and the girls screamed.

Cardinal Wolsey's study was a sunlit room on a floor above the women's quarters. Spread with braided rushes, the floor was littered over again with herbs, including fat fresh buds of cloves that crushed under her footfall, spreading a warm fragrance around her as she entered. The room smelled like a French perfumery and was decorated with so much gold and paint that it would rival any French woman. It comforted Anne to be in a room so familiar, even if she knew the man only by reputation.

Everyone in the French court knew of Cardinal Wolsey, who was the scorn of Martin Luther and the salvation of Henry's reign. Wolsey taught Henry to rule England and restrained Henry's appetites but then stamped Henry's thick wax seal on his own secret pleasures. Wolsey was one step away from becoming the Pope. Anne wondered what he would do with his mistresses and children when the appointment was announced. Men could forgive other men so easily. She sighed. Power was its own righteousness.

Cardinal Wolsey was working on his papers as she entered and did not look up until she stood before him. He rose and she knelt, biting her lip and pressing her eyes closed for one last prayer for mercy. Had he found the forbidden Hutchins book? It was outlawed here, but surely these laws did not apply to the court. She had not meant to offend these men. She had hoped she would be the friend whose company was sought after midnight, when girls with candles told stories and read aloud from books kept under mattresses. She had not known what powers it had, so she was afraid to throw it away, lest it mark her for vengeance and return. Her brother, George, was afraid of it. She should have listened.

"Anne Boleyn." He spoke it plainly, without question or accusation.

She felt it safe to reply and agree to it. "Yes."

"You have been in our court only a few weeks, returned from several years at court in France, is it?"

Anne nodded. So far there was no hint of her fate.

"Yet you have made a distinct impression on everyone you have met." His words were sour.

Anne could not help it. She tried to keep her face down so he would not see her cry, but her shoulders were shaking.

His heavy hand rested on her shoulder. He was a portly man, with jowls that began back behind his ears and fulminated in a point just under his chin that wobbled as he gestured. She looked up into his eyes, deeply etched with wrinkles and sagging skin, and saw they had a luminous, sweet quality she did not expect.

"My child." He patted her. "There is still time to repent." He gestured to a chair. "Sit down."

She sat in the chair pushed closest to his desk, and he paced as he continued. How could she repent? Anne thought to herself. Even her innocence must stink to God for Him to continually punish her for it. She wanted to unburden everything to the cardinal, to take confession and know forgiveness. She trusted his kind face. He was a man who could make anything right.

"I know your father. He has supported the church in every hour of need and has suffered under the indifferent treatment of this king."

Anne understood him to mean her sister, unworthy of a good match and financially dependent on a king who had grown completely tired of her after the first few nights.

"Anne, use your wits. Your family will be ruined by this." His voice was tender.

She started to declare a vow of repentance, but a page entered.

Wolsey rested his face in his hands before he spoke, rubbing his eyes before assuming a cold demeanor. "You are to inform Lord Percy that his betrothal to Anne Boleyn will not be recognized by King Henry. Percy must return the dowry. Next time, he should consult his monarch before making a match that would affect the alliances of the nobles."

The page nodded and scampered to his errand.

Before Anne could utter more than a strangled protest, Wolsey continued, to her, "You will no longer be housed with Catherine's ladies. You can thank me for this, for though Henry desires you, he does not consider how you must live. I have arranged private apartments on these grounds where you will be comfortable. Henry will allow you no visitors. Still, this is better than what the women will do to you when they find out."

"Find out what?" Anne asked.

"That you're Henry's mistress."

❊ ❊ ❊ ❊ ❊

I ground my teeth in frustration. Two-thousand dollars for retainers and hypnosis treatments had not cured me of that. "What an arrogant man! Claiming her like that and ruining her reputation. I'm glad I didn't live back then."

"It's much better to live today, to be the one who

steals and ruins?" the Scribe asked. "You have done so well with your liberty."

"I'm not going to talk about that."

"But why? You want people to know. You want them to understand what you felt, because it means so much to you. Emotion is law to this generation. I feel, therefore I act. I do not feel pain, therefore it must be okay. Tell me what you felt, Bridget. It matters so very much now, doesn't it?"

Hearing my name startled me.

"Not at all," I lied. "This is your story, not mine. Continue."

Chapter Seven

"I need fresh air," she pleaded. "This is a catacomb."

A Yeoman shut the door behind him as he left. He had appeared when Wolsey escorted her from his office and had not left her side yet. He was a man of considerable height, with a face red from the sun and white whiskers around his chin. His hair peeked out from his hat, and she could tell it was a reddish colour, though flecked also with white. His face was familiar to her, with deep lines under his eyes and around his mouth, a face made gentle by years of harsh treatment and bitter weather. He was, she decided, a true son of England, as content to serve others as to rule them.

The apartment was gilded in every possible way: Gold bullions ran along the ceiling, woods carved with delicate patterns set off by the gild. The chairs were set off in gold, with green silk cushions and tassels. The bed was monstrous, crafted of dark wood, with starbursts carved into the top finials and lions' feet resting on the floor at each corner. Anne pulled back the sheer curtains that ran along all four sides of the bed to peer in. Along the headboard, running along the highest beam, were the words *Dread God. Love God. Blessed be God!*

There were silk tapestries hung from the walls showing the great miracles of Christ and embroidered rugs at her feet showing Hercules' great deeds. In any direction she was wooed by the money fairly dripping from the place, and the first bloomed roses cut and displayed at her bedside and table and on perches throughout the apartment. She did not know where these had come from; someone must have ridden a distance to find a warmer garden in bloom. Anne breathed in deeply as she tried to steady her mind from this rapid turning of events.

Their fragrance was thick—and the first sweet thing she had found in England. She walked to the vase at the bedside and touched the cool petals. They were softer than any linen on her bed. Working only with mud and storms and heat, God crafted such wonder that no craftsman could duplicate, though he had all the materials in the world. Anne smiled and thought her life was misspent; she should have been a butterfly. Contented to fly for a few days, with nectar for wine and blossoms for blankets, she would not protest a short life. And she would not make so many mistakes.

"Anne," a deep voice said.

The voice startled her and she screamed, bumping against the table she leaned on so that the roses spilled onto the floor.

Henry entered, taking slow, circling, deliberate

steps, like a hunter watching a fallen deer to know how deep the arrow had gone. Anne grabbed the vase, lying on its side on the table, and hurled it at him.

He edged closer.

"Get away from me!" Anne screamed.

Other guards looked in, smiled at each other, and resumed their posts beside her Yeoman.

"I will have nothing to do with you!" she yelled.

"Sit down, Anne." Henry stopped and motioned for her to sit. The gesture carried the command of his office. She sat on the edge of the bed and cursed the table chair for being too far away. She didn't like even sitting on a bed in front of him. She wished there were no bed in the room at all, no suggestion of the things he must be thinking.

"What do you want from me?" he asked her.

She gasped without meaning to. "I don't want anything from you," she spat.

He waited. "Everyone wants something, Anne."

Anne's mouth twisted. "If I tell you what I want, will you let me have it?"

"Of course," he replied.

"I want to be sent away from here. I want to marry Lord Percy. And I never want to see you again."

"You can't return home, Anne. There are too many rumours circulating about you." He moved a little closer, and Anne sat up straight. "We'll have to repair that…. You don't love Lord Percy." He was only a few steps from her. "I didn't even need to meddle in that, save for canceling the marriage contract because you were too weak to do it yourself."

"I certainly don't love you," she said.

He turned to walk away.

"Wait!" she called out. "You promised to give me what I asked for!"

"No, Anne." He smiled. "I promised to give you what you want. And I will." He walked to the door, his hand on the frame when he looked back to her. "You are a true maid?"

She scrambled to grab something else from the desk to throw at him. He ducked as he pushed the door open. Anne listened to it lock from the outside.

The afternoon faded, and an unwelcome night spread around her. It was cold, the cold of a spring not fully resolved to allow summer to enter. Spring was inconstant in England, with all the charms and frustrations of pretty girls who flirt one day and play petulant the next. Still, all loved her and greedily awaited her favour.

Wolsey had sent her a few books, knowing that her years in France had given her a man's education, just one of the little scandals the French were known to cause. There was a book in the satchel from Sir Thomas More called *Utopia*. Anne found it a strange turn from a man well known for torturing men in his gatehouse when their ideologies conflicted with his own. One man had died before More could torture him properly, so More had dug him up and burned him, dead—yet still he publicly promoted his idea of a peaceable utopia.

There was a tract, in Latin, on repentance and the miracles Christ performed when saints turned back to

Him with their whole hearts. Anne wished the author had considered that sometimes Christ didn't want the saint back. This, at least, was what she felt.

Her own book, the forbidden Hutchins book, was not in her things. Someone had it. Someone knew her secret. The book would not forget her; she had a shadowy feeling the book was not done with her. She would see it again.

She sighed; none of these dead books inspired tonight. She tried to sleep but could not get warm. She blew out the candle and listened, shivering in her bed, tears evaporating on her cheeks, leaving her cold and miserable. There was an owl nearby who hooted to her and the insects keening together. No human voice could be heard, and Anne was glad. She fell asleep, still shivering, murmuring the prayers she had been taught in France.

Only once did she wake, when she had grown too warm under her blankets. In the darkness she heard the redwings singing as they flew away, the last of them leaving now that the weather was turning warmer. "See! Scc! See it!" they called, their tiny voices singing as they flew on.

Anne reached down to pull a blanket off, wondering dully how she had come to be under such a blanket, when there had been nothing but a silk coverlet she remembered seeing on the bed. But her mind was occupied with matters greater than blankets, and she returned to these thoughts in her sleep.

⚜

Three more days and nights passed. Every morning about five, when the sun was beginning to light the clouds that rested on the far horizon, Anne heard the horses and the men, saddling for a day of hunting. Henry was always among them. She could tell when he walked among them: their voices became soft, even as he thundered about. Every evening, near six, when the sun had made a start on its setting, she heard them return, the horses exhausted and breathing hard, Henry bellowing about what he shot or missed. He was escorted into the castle and all was quiet again. These glances through the glass windows with iron scrolls protecting her were her only glimpses of the world.

The eighth morning she sat at the table, brushing her black hair out, studying her face in the mirror. She didn't care much for the proportions or effect. The ladies of fashion had pale, powdered skin and fair hair, just as Queen Catherine had. Anne could not undo everything God had set in her, so she regarded herself with only fleeting care. She found greater pleasure in reading and sports, and neither activity required her to be beautiful.

She was still in her thin shift and had no time to cover herself when the door opened. He stood there.

"Anne."

She glared at him, once, before the view behind him drew her eye. She saw the sun was not yet too high, and the roses were all in bloom. The breeze entered, dancing past him and parading around her chamber.

"Come with me on a walk," he said.

She stood, shoving the chair back in her hurry.

He held up a hand. "You really should dress."

She ground her teeth in humiliation, keeping her eyes away from his. In court, no one was ever to look a king in the eyes, but Henry was known for his bald staring. He kept control this way, the servants said, for he watched every courtier to know their mind even before they spoke.

"Turn around," she said, meeting his eyes as she delivered the command.

He turned.

Anne slipped a petticoat on, crushing it between her knees so she could pull up the farthingale next. She yanked her bodice down after that, and noticed it was not as tight as last week. Days of anxiety in this prison had left her weak and thin. But she could walk. She would not have to talk, or listen, but she could walk in the open air. She was not altogether dressed, but there was no need to present her best self.

Within minutes, Anne was outside for the first time in eight days. She touched every new green leaf, ran her hands over every plant and along the rivers of bark running up and down the yew trees.

Henry watched her but said nothing, keeping a few paces away as she wandered through the garden, testing and inhaling the fragrances and turning her face up to the sun.

Bees swarmed the tall purple blossoms that edged the beds, and Anne could almost taste the honey that would be on the table in a few weeks. This was a spring thrown out into the world with abandon, every plant and creature catching its fever.

"Catherine's ladies say you are a witch," Henry said.

"They're fools and liars. No good Christian should listen to them," Anne retorted.

"You're a good Christian?" Henry asked.

"Yes."

"Yet you've listened to fools and liars about me, haven't you?"

"I've only listened to my sister. How do you classify her?"

Henry stopped to smell a bloom just beginning to split the green seams of its bud. He didn't answer.

"You've already taken what you wanted from my family," Anne finished. "Why must you ruin me, too? You should keep your word and send me away. Today."

"That night in the garden, what did you see?" he asked.

"If you're worried that I'll tell, I won't. Whatever troubled you can remain your secret."

"Why were my knees bloodied and my robe wet from tears, Anne? It was because I seek His will above my own. It is a lesson you could learn."

Anne frowned and took several steps ahead of him. The guards still kept their posts, following behind and lingering ahead on the path. Her Yeoman was there, and she was ashamed. She did not like being courted by a married king in front of him.

"You do not know me, Anne, and I suspect you do not know God, either. Have you wept with me as my sons have died in my arms, one after the other? I held each one and knew behind every wall in this miserable place was a man who rejoiced that I had no heir."

Anne did not want to hear of his sons. She would never soften her heart to him.

"Have you ever even prayed for me, good Christian that you are?" he asked, stopping beside her, facing her. "One day I thought, *If I am the cause for this suffering, I must amend it.* Six of my children have died, Anne."

"And? Many lose their children," Anne replied. "They do not repay God by committing grievous sins."

Henry stopped. "The Tower is overflowing with those who speak too freely."

Anne blanched and looked away.

"England will not be secure until I have an heir. Good people, Anne, good people would suffer if I died without an heir and civil war broke out for the throne. How many children would die, leaving their parents to suffer as I have? It is unbearable."

He began to walk again. Anne followed.

"I was determined to find a remedy. I read for days, taking no food or comfort until I had read every work or record pertaining to the matter. I went to the cross on my knees, bleeding and weeping for Christ's revelation."

"My king, I am sorry…."

"Anne, good Christian that you are, have you read Leviticus?"

"I know my prayers."

"Leviticus states that no man must take his brother's wife for his own, or they will die childless. It is a prophecy as sure as stone. The Pope granted a special dispensation for me to marry Catherine after her first husband, my brother, died. By doing so, the Pope has violated God's law and called down a curse on my throne. I must be free of my marriage; it has violated God's law. If I do not obey, God's wrath will break out, and England's sons will lie dead on a battlefield."

"Yet," Anne countered, "it is not a matter between us."

"It is a very great matter between us. You met me on my pilgrimage, washed my wounds, and spoke words of comfort. You were an angel sent to comfort me in that time of great distress. You were my unexpected answer, a promise to me if I will obey."

Anne knew her temper was flushing her cheeks. "I will not speak of that night, nor will I speak of the future. I will speak only on what I know today. I have not read this book of Leviticus, but I know my prayers. You have a wife. I will never consent to be a mistress."

"Perhaps you should pray about it," Henry replied, pulling out his dagger to cut a rose. He handed it to her without looking at her. "There is your family to think about."

"It is my family I think about. I will not partner with you to ruin our good name."

"I can save your name," Henry said, his voice soft and delicate with the words. "Your family has secrets. Your brother … he does not have a taste for the ladies, does he?"

Anne froze, cursing her sister silently for being so free with her body and words, letting this wolf through their door.

There were two groups who suffered vile, violent

deaths under Henry: heretics and unnatural men. It was great entertainment for the people to see such an offender hung until almost dead, then revived and tortured to death. Fear made a marvelous housekeeper for Henry, sweeping secrets neatly away and keeping a pristine order.

"My brother is not your concern, my sovereign," Anne replied steadily. "Let Your Grace consider only your servant Anne."

❊ ❊ ❊ ❊ ❊

"Henry's getting what he wants," the Scribe said to me. "How does that make you feel?"

"You already know," I replied.

"Oh, but I want you to write it down. It means so much more."

"I'm angry. Jealous. I didn't get what I wanted, and I played just as dirty as he did."

"You got what you asked for. You stole David's book."

"It wasn't good enough," I said.

"It was his best."

"No! He could have done better."

"But he didn't," the Scribe answered. "He was working on a love story for you. It can never be written now."

I closed my pen and sat back in bed. The walls, the sheets, and even bits of my chart were scribbled over with ink.

"I can't do this," I said. "I can't write this book by wrenching my heart out for your amusement."

"You are becoming a writer."

He handed me back the computer, and the words lifted and peeled away neatly from around the room, filing into the computer and appearing again on my screen.

I hated his smile.

Chapter Eight

Sir Thomas pushed back the double doors with the heavy iron hinges that guarded his private library. Rose followed, lifting each leg and setting it down with great effort, her body dead even as her stomach danced and her heart battered her ribs. Sir Thomas moved to one side to allow Rose to enter, and she saw him.

Rose began running the fingers of one hand along the walls. She had to touch the walls and know that this place had been real, that she had not dreamt this remission of suffering. She would lose it all.

Cardinal Wolsey stood, the parchment in his lap landing on the floor. He made no move to grasp it, staring at her.

"Rose, you have the extreme privilege of meeting Cardinal Wolsey. He is the highest official in all of England, whether in matters of court or church."

She couldn't move her arms. They were hanging, useless, at her sides.

"Rose." Sir Thomas prompted her.

Rose curtsied, staring too long at the little fibers in the rug, seeing flecks of the rushes Sir Thomas had carried in on his shoes and curling brown leaves from the garden. She took one last breath and lifted.

Sir Thomas was pleased; she could see it in his face.

"Cardinal Wolsey was telling me such stories that I could not believe," Sir Thomas said. "He says that the heretics have grown in numbers and fervour, infecting even the common parishes with their contagion. I myself thought these men to be more select—those rare scholars who crumple under the weight of rigorous studies, easy enough to extinguish one by one, their madness so plain that it would draw none to it. Wolsey needs my help to act."

Rose jerked her stare from the cardinal to Sir Thomas and tried to smile. She was afraid it was telling, so she stopped and cleared her throat. "How can I please you, Sir Thomas?"

"Well, tell the cardinal what you saw in church," he said and turned to Wolsey. "Rose has a heart of devotion unmatched by any noblewoman I've met. She gave everything to the church, even to the point of despairing of her life when she could not make a pilgrimage."

"Truly?" Wolsey replied.

"Go on, Rose. Did anyone ever read from the book of Hutchins? Tell us of the church you attended and if any of these madmen were about."

Rose's mind began the journey back to this story, but her mouth did not move. Her eyes remained on the floor as she saw the great spreading stain blurring her vision, turning even this peaceful refuge an angry red.

Long ago, he had lain there, troubling Rose with much talk. There was no place in his world for her class, and she resented him always drawing her in, prattering on every time about delicate troubles she would never be graced with. She wanted to stab him on mornings like this, when he arrived dejected, annoyed to be left alone for the day, annoyed that his name was always second on everyone's tongues, annoyed that the king's salt was moved out of his reach. He was like a child who needed constant kisses and plucky encouragements. Despite herself, she gave them both. She did not mind that the words rang false. They were, but he paid better when he was happy.

Her own troubles, what could she say of them? When her two little brothers took ill with the sweats, she begged his help, and he gave it. He arranged for them to be declared orphans and put into the king's charity hospital. They died before the week was out. She only knew they were dead when she saw another boy wearing their clothes. Her mother had been such a poor weaver that her work stood out, even among the pitiful. Her grief was like a mouth full of pebbles. She was dry and brittle from the choking dust of lost hope, and she had no tears. His petulant stories became a distraction, and his body a refuge.

"You can't live on the streets. You'll lose your looks within a year." The outbreak of sweats had alarmed him, she could tell. He swept his quill across a dry parchment, and she was established in an apartment. He saved her. She never saw her home again and remained indoors, waiting for him to return. She began to listen for the noises from the street, hearing her past through the filter of his money, which paid for these walls. It sounded so different to her. She was different. She was dead too.

He had other wives. She could tell their strident perfumes apart from the beckoning aromas of the court: the lavender sprinkled over the rushes, the breads rising on stone slabs in the open kitchens. She wondered how they all lived, which one he loved. Not that it mattered.

She rolled over with a sigh as he prattled. She was wedged tightly between the two worlds in London and wanted neither side as her own. The restlessness this fine and fancy man unburdened stayed with her, growing with every soft-spoken confession. She had given him no mercy, lying there in silence, making no move to invite his own sorrows to roost and tarry. But they had. The great crowing hunger pecked at her until she did what was once inconceivable.

She went to church. London was the city of God, he had told her, and it was true. Bells rang out at Mass when the host was elevated, choral chants floated through the streets, monks and priests milled about everywhere. Rose had never entered this world. Before this time, it had belonged to others … not to her. And why would she choose to be anchored to anything in this world? From her first cry as a baby she had awakened to hunger. Nothing ever satisfied. Life was a continual torment.

The cold cobbled path led her to two enormous

wood doors overlaid with iron bars and creeping ivy that
ate away at the wood and stone.

The world inside took her breath away. The ceiling
rose far above her. Towering beams of darkest timber
lined the ceiling, making a high sharp vault, with so
much air between her and the roof … air she couldn't
breathe. Jesus hung crucified above the altar, above it all,
and she averted her eyes from His shameful nakedness.
He was barely covered by a loose cloth, His frail body
bleeding and pierced.

He looked so weak. What right had she to lay her
burdens on Him as well? He looked to be a man who
needed mercy and salvation from men, not one who was
their only hope. Why had no one in this place saved
Him? How had they walked before Him every day, asking and pleading for little favours, while He hung there
in agony? Would it be so hard to bring Him down and
dress the wounds? His bleeding body disgusted her.

She looked away and saw Him alive, calling to His
disciples in a boat floating forever on a sea of cut glass.
In another window she saw Him standing with a great
book in His hand, the other hand extended to her. In
yet another He offered a chalice to men gathered at
a table—men eager to take anything He offered. To
turn in any direction in this place was to see that His
calling, His book, His cup, all pointed finally to this
brutal death. The gold and the damask, the linens and
silk were only a bright veneer that distracted from His
low, bloody end.

There was no glory in death. She knew it too intimately to be in awe of it: The weeping without comfort
when all were asleep; the stains that drew the flies;

the bitter stench and seeping ulcers that ridiculed the delight in young flesh, until one was heaped into a dark pit and forgotten. Every man met this fate, with or without God. She was here because she wanted something besides hunger and death.

She turned away.

A priest entered at that moment from a door at the back of the church and saw her dress, dirtied from wandering in the street, and her hands on the doors, ready to flee. He stood still. She saw his eyes move to her sleeves, and follow the curve of her frame, and she realized he understood her to be here for thieving, not mercy. If the authorities found her coin purse, it would be his word that sent her to a prison where she would die slowly, in ways that would make her wish for the briefer agony of a crucifixion.

From the corner of her eye she knew Christ held the chalice to her, too, and she sank to her knees in fear.

"I come to receive the Lord!" she cried out.

⚜

He attended to the candles burning at the altar, trimming the wicks as darkness fell outside.

"I am Father Grimbald," he said and gestured for her to retreat into the curtained box along the far wall on her right.

When he slid into the booth, pulling back the scalloped partition, she could not stop the flow of words that rushed out. It began as fear that he would not believe her and would still call the sheriff, but it swept through to the truth before she had her second gulp of air. She had thought the guilt was buried deep within, but it was at the surface … like a grime she skimmed from her heart, working faster and faster. He had listened in silence, but it was not the silence she had known and used herself. It encouraged her to go on, to root out every wicked, soiled thing, until she was purged.

There were many paths to this redemption she sought, he told her, but she did not have the money for a great pilgrimage, or for prayers to be said on her behalf. This was understandable. Perhaps she had only to show kindness to His servants and refrain from selling herself again, and the guilt would not return. She was a beautiful girl, he said, and she did not have to live this life in such misery.

When she stepped out, she wiped the last of the tears from her face and wept again. She was determined. She could sell scraps of wool that fell from the wagons, or find employ as a dyer of wool, or even a shearer.

Grimbald emerged from the confessional, touching her shoulder from behind. He turned her gently, and she saw his face in the candlelight. He was older than she, but not by many years. His mouth was full and his eyebrows dark and heavy, so that his small eyes were almost lost. Yet he was not unpleasant to look on, though she had spent her life turning her face away from the men who held her.

"You brought no coins to offer for the confession?" he asked.

"No," she lied. She needed every coin in her purse to eat and sleep safely off the streets tonight. If it turned cold again and froze, those coins could well keep her alive.

"I cannot let you go without payment. It is law." He reached to her hip and patted it before she could swat his hand away. He had heard the noise her pocket made. "You have stolen from the church, receiving confession with no payment."

"I cannot give you any coins," she said.

He dropped his hands and took a step back, his face setting into hard lines as he turned on a heel to walk. She knew where he would go. She reached for his hand and stopped him, then drew it slowly to her face, kissing it.

"What have I that pleases you? Take that," she said.

What roosted next in her heart was a grief so unbearable it had no name.

Later, when she hesitated to die on a rain-soaked, twisted path, she watched him hound to hell one good man already long dead. She knew then she had no hope for peace, even in death. She was of those who are forever cursed. The hope of redemption was gone and she ran to meet her death. The searing iron strength of the grace that saved her gave her hope for her son.

She remembered her newborn child, his breath shallow, his chest moving in and out in flurries of raspy gulps. He would not live to see his first sunrise. She had little money, only what the local women had helped her earn by sending her out on errands for merchants. Wolsey had thrown her into the street when he had discovered her secret. He had other wives to comfort him in his tribulations at court; he did not want one who brought her own troubles. He took vengeance on Grimbald as well; the man was driven from his parish with blows and scourges.

She held her head straight ahead as she walked in the street and still wore a ribbon in her hair, even when she hadn't eaten for days. But she was terrified. A seamstress admired her blue silk dress, mistaking her for a woman of quality, and had allowed her to sleep on the floor of her shop, but the miserable work piecing pearls on gowns could not feed two mouths, nor drive away the wet, fevered coughs that claimed so many children here.

The child needed a baptism and a doctor. The doctor could bring medicine, but she would not have the money for this and his baptism. Purgatory was a danger more real to her than death. She had lived in purgatory; she could not sentence her son to an eternity there.

She watched the baby breathe. His eyes were closed, the lashes dark little tendrils that nearly touched his cheeks. His fingers were impossibly small and perfect. She kissed him and held him against her breasts, rocking him as she draped her robe around them both. His flesh was so sweet and soft and new. She would not let him go even as death, a tender, shadowed nurse, came gently for him.

"Please," she whispered, "a little more time. I must find a priest." She sensed Death pause for her, and though it was near, she was not afraid. She called for a neighbour, and when the woman poked her head through the thin curtain sheltering Rose from the others, Rose told her to find the priest.

The baby's movements grew less frequent. When

the priest came, she held the baby firmly in her arms for the baptism. Then she had slept, feeling strong arms encircling them both, pressing them together so she could not separate the baby's heart from hers. She never felt it cease, only that it joined hers and beat on and on. She had held him until their hearts and breath aligned, his growing fainter and freer. She knew the instant his soul had flown away like a little bird in winter. She did not know if she had dreamed this.

This is why Christ hung there and never came down, she thought. He hung in agony so that those in grief could not accuse Him of less. He hung, rent open, and men were comforted by the sight. In this bitter life, who could love a God who did not suffer?

She hoped she would never see Wolsey again, or Grimbald, or the inside of a church. She was done with men and their God.

Rose realized Sir Thomas's foot was tapping. These memories fled, and she faced the men as if she had forgotten it all. "Madmen?" she answered. "Yes, there were madmen. And sinners and thieves. The church welcomed them all. This is what I saw."

She didn't know why she said it. Wolsey's face, hard-set and ready to defend himself against the truth, softened into the face she had once glimpsed and dared to hope in. He smiled at her, and she knew, the way women who have given themselves do, that he desperately wanted a smile in return.

"Sir Thomas has given you a chance for a new life,"

he said to her. "May his name be praised. I pray you, make good use of it."

"Yes, but Rose," More continued, his thoughts plainly too far away to see what was happening in his study. "Were there any heretics among you? Those who read Hutchins?"

Rose held Wolsey's gaze.

"Yes."

She didn't know why she had done that. Was she a weak woman, or a fool? Later she wanted that moment back, wanted to crush Wolsey with her words, wanted to scream her truth and hear the words out loud.

But she knew the truth. She wanted this new life more than she wanted revenge for the old. She wanted another chance, and she feared her only way to get it was to give one to Wolsey, too. She prayed, the second surprise of the day.

Jesus.

It was the only word she knew, the only word not spoken in Latin in the Masses she had attended. *I cannot stop sinning,* she prayed. *I just sinned to buy grace. I let my son die to buy him grace. I let my brothers die to find them a cure. Everywhere, grace and redemption are soiled by my hands. Help me. Help me stop.*

The next morning she sat on her bed looking out the window. It was late in the morning, but water still beaded on the panes, making her crane her neck to catch sight of the trees below. Though it was the end of April, winter and spring still wrestled for the trees. Green leaves had unfolded on all the trees, and only a few had dead brown branches—the stragglers that the last frost had bitten. There were several boulders placed below the trees in her view. She wondered how the men had moved them all into place, for they were large and rough-edged. Moss and green tendrils grew up all around them, content that the boulders would be unmovable features of their world.

A knock at Rose's door made her jerk, and she grabbed her skirt to be sure she was modestly covered, with no calve or ankle showing.

"Margaret!" she exclaimed, opening her arms as the girl walked in. She was a sweet sight after a night of tears. Margaret rested in Rose's arms for a moment as Rose inhaled the scent of her hair, powdered and perfumed with roses. Rose relaxed in the softness of the girl, her warm, steady breath, and was surprised love was again in her heart. It had been gone for years and its return made her laugh out loud.

Margaret pushed away, her face serious. "Who does Father whip at the gatehouse?"

"What?" Rose asked.

"I saw him. There is another man at the gatehouse. He was whipped last night, lashed to Father's Tree of Truth. Did you not hear his cries to God?"

Rose shook her head. She had heard only her own. She wondered who God would answer first. "Has it happened before?" she asked.

"Sometimes. Father says it is a great mercy, for if he turned the men over to Wolsey, they'd be racked. At least here their punishment is over swiftly, and they have much time to recant. Father thinks everyone will worship properly again if they can be broken first."

The prisons she had seen in Southwark were visions of hell. A whipping here would end; those who entered the gates of a prison were lost forever. Only a gravecloth was ever returned, and this went to the priest as payment for his final services. Guards stole the boots and cloaks.

"I don't understand, Margaret. What is their crime?"

Margaret sat next to her on the bed. "Can you keep a secret?"

"Yes," Rose replied.

"They are guilty of reading a book, that's all. A book by a man named Hutchins. Father knew him. He even visited us the summer that Mother died. Hutchins believed every person could approach God and know Him intimately. Father said God could make no sense to the average man. We must be led by wiser men."

"If they are being whipped for reading it, it is no secret," Rose replied.

Margaret squirmed, biting at her cheek.

Rose frowned and reached to assure Margaret, but Margaret pulled away. "Margaret, what is the real secret?"

Margaret grew still and set her face in a cold frown. "I am a little bit afraid, although he promises to keep me safe."

"Margaret!" Rose shook her. "What is your secret?"

"He is like Father in many ways, you know. Father hates him, but he does not know him like I do. The book is superb, Rose. It will open your eyes. You'll never think of God the same way again."

Rose's stomach turned. She had smelled death when she had first cracked open the spine of a book.

She wondered what man would be so bold—or so careless—as to leave such a record of his thoughts and heart so that any man, anywhere, could know them. To see a book open was to see a shield laid down. It made no sense to Rose why anyone would wish to be exposed to their enemies this way. If men could see what was in the heart of the world, they would leave the books closed and the inkwells dry.

Rose jumped from the bed and grabbed the horn-book from her table. Racing into Margaret's room, she began pulling as many books from the shelves as she could, lifting her skirts to carry them in. She ran to the family room, throwing them into the fireplace, which roared and sprang up, nearly catching the edge of her skirts as she worked. Margaret screamed when she saw what Rose was doing, and the children came running, Sir Thomas just behind them. The fire was blazing out, high and hungry, when Sir Thomas pinned Rose's arms to her sides, dragging her back from the flames. A book fell from the fire, its pages lined in burning red, sparks biting along its edges as it smoked.

"What are you doing?" he demanded.

Margaret was crying. Rose looked around at the children and the other servants, all staring at her with furrowed brows and deep, angry frowns.

"All of you, to your rooms," he ordered.

Alone, he stared at her but did not release his grip. She didn't want him to; she wanted to be shaken from her fear, her dread broken by his hands.

"It is the books, Sir Thomas," Rose began. "A man in your gatehouse is paying in blood for this man Hutchins, and your own children are curious about the book! I burned these books, and I would burn more, if it can save the children from their influence! They must not be tempted by the world beyond this one."

She didn't notice his crushing grip on her arms; it would be only later she would see the bruising. His face was so near hers that his breath washed over her neck and bodice. She had been overpowered by men in a life that was far away. She had never been forced to stillness at that moment so that a man could see what was in her eyes.

"You are salvation to me," she whispered.

For a long moment they stared at each other, his heart beating through his doublet, the heat of his body touching hers. He was pulling her closer in so that she was pressed against him, the distances between them being sealed off and forgotten.

Her knees were weak, but she did not fall; his grip on her was too tight. She stopped trying to stand on her own and let him take her weight, lifting her face to kiss him on the mouth. She needed this kiss, needed to be taken hold of and firmly fixed in his world of grace. She could see his lips parting as he leaned down, and she closed her eyes.

Then Sir Thomas shoved her away, a push so fierce it landed her on the floor. He did not look down as he left the room.

Rose didn't move from her bed, not for supper or evening prayers. No one came to fetch her. She watched as the red sunset faded through the garden and she could no longer see the trees that danced in the night breeze. Only the birds, still singing, were oblivious to the boundaries of More's home. She wondered what they had seen today in London. Had they seen madmen and lost women, or mothers whose arms were as empty as their stomachs? Where would they go when they left here? She hoped they would fly to the bosom of God and tell. She wished she could follow, but she saw the world and doubted God would receive her. She stank of it.

How long she lay in this position, curled into a ball, her face towards the garden, she did not know. In total darkness a noise had stirred her mind and she awoke.

It was a dull keening, the soft groaning of a man. The hairs on her arm lifted, and Rose closed her eyes, listening hard to know where the sound came from. It was somewhere beyond her room, beyond perhaps the walls of the house. She eased her feet off the bed and pried the door back, careful to make no noise. As she crept down the hall, she saw that everyone was asleep and in several rooms the candles had burned out. The servants snored like drunks; Rose did not doubt a few of them kept refreshments under their mattresses for lonely nights such as this.

Rose crossed through the servants' wing and peered down the hall that would lead her to the children, but it was as dark and quiet as a closet. She went down the stairs next and peered into Sir Thomas's study. It was empty. A candle burned before an open book, and a crucifix hung on the wall above his desk. In the shadows it appeared as if Christ moved upon His cross, and Rose fled the room. There was no movement or noise on this floor, so she looked at the heavy double doors leading to the garden, a side entrance for the household. She was debating the wisdom of leaving the house on a dark night, just after a man had been whipped there, but she saw she would not be the first to do so. One door stood slightly back from the other, not having been closed all the way after someone's exit. She took a deep silent breath and decided.

The door slid quietly, but the cold air that met her made her gasp. She hunched down, drawing herself in tightly, and stepped out into the garden. The dull keening continued but sounded wet, and there were not so many moans.

She followed the path down through the gardens, the rows and plots of plants marked into squares, each for its own kind, going farther down the path until the house was nearly out of her sight. The voice grew louder, and she heard whispers of Latin, a man's pleas punctuated by a long cry for mercy. This word, *mercy,* was the only one she knew, for it was the only one in English. She held her breath, waiting for the last cry, which would surely be a wail of death. The dull pounding continued.

"I have made a covenant with mine eyes!" he cried out, his teeth grinding down on the last two words as a bolt of pain hit.

Rose crept a few more paces, keeping to the side of the path, shrinking into the shadow as best she could, willing herself to make no noise no matter what she should see. As she came around one last curve, she saw the Tree of Truth. A man was beneath it, with a heavy stone in his hand, and a scourging whip in the other. In the moonlight, he glistened. It was the black glistening of blood. Stepping closer, she knew him.

It was Sir Thomas.

She stumbled back, her steps making the stones of the path scratch together.

Sir Thomas stopped and stared into the darkness. "Who goes there?"

Rose held her breath, mouthing a silent prayer that she would not be discovered.

A rabbit jumped from behind a tree in between them and ran down past the gatehouse. Sir Thomas watched it go, and Rose watched him. He exhaled and raised his scourge again. Rose was more careful with her next steps and made it back to her room undiscovered. She eased the door closed and hung her head.

She lay on her bed but could not face the garden, for she knew another of its secrets. Instead, restless, she turned to face the door, her mind exhausting itself of what might happen next. She could be thrown out or demoted to tending animals instead of children. She would certainly lose Margaret's affection, and Margaret was a girl thirsty for affection. What would happen to the girl if Rose was thrown out?

There were so many worries and visions that Rose could not tend to them all before sleep found her. It was a deep and dreamless sleep, and when she awoke, unsettled and unsafe, sleep having done nothing to put distance between her and her fears.

She noticed her door was ajar. She rose and shut it. Perhaps it had swung open of its own accord, a breeze from an open window somewhere doing this.

There was no breeze in the house. She opened it again, perplexed, and stepped into the hall to see if anyone had been there. Perhaps another servant had been trying to summon her to breakfast. The hall was empty. She heard the other servants just beginning to stir.

A pebble on the wooden plank floor caught her eye. Bending to pick it up, she saw that it smeared in her hands. The stain was rust coloured, a stitch of bright red breaking through.

Chapter Nine

"Show me Germany," Margaret asked again, shoving the map once more to Rose. Rose had no more idea about Germany than the moon, and she lost her patience.

"Goodness and mercy, but you're restless," Rose chided. "Set about another lesson."

Their lives had resumed as if nothing had happened. Sir Thomas replaced the lost books, and the children found it amusing that Rose had burnt books on proper cookery and gardening. Rose had worked harder on her own lessons.

Margaret pulled the map to her chest and sighed. She showed no signs of working.

"What is it about Germany?" Rose whispered. "Why are you pulling a face like a moonstruck calf? Here. The English love stories, the Germans love beer, and the French love anything in a skirt. There. I've just explained the world. Quit wondering about it."

Margaret, still clutching the map, leaned in to Rose.

The other children looked up from their work, and their tutor switched them with a feather. He was teaching the youngest to count money, and each child had a stack of coins in front of him, to practice counting and making change.

"Margaret!" the tutor called. "Let the servants alone and finish your work!"

Margaret blushed and set her mouth in that firm way of her father's. "I'm going to my room to lie down. I'm not up to my lessons today."

Rose watched as Margaret stood and marched out, her soft shoes not yet having their wooden heels strapped on for the garden walk to follow the morning work. Margaret stopped only to kiss her little brother John on the head and wrap her arms around him for a quick hug. He giggled and pushed her away.

Seeing there was to be no further dramatics, Cicely, Elizabeth, and John returned to their work as their tutor, Candice, watched. They enjoyed the routine and never made a peep as they sifted through books upon books upon papers and lessons. Only Margaret was unwilling to devote all her mind to the work. She scored brilliantly on her tests, and the tutors marked this as progress, but Rose could see there was nothing in this class that held her attention. Something was speaking to her, stirring her, and Rose knew its name.

She followed Margaret's exit with her own, making sure to close the door behind her so that no eyes would be on her. She crept from the study room, past More's empty office, through the family sitting room, looking for Margaret but not seeing her. She moved on towards Margaret's bedroom.

The door was cracked open. Rose pressed against the wall and slid closer to the opening, leaning her head in to get a sly view. Margaret was standing with her back to the door, her hand in her skirt's pocket. She pulled something out and crouched on the floor. Sliding her arm deep under her feather mattress, she began pulling back, and Rose could hear a familiar crackle. Margaret had been hiding a leather pouch under her mattress and it contained papers. She removed a sheet, a feather, and set to work. She placed the paper on the bed and grabbed a tiny well of ink from her night table. Her hand was fast and skilled, scratching out the words without careful deliberation. Dropping a few coins into the center of the paper, she folded it, again and again, until it was a tight parcel. She slipped it between her bosom and her bodice.

"I did not!"

John protested so loudly to the tutor that his words reached Margaret's room. Rose stiffened against the wall as Margaret spun to face the door.

"You counted wrong! You gave me less than the girls!"

Margaret laughed, a nervous laugh.

Rose shook her head. Whatever mischief Margaret dreamed of, it was in Germany and she was stealing for it.

Rose wondered if she dared confront Margaret. She was probably taken with a soldier she had seen in town who was traveling in Germany on some errand for Sir Thomas or the king. Or a past tutor who had moved on when his commission for More was finished. But what harm could come from a boy so far away, Rose thought, when Sir Thomas locked his daughters away behind three guard houses and acres of protected gardens. Even the squirrels only got in by More's grace.

The thought took her breath for a moment. More knew the world as she did. He would never know the role she had played, but he knew what was beyond his home. He had built these walls, not to keep his children in, but to keep this world out. And he had brought her in, brought her here, to save her from it. What puzzled Rose was that he required nothing for it. Even her body, freely offered, was rejected.

"Rose."

His voice startled her and she cried out, stupidly, she thought.

Margaret was at her door in a flash and the pair stared at her, father and daughter.

Rose touched the cross on her neck and gathered her wits. "I was coming to check on Margaret. She was unwell during morning lessons."

Margaret glared at her, then softened her face to smile at her father. Rose noted how she shifted a bit, as if something were poking her in her bodice.

"I did leave morning lessons, Father, forgive me. I must have spent too long in the garden yesterday and the sun was too much. Summer is coming early, I should think. The falcons were restless to fly. It would have been good if you had joined us."

Sir Thomas spoke to Rose but did not look at her. He had not looked at her since that night she had burned the books. She saw that there was a stain creeping above his doublet vest, turning his linen undershirt a dark red colour. She could say nothing.

"Well, Margaret, take your rest this afternoon but join us for evensong prayers. And you, Rose, take care not to go creeping down these halls unannounced, even if your intentions are pure."

Rose walked heavily back to the servants' wing, her shoulders feeling like two great hands were pressing down, driving the sorrows into her frame and expelling lighter breaths.

She thought of her son ... his sweet soft skin, the pursed lips that moved as he slept. God was right to have taken him from her. All she could do was pray that her offering had bought his freedom from purgatory. That when she died, she would have no fear to meet him. She had wanted salvation for her son. She had purchased it with what she had, but she had never known how far above her Christ hung. She could not reach Him. All of her troubles—were they not of her own making? Here she was in this place of second chances, of unending devotion, where prayers and matins were said morning and night and she was given children to love, and she was making a wretched mess of it. Death was stealing in, she was sure. It had found her here, too, and was stealing in on the pages of a book, leering at her in her dreams.

She passed his office and drew herself up, taking a deep breath. She could be worthy of salvation herself if only she tried. She could wash the past off and please Sir Thomas. She would stop death from claiming anyone else she loved.

As she passed, she heard a man's voice peppering Sir Thomas with spicy words and invective.

"I swear this is it! Our moment! The printer's men were dead drunk, drowning in their barrels, they were, and our wolf spared no expense to keep them in their cups all night until at last one talked. Hutchins has completed the diabolical work, and it's on its way to our shores! We've had only scraps of it until now. When the whole thing is here, chaos will destroy the city!"

Rose heard Sir Thomas make a gruff noise. The man rose to his own defense.

"But I ain't lying! This time we've got him! The printers are working night and day to set up the presses, and Hutchins hovers over them like a fussy nursemaid pecking at a new babe. And this time, it's not just one chapter. It's the whole thing!"

Rose knew she shouldn't stop at this door and listen.

"How will it come into the country?" Sir Thomas asked.

"Aye, the usual way. New book, same tricks. They'll smuggle it in at the ports, each bundle marked with a blue cloth tied around it. Thomas … we can bring him in before the damage is done."

"All right. Give the order to raid the printer's shop. Confiscate everything. I doubt your men can read, so I don't want them choosing what it is that I want. Confiscate the presses, the dyes, the letters, the papers, and above all else, get me Hutchins."

"Alive?"

There was a silence, and the hairs on Rose's neck began to rise.

"Aye, alive. He should die in full view of the English

people. A fire consuming the flesh is a mercy to these types, purging them of their sin before they meet the Almighty, who will show them so much less grace. And perchance his miserable screaming death will save a good citizen from ruin. The commonwealth does not know the pestilence this man brings. It will be my honour to save them from it."

A hand on Rose's arm made her jump, but another shot out and clasped itself on her mouth. Rose spun and saw Margaret. Margaret released her, motioning for silence, and fled to the garden.

❧

"What is it they said?" Margaret demanded.

"What were you doing in the hall?" Rose asked.

"Oh, pox! What is it they said?"

The air was chilly, a late-morning rain still playing on the extravagantly green leaves, and Rose frowned. The wind blew raindrops into her face.

"If I tell you, can we go inside?" Rose replied.

Margaret nodded and leaned in. Seeing her father exit the house with a man dressed in the red livery of a law clerk, she wrapped her arm through Rose's and pretended to stroll about. Neither man paid them notice though the rain grew heavier.

"There is to be a raid on a printer's press, and Hutchins is going to be captured alive, to be brought here for burning."

Margaret chewed her lips. "All right" was all she said as she released Rose's arm and turned to run back to the house.

Rose caught her. "What's going on?"

"Go back to your quarters, Rose. This does not concern you. It is simply his work, and you should see to yours."

Rose pressed in close to her, looking down with a stern grimace. "You are my work. Something is going on which I suspect your father would be displeased by. You're young and stupid. There is nothing beyond those walls that you want, Margaret."

Margaret looked pale. "Whatever you think you know, Rose, keep it to yourself, I beg you. My father could be ruined."

"What on earth are you up to that could ruin him?"

Margaret wouldn't answer. She turned her attention to her shoes, wiggling her toes and watching them in earnest.

"All right," Rose finished. "I'll not say a word on one condition."

Margaret looked at her.

"Move me to your bedroom. I'll sleep on the trundle."

Margaret started to protest, but Rose waved her off. "Servants know how to give orders too. I am decided in this. You need to be watched. And Margaret, I have mastered my letters. I want to read everything you touch: every book, every letter."

Margaret went limp, her mouth opening as she pointed beyond Rose. "It's the queen!"

❀ ❀ ❀ ❀ ❀

I shook my hands out. "I agreed to take down one story, not two. What are you trying to do, kill me?"

"There is only one story," he said.

The joke was lost on him.

"Why Anne Boleyn?" I asked. "Everyone and their brother has written an Anne Boleyn story. You might be a great angel, but you'd starve as a writer."

He paid no mind. "There are angels in England. The air in London is thick with them in this age. It is they who move the women into place, who move about positioning the players so that His will may be done."

I frowned. "Thank you for giving me my computer back."

"Yours?" he asked.

I blushed.

"I forgot how easily you forget what is stolen."

My face went pale; the fear and dread made my head swim. I didn't want to live to see tomorrow.

"You are afraid?" he asked.

I nodded.

"Do not be afraid for the women in our stories, though the pageantry is about to turn bloody and wild. Angels with drawn swords will shepherd them across this stage."

I had no idea what he meant. But I knew he couldn't read my mind, which surprised me. I called him fat in my head.

"Who was William Hutchins?" he asked me, in a tone that said he did not expect an answer. "What is the rock they break themselves upon?"

I shook my head.

Chapter Ten

May had by now faded and was being daily persuaded to give way to summer. The sun stretched its rays further and stronger, like a thousand lances determined to strike a strong blow and leave a red mark. The sun was the only challenge to his glory that Henry could not conquer, Anne thought with a wry smile.

He caught her smile and laughed. "How do I amuse you, mistress?"

"I am not your mistress! Nor your wife!" Anne yelled, being careful to keep the reins in hand. This horse was much different than the courser she had in France. She did not care for his churlish temper.

"For a good Christian, you have little faith!"

Henry motioned to his privy guard to hand him a pike, which the boy did with great trouble, being similarly mounted just beside Henry. Henry took the long weapon and dealt Anne's horse a glancing blow on the rump. The animal ran with great spirit, and Anne cursed this king who was determined to spur her from comfort.

She pulled tightly on the reins, careful not to unseat herself, with her thick bodice and train making any movement difficult. At least Catherine and her court were not on this procession to see her humiliation. Henry spoke out loud as if intimacies had passed between them. Anne hated the taint it bore her, the dirty feeling in her spirit that anyone would think she was unfaithful to Lord Percy or to her Christian duty. Yet what could she say? Henry was master of the realm, and every knee bowed in reverence, making him wholly incapable of understanding anyone else.

"Au premier, L' Pleazaunce!" she heard him call behind her, and as her horse steadied and slowed, taking a turn in the road, she beheld it: Greenwich Castle, "the pleasant manor," as Henry called it. Indeed, it was different than his castle at Windsor. Windsor was a grand lady that impressed every visitor with the weight of her history, like a grandmother pouring an old, heavy necklace into the palm of a young girl.

Greenwich was much freer. There were many small buildings, but their charm was not their construction, for they each had small angled eaves and only a few rose above them with spires. But there was an endless army of trees, decked in green and glittering with birds, whose songs filled the air as the royal party entered, her train being lifted by a gentle breeze as she dismounted. Her servants jumped from their horses to assist her, lest the king order them lashed, but she was faster than they

were and was off her mount and walking about before
they even reached her.

Anne was immediately surrounded by great, tall
magical yews and thick, full, long-suffering beeches.
Peace lived here; she knew it.

Henry had dismounted and joined her. His face
beamed with great pride and appetite. Anne sensed he
was hungry after this ride. She hoped he would restrain
himself to merely his appetite for victuals. She hadn't the
energy to stay awake through the night and keep watch
over her door to prevent his entry yet again.

"The palace sits on the River Thames," he said,
motioning beyond the cluster of red brick-and-plaster
buildings. "When the tide turns every seven hours or so,
you can catch a barge to any other estate."

Wolsey was not far behind them. "Yes, Henry was
born here ... his mother's most perfect consolation after
a hard and difficult labor."

"Yes." Henry nodded, but to Anne, not Wolsey. "It
is the home of many revelries. I am a king of the people,
am I not? All comers are welcome here for jousts, if they
do not mind a sore stripe and broken lance!"

Why was everything directed at her? Anne grum-
bled inwardly. Did she want these prizes? He went to
great trouble to present her with these affections, but
they were unwholesome. Any move she made only
encouraged. To protest gave him license to overcome her
disdain. Heaven forbid she praise him, for there'd be no
end to his great leapings and posturings.

She had found no way yet to dissuade him in his
attentions, to allow her to return to Percy. She reached
in her pocket and patted her prayer beads. They were

there, as always. She had rubbed them through her fingers so often these last weeks that she feared one day she would reach into her pocket and they would crumble beneath her touch. No prayer beads were meant to withstand this much use, she was sure. When she was alone, she sank to her knees and said her prayers aloud, and when she was attended, she kept the beads in her pocket and said them silently. Once she had fallen asleep in her bed, saying her prayers, and was awakened when the beads hit the floor. She had sat upright in bed and saw a sudden fluttering of the curtains drawn closed around her bed.

⚜

"Leave us!" Henry bellowed, and the attendants fled back to their mounts.

"Wolsey, you as well," Henry said. Wolsey bowed and fell back.

Henry grasped her hand and tried to lean against a trunk, but Anne's head began to ache. She thought it was the strong sunlight so she moved deeper in the shadows, the woods that surrounded the palace grounds. She hoped Henry would notice her discomfort and not take this retreat into shadow as a sign of encouragement.

The earth was so soft under her feet and, unsteady after a hard ride, she leaned into his grasp ... then wished she hadn't. Henry slipped his arm around her side, dropping her hand, glad to have reason to touch more of her. The birds still sang, and there were so many varieties here that their trilling overlapped and wove together a song unique to this place.

"Everyone in the court observes the order I set," Henry said. "How many dishes they may eat, and when, and where they may sit, where they may stand, and what clothes they may wear, what they may say and when."

Anne continued her walk. It was misery. She wanted a still bed and a dark room.

"Only here do I know what it is to be a subject. How small I am against this king." Perhaps he meant it to affect righteousness, but he sounded depressed, as if he would rule this world too if he could.

Anne bit her lip and kept walking.

"Anne," he said, pulling against her, stopping her in the path.

She turned to look at him, and his face was that of a boy, lit with desire for some great prize. She noticed her stomach had turned sour and didn't know if her head or her sovereign was to blame.

"Anne, I am your servant too." He pulled a velvet drawstring from the pocket of his cloak and reached for her hand. She held it there stupidly, confused why this monarch would abase himself before her, when her sober judgment of him was so plainly spoken between them. But men had lost their lives for scorning his charity. She would at least not make their mistake.

He loosened the sack and dropped a fat green emerald ring into his palm before lifting it to set it on her ring finger on the right hand. It was a square-cut emerald, as big as a walnut. It weighed her hand down.

"Henry, I cannot accept this." She took hold of the ring to pull it off. "This gift belongs to your wife, not me."

His shoulders fell and he looked away from her. Shaking his head, he walked off a few paces. "Is there no one at this court who believes in me?" he muttered. "Anne, you have read the papers I delivered?"

"Of course," she lied. These were endless technical papers drawn up by lawyers attesting that his marriage to Catherine was invalid.

"There can be no greater danger than a monarch ruling in dishonour. When I die, civil war would break out, a hundred different nobles claiming the throne for themselves. And who would die, Anne? Is it not the poorest, who send their sons into service when the grain gets low?"

"You have a daughter from Catherine to rule England when you're gone," Anne reminded him.

"What woman could rule England?" Henry bellowed.

"What does Queen Catherine say to the papers?"

He shrugged, coming back to her and taking her hands. "She will not read the papers, but she knows my intention. She will woo me back, or turn everyone against me."

Anne tried to pull her hands out from his but he drew her closer yet. She was crushed against his chest, his arms wrapping around her waist, with her looking up at him, the sunlight burnishing his red hair and making his eyes glisten like embers.

"I will not be won. Only, do not abandon me, Anne. Swear it. Swear allegiance to your king."

"Do not say that, my lord," she whispered.

He crushed her tighter. "Swear allegiance to your king!"

"I swear my allegiance," she said under her breath, thinking the pressure would cause her to black out.

She could smell his robes, anointed with cinnamon oil and spices, as the heavy gold and jeweled chain around his shoulders crushed into her skin. The shining hurt her eyes, and the world spun. She let him take more of her weight.

"Wolsey, More, the men of the Star Chamber, they would choose tranquility with her over my conscience," he said. "I am suffering, but do you see me complaining in the streets? No. As a man, I do not matter. I do not exist. It is as king that I must act, and I must do what is right."

"As must I," she said, finally pushing him away. "I cannot lie with you. I cannot receive your gifts. You must not try to persuade me again. Let me return to the court and marry Lord Percy."

He looked stung, but the look deepened as if the venom found a quick vein. "Lord Percy does not wait for you. He married another last week, did you not hear? A woman of excellent name."

Anne gasped, her mouth hanging foolishly. She prayed she would not cry in front of him and bit her lip.

"I have brought you to my table, Anne, and given you a brace of cards. Whether you lose or win is your decision, but you are in the game. And you *will* wear that," he said, pointing to the ring.

They walked back out into the sunlight, Anne clutching him harder. Her legs were weakening, and she had no energy to support her throbbing head. The guards and courtiers all averted their eyes. Wolsey walked to them.

Henry grabbed her hand and presented it, with the fat emerald upon it.

Wolsey's mouth puckered. "Well."

Henry burst out laughing. "*Well*," he mimicked.

"You will not be dissuaded? You know the type of woman she is. You know what she brought into your courts," Wolsey said with a shake of his head.

Henry bowed to her, a great embarrassment in front of the malicious court, and began his walk into the palace.

Wolsey began to follow him, but Anne grabbed his hand. It was cool in comparison to her own. Wolsey's eyes narrowed, and he shook himself free.

"Please, Cardinal," Anne said, "this is not my work."

"What do you want from me, Anne? You have more influence with the king than I in this matter."

"No! You have more influence," she replied. "And you have the Pope's ear."

He studied her. "I thought you did not want to be a queen."

"I do not want to be a mistress! Only you can protect his name, and mine."

Wolsey looked at her, his eyes watery and soft in the bright sun. He had a kind face, Anne thought, too kind for this work. This was not the age for men of compassion.

"You have shown yourself as an enemy of the realm, Anne. In time Henry will see it too. This is a prophecy as certain as anything in that black book you secreted away in your trunk."

He took his leave of her without another word, and

Anne was left alone while yet surrounded by courtiers and guards who did not speak to her as they moved past. She waited for her attendant to find her and show her which room at Greenwich was to be hers and tried to keep from crying in front of any of them. She bit down on the inside of her cheek and clenched her lips together.

The sun bore down strangely, and sweat beaded along her lip and down between her breasts. She shrugged, trying to make herself comfortable as the heat grew remorseless. A cough rattled her chest—not the deep cough of a winter cold, but a choking, bloody cough. She saw the sleeves of her dress speckle with red as she covered her mouth.

The last thing she remembered was hearing Catherine's courtiers arriving behind Henry's procession. Henry had brought his queen in on the progress after all. Anne fell to the ground, thinking of this doomed queen who held everyone's heart but his. She wished to be trampled under the hooves of a fast horse so she could be absent at last from this world.

She was aware of voices, warm and whispering, all around her. She laid there, listening for the one voice she always heard in her dreams, but it was not among them. Instead, she recognized the clipped, short speech of Dr. Butts, the court physician, a man of many remedies and few words. She felt his hand on her forehead and heard him whisper.

"Graces, no!" another voice said.

Anne opened her eyes. She grabbed his hand and jerked it from her forehead and sank back, lifeless, onto the pillows. Why was she so weak?

The men stared at her dispassionately. She tried to make her gaze fierce but began to shake, as helpless before them as a bent old woman. She shook so hard the linens quaked all around her and slipped down, revealing an immodest view of her bosom. She saw she was in her linen shift and it afforded a generous view at the moment. She saw her chest was spattered with blood.

Dr. Butts began putting his bottles back into his bag and spoke to the other man, not to her. "We'll have to inform the king of this. You know how he detests sickness, especially the sweats. The Boleyn name pollutes everyone it touches. Her attendant, Jane, has fallen too. Send Miss Boleyn away from court, back to her parents at Hever Castle. We're done with her."

She watched them leave, without giving her even so much as the dignity of a nod or bothering to adjust the linens so she was not exposed. She tasted something—old blood?—in her mouth. She wished for the crown, thinking how she would use it to crush this man. She had been indifferent to the promise of power until she had someone to hurt. Now she was tasting revenge.

A violent tremor shook her, and warmth moved through her body. She thought she was dying, and it was clean and tasted sweet. She slipped away.

The room was dark when she awoke. Anne did not know how many hours, or days, had passed. Her tongue was thick and dry. Everything within her cried out for a drink. Her very bones were made of sawdust and brimstone; the fever burned through her thoroughly. She groped about in the dark, finding the table next to her bed but no bell upon it.

"Help," she called, with no energy behind it. No one came.

"Help me!" she called again, but nothing beyond her door stirred. She sank back onto the pillows and fell back into unconsciousness.

When she awoke again, the sun was piercing the curtains, splitting the mattress she was lying upon into light and shadow. Strength was returning to her flesh, though her tongue remained swollen and cracked. It burned as she opened her mouth to call for help, but no noise came out that would bring anyone to her door. Hoisting herself into an upright position, she banged her head against the wall above her bed, wincing from the pain it caused and the halos she saw as the room doubled and spun around her.

The door swung open and her brother cried out when she saw her. "She's alive!"

Anne sank down as George rushed to her side, touching her forehead and calling for others to come and help. Her father poked his head in the room.

"Fetch wine and some cool rags—hurry!" George commanded him.

Anne did not remember the next few days that passed, only the comforts they brought. She remembered the sweet stinging warmth of the wine flowing over her cracked mouth and tongue, filling her empty belly and making the pain in her joints and head less worrisome. She remembered soft rags dipped in cool water from great bowls of copper, brought to her bedside and laid over her forehead and face. She remembered her first appetite for food, the way the smashed berries, so early in the harvest, tasted on her tongue. She didn't care that the juice ran down her mouth and stained her shift. All of her bedclothes would be burned anyway.

Her brother slept on the trundle that pulled free from under her bed. He did not mind that this was a duty most often left to women. He loved Anne better than himself, he told everyone, and would trust none to care for her as he would.

Her tongue was healing, but her lips broke their cracks whenever she tried to speak, bringing tears to her eyes. She had not tried to say much, only pointing to what she needed as her brother attended her every day. But there was one name she must speak, one question she had to know. She prayed it was over, and she was home to stay.

"Henry?" Anne asked, her voice like a rusted spit grinding against its stake.

George went back to wetting rags. He laid one on Anne's head and attempted to cover her face next, but Anne shook it off.

"Henry?" she asked again. She had to know. Perchance God had delivered her while she slept.

"He fled to his estate in Essex the moment he knew you were ill. We sent word when the fever broke. You recovered against all hope, a sign of God's favour. The king's heart rejoices with us. They say he has burned with a desire to know of your health, to see you once more." He sounded flat as he recounted all this, and Anne saw tears in his eyes.

"George," she whispered. Her heart was dead at this news.

"Why, Anne? Why did you let yourself be pulled into this? Was it not enough that he ruined our sister? Why must he have you, too? Why did you not protect us from this disgrace?"

Anne wanted to cry, but she had no tears. Her body was so dry from the fever, so used and parched, that it took great effort to deliberately wet her tongue enough to speak. George continued, busying himself with the rags, a cold, indifferent tone in his voice.

"The queen and her daughter, Mary, left the court, following the king. They are with him right now. They were not touched by the sweating sickness."

There was still hope. Anne took her hand, the movement exhausting her once again. She raised her chin, trying to get George to stay close so she wouldn't have to use too much energy to talk. "There is a nun. She speaks for God. Send for her."

"The Mad Nun?" George asked, standing back, chewing his lip.

"Go!" Anne commanded.

Chapter Eleven

The scent of earth and roots woke her, and as her eyes focused, she could see a tiny figure draped in black, hunched over a bedside table, crushing something with a mortar and pestle, quietly singing a chant. Anne had heard these chants from the monasteries and found them comforting, but this one thin voice stripped the piece of its charm. Anne was cold.

Liber scriptus proferetur,
In quo totum continetur,
Unde mundus judicetur.
Recordare, Jesu pie,
Quod sum causa tuae viae:
Ne me perdas illa die.

The nun turned. The black wimple draped over her head, the black sleeves that spread as she raised her arms in greeting, unnerved Anne. She saw something in her mind—a black bird in a place of desolation—and shifted in fear, attempting to dislodge the vision.

The nun smiled. "'Tis the skullcap. I have already spread it around thy bed."

Anne looked and saw that the floor was strewn with green leaves and purple buds, plus something else with a strong odour of old meat.

"It reeks," Anne said.

"Not many survive the sweats," the nun said as she worked. "Why did God spare ye?"

"I don't know."

"Why did God inflict it upon ye?"

"I don't know."

"'Tis why ye called me."

She went back to grinding at her mortar, turning a bit to keep an eye on Anne as she worked. Removing a black bottle from her robe, she poured a green oil into the crushed powder and began to stir. She dipped a finger in it and tasted it, nodding in approval.

"Here," she said to Anne, thrusting out the pestle covered in thick green sludge.

"What is it?" Anne asked.

"Eat it. For strength."

Anne tasted it. The taste was of lettuce and onions. The nun went to work setting onions in the foot of her bed, placing them deep within her sheets. Anne knew they would balance her humours and return her energy. She handed her back the pestle, and the nun scooped more of the green paste onto it and gave it to Anne.

"Why do they call you the Mad Nun?" Anne asked her, in between little tastings.

The woman held up a finger for silence and went to check the door. Finding George just beyond it, she clucked at him and shut the door firmly. She moved back to Anne's bedside and lay on the floor. Anne sat up in bed to watch.

The nun was a puddle of black, arms extended at her sides and feet on top of each other. She shut her eyes, murmuring under her breath. "What is it you want to know, mistress? My mind is a whirl of confusion and voices today. If we want a clear sign, we must ask a clear question."

The nun lay lifeless on the floor, waiting for her. Anne had never asked such questions before. All matters of faith were contained in her prayer books and Masses. People were born and they died and God gave them sun and wine to soothe the journey of days between each. But how to tell devil from angel? She could sense the importance of her decisions at every turn, but no one told her how to discern the right path.

"Have I angered God, or am I used by Him for good? Whose word do I trust?"

The nun opened her eyes and stared at her, making Anne cold and frightened. Standing, the nun placed her hands over her heart, tears falling down her cheeks. "There is great darkness around you, mistress. I have no light from God on this."

"You told me to ask a question!" Anne protested.

The nun moved to her, her feet shuffling softly across the floor, her voice dropping to a low whisper. "Merlin spoke of these days."

"Merlin was a madman!" Anne said.

"Aye, madness is of God. Merlin prophesied of a

mouldwarp, a ruler who would lead England to a bitter break, rending the kingdom, tearing mother from child." She grabbed Anne's hands and pressed them to her beating heart, pounding wildly. Anne recoiled, but the nun held firm.

"You speak of Henry?" Anne asked.

"No. May the angels guard your path, my daughter."

"But you speak for God! Tell me what I am to do!"

A knock on the door startled them and the nun dropped her hands. Her brother entered, pulling a face at the nun. He presented Anne with a great parchment, sealed in red with a fat waxy center, the impression of Henry's Great Seal of State upon it. Her fingers were stained red as she rubbed it in wonder.

She looked up, her brother watching her with an accusing stare. The nun was gone.

Anne,

> *I and my heart put ourselves in your hands, begging you to have them as suitors for your good favour, and that your affection for them should not grow less through absence. For it would be a great pity to increase my sorrow since absence does it sufficiently, and more than ever I could have thought possible, reminding us of a point in astronomy, which is, that the longer the days are, the farther off is the sun, and yet the more hot.*

> *So it is with our love, for by absence we are parted, yet nevertheless it keeps its*

fervour, at least on my side, and I hope on yours also: assuring you that on my side the ennui of absence is already too much for me: and when I think of the increase of what I must needs suffer, it would be well nigh unbearable for me, were it not for the firm hope I have. And as I cannot be with you in person, I am sending you the nearest possible thing, namely, my picture set in a bracelet.

Wishing myself in their place when it shall please you.

This by the hand of your loyal servant and friend,

Henry

George produced a black velvet bag, which made a clinking noise as he set it in her hand. She pulled open the drawstring, pouring out a gold bracelet made of interlocking roses, Henry's portrait set in the center, with gold filigree all around him. Anne touched it gently with her fingers, the gold making the red stains darker on her hands.

"A reply?" George asked.

"No reply," she answered. "There is no reply."

Two more days passed and more strength returned, pouring into her bones like sunlight flooding through an eastern window, her body warming and springing back to life. She took nothing for granted, drinking wine more slowly, letting it sit on her tongue and tasting it with relish. A cook made her the most delicious pies, brought trays to her bed, still steaming from the ovens below. She loved to cut a slit into the top crust, peeling it off to set it aside, watching the steam roil up and away, inhaling the scent of thyme and venison. Even her sweetmeats, the perfect little bubbles of berries set into silver dishes, made her groan with the pleasure of life. Anne turned her face towards the sun as it rose above her room and sighed. She would find her footing. God's graces were so many, so rich, and so sustaining that they left no room for rotten fears.

On the third day, George entered, once more holding again a letter bearing the Great Seal.

> *I beseech you now with all my heart definitely to let me know your whole mind as to the love between us; for necessity compels me to plague you for a reply, having been struck by the dart of love, and being uncertain either of failure or of finding a place in your heart and affection, which point has certainly kept me for some time from naming you my mistress, since if you only love me with an ordinary love the name is not appropriate to you, seeing that it stands*

*for an uncommon position very remote
from the ordinary. But if it pleases you
to do the duty of a true loyal mistress and
friend, and to give yourself body and
heart to me, who have been, and will
be, your very loyal servant, I promise you
that not only the name will be due to you,
but also to take you as my sole mistress,
casting off all others than yourself out
of mind and affection, and to serve you
only; begging you to make me a complete
reply to this, my rude letter, as to how far
and in what I can trust; and if it does not
please you to reply in writing, to let me
know of some place where I can have it
by word of mouth, the which place I will
seek out with all my heart. No more for
fear of wearying you.*

*Written by the hand of him who
would willingly remain yours.*

Henry

What was Anne to do with this? There was no word
of Catherine or her fate. There was no word from the
nun.

She called for a writing desk, which was brought
and laid across her lap. Carefully she peeled back the
wax seal over the inkwell, took her quill, and began
to write. Her graceful hand failed her today, though,
and she threw several attempts at letters away.

My king:

For your letters I am grateful, though I wonder that a poor servant of the king should find such favour. I am obediently yours in all matters, but you must not ask me to do that which I cannot, for in pleasing you I may offend God, who constrains me. I must save my bed for my husband; it is his rightful gift and service from me, and you must not ask me to surrender what can only belong to him. Forgive me for when I have seemed cold, for I do not know how to secure my position in this court, being moved about, without assurance of a future, and wanting only to be a servant of both God and king.

But I honour the king with my whole heart and am ready to do his will as a loyal subject, so I find I am tossed about, like a damsel lost upon rough waters. Take this, therefore, as a token of my esteem and my pleading for your protection, for I am helpless to stand before you. Give me your full assurance of protection from the storms that surround me, the dark clouds that rise unbidden from the depths of the sea. To please you as you ask would offend God and do no good service to your kingdom, incurring His great wrath for my wickedness. I must obey your command, as

your servant, and I plead with you to be a
gentle monarch. I am at your mercy.

Anne wrote, the quill scratching against the paper, the feather shaking as she wrote, so that it resembled a quivering bird in her hand. In the letter she set a little charm, a wooden ship in which she had placed a loose diamond.

Henry's reply came so fast he could not have had time to digest her letter completely. She had heard the horses burst down the last stretch of path and she ran to the window. She watched the rider, so unsteady when he dismounted that he grasped the horse's mane for support. The great beast was going white at the mouth.

Anne,

The proofs of your affection are such, the fine phrases of the letters so warmly couched, that they constrain me ever truly to honour, love, and serve you, praying that you will continue in this same firm and constant purpose.

Praying also that if ever before I have in any way done you offence, that you will give me the same absolution that you ask, ensuring you that henceforth my heart shall be dedicated to you alone, greatly desirous that so my body could be as well, as God can bring to pass if it pleaseth Him, whom I entreat each day for the accomplishment thereof, trusting that at length my prayer will be heard, wishing the time brief, and thinking it but long until we shall see each other again.

Written with the hand of that secretary who in heart, body, and will is

Your loyal servant and most ensured servant,

Henry

George stood at the door, stealing scouring looks at her. "The king is sending a carriage. He is sending you back to court. You will lodge at Cardinal Wosley's Hampton palace."

"Send me with your blessing," she said. "I am afraid."

He did not reply.

"If I am close to the king, no one will question you."

George shook his head, frowning. "We both know the law of the land. And we both know who I am."

Anne's heart beat faster. She did not like his secret spoken of so plainly. She did not like to see it so close to the surface of the waters; she wanted it buried and unspoken.

"Be careful how you speak, George, and do not give up on your prayers."

She moved to the doorway and embraced him, waiting until he held her back, each clinging to their childhood for one last moment. A rider sent from the king's court entered the home and watched their good-bye from the entryway below. Anne thought she saw a cold smirk play upon the rider's face. It did not matter.

She was ready.

Chapter Twelve

A great carriage had entered through the main gates and was coming down the path. As it took the gentle turns, the girls could see the badge that identified it, a coat of arms with a ripe pomegranate spilt open, its seeds too many to count, set below a magnificent crown. The wood was polished and dark, and its wheels turned without noise. Rose had never seen such money in one carriage.

There were several litters behind it, smaller carriages with cloth canopies. When the queen's carriage stopped, these stopped too. Rose laughed to see the attendants popping out like baby birds, with their high-pitched voices and bobbing heads, their straining eyes taking in Rose and the estate with wild interest.

Catherine waved them off and walked alone to the house. Sir Thomas and his attendants rushed to receive her. She looked to be a woman in a dream, ignoring their attempts to escort and support her, and simply walking into the house as if it were her own. When she was inside, the birdlike attendants began their twittering and fussing again, and Rose stole a last look at them as she followed in behind Margaret.

They found the queen in the family room, hastily swept clear from the lessons that had been in progress. Rose could hear the cook flying about in the kitchen to prepare something suitable, and the servants of the household stood about stupidly. The royal family had visited before, but always with notice, and always with enough time to remove traces of their everyday lives. To be seen like this, without preparation, was to be unmasked in an unnatural way. Rose noted that no one was comfortable, save the queen.

She looked entirely mortal, which surprised Rose, who kept searching her face and person for some hint as to who she truly was. She was a daughter of kings, which should have imbued her with great mystic quality, but Rose could not pinpoint it. It was enough, she decided, that this woman had seen what she had not and lived a life she would never know. To Rose, Catherine was a mystic—one who inhabited another place. Rose hung on every word and gesture as if it had great meaning.

The queen was not terribly big, but beneath the enormous skirts and great pointed hat with a train, she filled the family room disproportionately. Her forehead was broad and tall, with the hairline plucked for several inches so that her hat sat upon her hair but revealed none of it. She had a tiny nose, with a slight bump and upturn at the end. It must have been a darling effect as a young girl, but it was offset by a frown etched below it and deep wrinkles around the puffy eyes. She absently pulled at her eyebrows and wiped her eyes again and again. Rose realized the queen was waiting for everyone to finish staring.

Sir Thomas ushered everyone from the room, sweeping them from it like they were children. Only Margaret did he allow to stay, when she gave him a heartfelt look, and since Margaret held close to Rose's hand, Rose did not move. All others were gently banished and Sir Thomas closed the door behind them.

"There is a man being dragged through the streets behind a horse," the queen began, looking only at her skirt and picking at it. "He carries a faggot of wood for burning, and a placard around his neck saying he is guilty of heresy."

Sir Thomas nodded.

The queen stared at him. "You are too merciful."

Sir Thomas bit his lip and nodded. Rose did not think he nodded to agree, but to encourage the queen to speak more.

"Do you know the source of my troubles?" The queen stood, looking at the girls as if she had just noticed them. She spoke to them directly. "Do you know the source of my troubles?"

No one moved or spoke. Catherine continued, her voice gaining edge and pitch. "I have lost children. What woman has not?"

Rose's joints went cold, fearing the queen's gaze would linger on her.

"I have borne the king many children and God's mercy has been to receive them. Am I to blame for God's will? Do I stand in His place? No. I stand in my place, beside Henry, doing Henry's will. I am a good wife and a good queen. Am I not a good queen?"

"Your Majesty," Sir Thomas began, but she cut him off. Rose wondered how Sir Thomas thought that was a real question. For a man of learning, he was woefully ignorant in this subject.

"Henry was content to obey God and honour me as queen until he found this verse, this one verse, in Leviticus, and claims the marriage has been inalterably voided by God's Word. The Pope himself validated our marriage, and Henry thinks to upturn it because of one sentence! He is a learned man, but he read without instruction and will not take counsel from the church on its meaning. He is like a crazed dog with a bone. No one can reach him on this."

She was wandering about the room, looking at their lessons thrown into haphazard piles, turning vases and adjusting the decorations. She was setting the room in order with a vengeance.

"You were too gentle with that heretic. I want them burned alive with all their books. Find them and destroy them, every last one."

"My queen!" Sir Thomas said.

She burst into tears and sat. "I am the daughter of Isabella, no less. I know what things must happen to preserve an empire. These books, most especially this book by Hutchins, do you not see? What has happened to my home will happen in every home, until the realm is destroyed from within! We are in such danger!" She cried for a few moments.

No one knew what protocol would allow to comfort her, so they all watched her cry but did not move.

"I have lost him. He has decided to send me away to a nunnery, to pretend he never loved me, to pretend we have not spent a thousand nights and more together. He wants a new wife, a wife young and able to give him sons. I am finished bearing children—this is what Dr. Butts has confirmed. I cannot compete with a young girl like that Boleyn witch."

Sir Thomas waited a long moment before speaking. Rose thought it demonstrated wisdom.

"My queen," he began, "you are a gentle and good monarch, well loved by the people. They have wept with you as you buried your sons and would never consent to be ruled by another woman in your place if they knew how cruelly you were handled. I cannot judge between you and our king in matters of marriage; it is not my place. But I can speak of this Boleyn girl and the mischief she is causing. My counsel to you is to find evidence that she is meddling in the royal marriage, evidence that her intention is to steal Henry from you and you from the people. Bring this to me. With the Pope's decree that the marriage is lawful and the people's outrage at Anne Boleyn, will you not be secured?"

Rose knew the servants would be straining outside to hear every word. His voice was so low they would hear none of it.

"And the heretics?" the queen whispered back. "This man … Hutchins?"

Sir Thomas began to speak, but she cut him off.

"Do not be weak. This is the work of an empire. You will burn them all and their poisonous books. I will leave you with a sum—" and here she removed a sack of coins from her skirts—"to begin. Pay anyone who can help us. I do not care if my money lines the pocket of a filthy tramp in Southwark if it buys me a heretic. I have set aside another sum of cash for you, which will be delivered by messenger every fortnight, until the country is cleansed. And for Hutchins, for his arrest and a very public death, I have set aside a sum that will stagger you."

She whispered it to him and his eyes grew wide.

"Keep what you do not use," she said, "and may it bless your family."

❈ ❈ ❈ ❈ ❈

"Am I Catherine's heir?" I asked the Scribe. "Is that why you're giving me this story? Because of what I did?"

"Let's write your story together. David brought you his best work—"

"It wasn't good enough. Not for David. He was brilliant. I loved him too much to let him settle."

"So?"

"So I stole the galleys and sold them to a tabloid. They ran them, watered down, stripped clean, in monthly installments under someone else's name. I thought if he saw his work watered down, stripped to the bone, he'd see its flaws. He'd write again—bigger, bolder. We'd both make a killing."

"Oh, you did."

"What do you mean?" I asked.

He didn't answer.

"What has happened to David?" I cried out.

But the story burst into play again, and my scream was lost.

Chapter Thirteen

She could hear church bells ringing as she studied the Exodus scene of the tapestry. Somewhere in the distance at noon Mass, a church was elevating the bread, and Christ was again present among them. She bowed her head and blessed His name, asking favour for this mission. She looked at Miriam and the dancing, free women one last time and moved up the stairs.

Hampton Court was so different from the other residences she had been in. In Greenwich, the staircases were narrow and canted at an angle, making you dizzy before you reached your room. Here, the stairs were straight, with every step wide and low, perfect for women in such skirts as hers. *But of course,* Anne thought, *Wolsey wore great robes of office.* He must have designed these stairs to suit himself, not others. Only Henry liked short robes, having broken with the tradition of long robes for monarchs, because no monarch had ever had legs as powerful and shapely as his own.

If Wolsey had given such attention to the stairs, he had spent so much longer overseeing the rooms themselves. The doorway to her room was nearly twice her height, and her Yeoman had to give a great heave to open it. The room was dazzling, no doubt meant to woo a woman.

"Oh!" Anne gasped, unable to pair words to the vision. The bed rose above her at the end of the room, a great red giant, as tall as three men standing on each other's shoulders, with cascades of shimmering silks floating down to surround the sleeper. The walls were a dark wood, polished and glistening, and as Anne looked up to the ceiling, she saw a fresco of sweet cherubs, its soft blues and whites reminding her of the sky in spring, when the clouds have just begun to turn from grey to white, and the sun has found its strength once more.

Anne hugged her arms to herself, unable to step into the room. A perfume still lingered, of deep spicy scents, so unlike her own rosewater. Servants clambering down the hall behind her were carrying her goods, and she stepped aside to let them enter. They and her bags disappeared into the room.

Wolsey appeared behind her, his robes masking his footsteps. Anne saw her Yeoman's jaw set in disdain. He did not speak, she thought, but his thoughts were made plain enough.

"Forgive me, my lady," Wolsey began. "I was preparing for Henry's arrival."

"He will be here?" she asked.

"Yes, and since the sweating sickness has passed,

more courtiers will be returning. After this I expect him to move on to another residence."

"It is good of you to receive me," Anne said.

Wolsey's eyes went cold. "It has displaced no one to have you."

Anne bowed her head to end the conversation, embarrassed to have drawn Wolsey out on this point.

"Please explore the gardens as you like, and you may enjoy whatever charms you. Only do not enter my personal rooms, Anne, and do not disturb me after supper."

"But you know my secrets, Wolsey. Why should I not know yours?"

She touched her neck, fingering her necklace, making sure the fat green emerald ring sat accusingly on her hand before him.

❧

The estate was so quiet while it awaited the court. Anne hadn't realized how such a crowd of people, with their pecking and preening, their dignities and spites, kept her on edge and rolled into a tight, brittle woman. In the quiet her heart unfolded, her breaths grew deeper and slower, and her courage was a little quicker to rise to the top.

Why was she here? God had allowed all this to happen to her, had He not? So what did He want her to do? Anne tried to reason well. She was being elevated; Catherine was being cast out. Henry insisted the marriage was void, a disgrace to God, which only annulment, a clean washing away, would remedy.

Henry's only interests, Anne saw, were his conscience before God and heirs for the realm. Heirs God would only grant in a lawful, honourable marriage.

Wandering outside her room, she gave a little dismissive nod to her Yeoman guard, who allowed her to pass. She lingered at the image of Miriam again, her thoughts lost and loose, weaving between the delicate stitches before her, moving in and out of little threaded bits and pieces, shadows of thought. She had obeyed God in everything, committing to the seven virtues, shunning the seven sins. She had guided Henry's early passion for her into something more noble and God had honoured her obedience, setting before her the throne and its powers.

A distant song caught her attention. It was voices singing but one word, over and over. Anne could not understand it but sensed the drumbeat, low and steady, in her bones. Then something pushed against her, setting her off balance. All at once unsteady, she braced the wall beside the tapestry for support, as if the ground beneath her was shifting. A thought came to her and lodged in her mind like an errant bow striking a green young tree and sending little shivers down its trunk. She shook herself and walked on, suddenly compelled to commit a tiny treason.

Anne held her breath, but the halls were quiet. Her Yeoman had not followed her, but she caught his scent, lye soap and rosemary, near her anyway. It comforted her for what she was about to do.

⚜

The doors were not locked, but no light was set in the room. It smelled of leather and linen, of candles that had burned throughout the night, and of wax seals poured onto dry parchments. Her stomach lurched and tingled as the voices grew louder in her ears. It was here. She knew it. But looking around the room in the dim light from the hallway, she could see only bales of wool, marked at the ports as they came in. Why Wolsey would be impounding these imports was not a mystery in itself; these could infringe on the English trade. But this was not a matter for priests and cardinals.

They held her attention, and her heart beat faster. Without knowing why, she took a knife from Wolsey's desk, meant to split seals, and loosened the tie holding one bundle together.

A dozen of the forbidden book spilled out across her feet in the darkness. She cried out from the touch of cold leather against her skin. Every one of these bundles contained them, no doubt—hundreds in this little room alone. Each book was like an accusation, a reminder that she had failed to read it, failed to trust it. She picked one up, reading the marks on the inside page. It was indeed from William Hutchins. She flipped through the pages, eyeing the new woodcuts Hutchins was using. One line caught her eye. It said she was surrounded by invisible witnesses.

The room was still, but not empty. Trembling, she dropped the book, spying on Wolsey's desk shipping papers and documents that had broken seals.

Checking to be sure no one approached, she picked up a letter. It had only names—a long list of men and women. Her name was on it, hastily scribbled along the bottom.

"He approaches!" a guard called below.

A loud burst of activity made Anne jump. She grabbed the letter—and on impulse took one of the books too—determined to silence it. She ran out of the room and saw servants springing out from all directions, rushing to be in place and presented well as he arrived. Only her Yeoman was unruffled by the king's arrival.

Anne ran down the hall to a window that afforded her a view of the great path leading into the estate. She saw a line of carriages and litters, with riders accompanying them bearing the flag of England and the Tudor coat of arms.

She ran back to her room to check her mirror, licking her lips and setting a diamond pin in her hair to pull the dark curls off her shoulders. She hid the letter she had stolen from Wolsey and rushed downstairs.

Henry was in the courtyard, towering above the servants and guards who scurried about, trying to scrape and bow and never look directly at him while they carried out their business. His red hair pierced her vision, and she looked at him for a moment as she stood in the shadows on the stairs, peering out into the courtyard. He was indeed handsome, and today he looked free and happy, like a man pleased with a change of winds.

He was laughing at a young servant who was having trouble grabbing the reins of a temperamental black mare. She showed him her teeth every time he lunged for the reins, and the boy began to sweat profusely, understanding himself to be sudden entertainment for the king. Henry stopped laughing and turned, facing her where she was hidden. Anne swallowed nervously and touched her hair. He extended a hand in her

direction, and a curious silence whipped through the
men. The young boy seized the opportunity to lunge for
the reins and caught them, yanking the horse hard in the
direction of the stables.

Anne stepped from shadow into light, smiling at
Henry, her body softening to anticipate his embrace.
Henry did not take his eyes from her but held his hand
out still, and she crossed the courtyard. All the men
were so startled by her sudden appearance that they
scrambled to observe protocol. Anne knew that none
were entirely sure what this was, as their official queen
was not in residence, and Anne was known to be more
than a temporary mistress. They averted their eyes and
bowed their heads.

As the wave of men submitted to the king's wishes,
Anne's weak knees made the slick stones treacherous.
She placed her hand in Henry's.

He pulled her in, his other hand circling around her
waist. He was a full foot taller and bent to her, not for a
full kiss on the mouth, but a gentle, lingering kiss on her
cheek. His breath was hot on her neck, and his whiskers
scraped against her face. He held her there, inhaling deeply,
until she rested her head against him and exhaled.

"When can I see you?" he whispered in her ear. His
voice brought up goosebumps all over her skin. This was
not the monarch who had sought her company only for
his bed. That she was surprised, even a little, made her
ashamed. She had much less faith than she imagined.

"I have something I must show you," she said.

He bowed to her and replied, "The gardens. Tonight."

⚜

Anne sat on a bench, its stone still warm from the sun. But the sun was gone, and a rich black night blanketed the garden, punctuated by scattered torches at the far ends. A perfect breeze, like cool silk on her skin, brushed her face and shoulders, and Anne lifted her skirts a fraction to let it relieve her feet and calves. In July, the garden was in full bloom, even while the ladies wilted. The wisteria released a strong sweetness that the breeze carried through the garden, and Anne smiled to see a ladybug land on her skirt. She let it explore the folds of material until it decided to fly away. Ladybugs were good omens, the seven dots on their shells representing the seven sorrows and seven joys of Mary, the holy mother, and their red shells representing her red cloak.

Anne reflected on the meaning of such blessing—of being visited by a ladybug even so late, well after ten o'clock at night. Mary had suffered much but borne the child who would save all men from their sins.

The thought sent shivers down her arms. Perhaps there were travails ahead, or God was acknowledging the rough path she had just left, but the message was the same: God would use Anne to send peace at last to England.

A few birds still sang, their long trills punctuated by sharp short bursts. The garden was packed with life yet still quiet. How was it the palaces were packed with quiet people, yet were so stressful? The natural world was no less crowded, and the animals had no guarantee of survival. Even one of these birds in the garden could well be eaten tonight by a snake or hawk, yet there was a tranquility here, an acceptance of order and destiny.

Men were not content with their place in the order,

Anne decided. This was why people made the palaces uninhabitable. Their discomfort, angling, grasping, and ambition ruined the place.

Henry's hand was warm on her shoulder, but it did not startle her. Reaching up to lay her hand on his, she turned her neck to allow the breeze to reach more of her skin and did not mind that Henry watched.

"When I thought you might die," Henry began. He gripped her shoulder. "When I thought you might die, I was lost."

"God did not let me die," she replied.

He moved to pull her up to him but she resisted. "Henry, what do these names mean to you: Thomas Garrett, John Frith, John Clarke, Anne Askew?"

Henry removed his hand and grunted. "Enemies. Thomas More wants to burn them. Wolsey asks for mercy. Says they may yet repent."

Anne felt fear. Her name was on that list. "But Henry, why would Wolsey have mercy on your enemies?"

"He is a merciful man."

"He is going to be Pope, is he not? Do you trust him?"

"Do not speak of him like this. Wolsey is not stupid, and he is not a traitor."

"It may not be treason. It may be faith. He has not worked with all haste to secure your annulment."

"This pertains to the Hutchins book, not my annulment."

"Hutchins pertains to you, Henry. He offers the people a new path to God, one that has not so much need for the Church. The realm will be in an uproar. Their faith will be shaken, their king will be held in disdain, and Wolsey will be Pope in another land, another land that stands ready to invade. Maybe More will burn these people; it can only work in Wolsey's favour. He will be the kind saviour."

"Wolsey banned these books," Henry corrected her, "because of a violent uprising in Germany, attacks on the princes and nobility. This man Hutchins incites fury against establishment. I will not tolerate this book in my realm, and I've no more patience for the matter."

He pulled her up and she turned into his arms.

"The Spanish, the French, and the Pope," he said, "all these want one thing: power. As long as I am without an heir, I am weak. Without a queen in my bed, Anne, I do not think I will have much luck producing one."

"I do not want to refuse you, Henry, and harp like a shrew night after night."

"Do not make me wait. I have no marriage in the eyes of God."

"Neither do I."

He released her and pushed her away.

Anne reached for his arm, to put her hand upon it and so soften her words, but Henry jerked his arm away and would not look at her.

"The law serves the king," he retorted. "I suggest you adopt the same attitude. I will speed this matter to its conclusion, but I will not take a shrew for a wife."

"Henry," Anne began.

But Henry yelled, "Back to your chambers! You'll wait for me in the city, where the heat and stench will remind you to cherish the respites I offer."

He turned his back. Anne did not know how to make a dignified exit, being swept from under his feet like a kitchen dog. She picked up her skirts and walked back to her room, her tears glistening as they fell to her bodice, a thousand tiny stars falling on this dark night.

In her chambers, her tears still fell. She berated herself for not understanding the king better, for provoking him, though she had tried to do what was right. There was only one other woman who could offer her counsel, and this was the very woman Anne was destroying. Catherine had survived years under Henry's thumb. Anne doubted she could survive a week without ruin.

She yearned for his softer words and lifted the lid of her trunk to fish out his letters, kept safe at the bottom, where no one dared disturb her private treasures.

They were gone. A stab of panic made her cry out, and she began removing the items one by one, setting them on the enormous bed, until the trunk was empty and there were indeed no letters.

She had committed treason in those letters, asking for the crown when another woman, very much alive, still wore it. Anne was sweating, a cold sweat that stung her brow. She shivered, wrapping her arms around herself, pressing in hard on her roiling stomach to calm it. Those lovely white papers bared at this moment before some enemy—they were no less than her neck. Is this what Hutchins must fear? Were they all doomed by ink and presses?

Anne shook herself awake from these terrors. She had to think. Who had access to her trunk, and who would want her in such a vulnerable state? It was either Wolsey or Henry, she decided. Henry could blackmail her to get her into his bed, and the law would still be on his side. Wolsey might not have known what he was looking for in her chambers, but if he was the thief, he had found the papers that would cause such outrage against her that Henry would have no choice but to dismiss her from court and remain with Catherine. Wolsey's life, and his fortune, would be secure if there were no troubles with Catherine and the Pope.

Either man could be the thief. Both could be her adversary.

She paced in little turns, trying to find a spot that would stop her stomach from flipping and twisting. She accidentally knocked the book to the floor, and as she bent to retrieve it, her eyes fell upon the same words. But this time, the words were balm, and she pressed the book against her stomach, cradling it, murmuring the words again to herself. The words, spoken into thin air, did not disappear but lingered, settling in around her chamber, steadying her nerves as a friend might who sits with you on a night of fevers and dreams.

"I am surrounded by invisible witnesses," Anne murmured.

A tapestry against the wall fluttered.

Chapter Fourteen

The crowds made progress through London tedious. The shop on Honey Lane was not so far that Rose and Margaret were compelled to travel by barge but had instead taken the litter drawn by two great mares. The horses, in their snorting, belligerent impatience, strained to make quick work of the journey, but the slow-footed, dim-witted commoners impeded them at every turn. That is how they looked to Rose, at least—throngs of oily stained people who lacked the wits to let the quick-moving nobility pass. Once Rose had resented these litters darting through London's streets, making hazards for children and the infirm. But it was clear that bearing down on the people produced no ill effect, nor did it encourage them to move. Rose and Margaret were stuck, forced to submit at points to the indifferent will of the people.

As they took the turn at Honey Lane, they were

again stopped by a gaggle of commoners. The horses pawed the ground, but no one in the crowd paid them mind. Rose lifted the curtain drawn round the litter ever so slightly, fighting back the duststorm that rose to meet her. The stink was overpowering with no curtain to filter it. The city streets stank of beer and urine and of unwashed bodies sweating in the August heat. The usual heat in August was not bad, but the drought that had cursed them took with it all the comforts of summer. There was no relief, not from the poor and their odours, nor for the farmers and their crops. Stalls should have lined this street with vendors selling the early harvest, blackberries being here by now, cheeses and herbs. Nothing lined the street today except these dread people and some amusement parading before them that had stopped them all dead in the street.

Rose leaned out of the litter, lifting herself a bit to see what amused them, and how long this delay would last. Margaret peered out the other side.

"Margaret! Stay inside!" Rose called to her.

Both women strained for a good view above the crowd. A group of men and women were being led down the street, their hands tied behind them, each with a bundle of wood tucked into their grasp. Their faces were red and pocked, ravaged by disease once and ravaged again by something new, some unknown shame. After them came several men on horseback, but it took Rose a moment to comprehend this sight, for the men rode backwards, and on their backs was painted a placard describing their crime. Rose tried to work the letters, but it was hard to read with the signs being jostled and the letters written in a loose hand.

She stopped and ducked back into the litter, grabbing Margaret and pulling her in.

Margaret did not look well. Perhaps the stench and heat were too much for her. She looked for a cotton veil Margaret could wear, one with tiny holes cut for the eyes. It would give her another layer of protection.

But Margaret did not want to wear it. She told Rose to stop. "Rose, why don't we shop for our fabric on another day? The heat is too much for me."

Rose would have consented, but she saw that Margaret was not sweating much. Her face was not flushed with red, but was instead pale and distant, as if the oppression came from within. Rose began to be nervous, her stomach pierced through by darts of panic.

"Who were those people, Margaret? You could read the signs; I could not."

Margaret cut her cold stare from the flapping curtain back to Rose.

"They were heretics, Rose, guilty of owning one of the books Father has banned. The wood they carry is the wood that will be used to light the fires at Smithfield, the fire that will burn them to death if they commit the same offense again."

"But they did not read it? They are condemned for owning it?" Rose wondered that those men and women she saw could read; not many could, even among the nobility and clergy.

"Owning it is the same as reading it, Rose. Father and Wolsey, they say a book can infect a house with a thousand devils even if the words are not loosed."

The litter broke free and the women lurched forward, startled by the sudden return to the journey. Rose lost

the question that was next on her tongue, and Margaret
said nothing else. She still did not look well. They arrived
in short order at Goodwife Grisham's fabric shop. The
store was hard to find, tucked between the rows of shops
on Honey Lane, but once inside, Rose was glad to be
free of the streets and crowds. The air in here was better,
from dyes made of flowers, clean cottons, linens, and
rich damasks. There were fabrics hanging along the walls
to display their patterns, great bolts of fabric stacked on
tables and against benches, and fabrics lining the stairs
that led to what Rose supposed was the workroom.
Tailors bustled up and down the stairs, checking the
books that were opened to numbers and names, often
grabbing fabric when they went back upstairs.

A fabric caught her eye, a deep navy with swirls
of gold and a leaping unicorn flying through the inky
folds. A woman, sweating heavily and taking generous
slurps from a pot of beer, bustled towards them.

"Mistress Margaret! Child, dear one, lovey, come in,
come in! What ye be needing today, hmm? What ye be
needing, love?"

Rose wondered if the woman always repeated herself
or if the beer and the heat were poor bedfellows.

"Goodwife Grisham! 'Tis so good to see you again,"
Margaret said, pecking her on her cheek. "This is my
maidservant, Rose."

Goodwife Grisham squealed and took Rose's hand,
dragging her closer to look at her face. "Such pretty eyes!
Very pretty! You're a marvelous girl!"

Rose tried to smile but was afraid to part her lips
even a bit for fear of inhaling near the woman. The beer
smelled as sour as her bosom in this heat.

"Goodie, we're attending a revelry at His Majesty's request, in honour of my father accepting the title of Chancellor."

"Yes, yes, he's moving up, isn't he? Won't this be marvelous? The king's inner circle. What nobleman won't be fighting for your hand? What man won't fight for you?" Goodie Grisham's voice kept rising higher, like an expired ash that floats up and away from the fire.

Margaret began to say something, but Goodie's face changed into a menacing dark pageant, twitching and glowering. Rose was convinced that the woman was mad, until Margaret pulled on her hand and pointed to the door. A royal guard, a tall redheaded man in a Yeoman's brace, stood at attention. Behind him was a carriage with a coat of arms Margaret must have recognized from the rose.

"It's her," Margaret whispered. "Anne Boleyn."

Goodie Grisham bustled her way to the guard. "I'm not open for business, you may tell your mistress. Not open."

The guard looked at Goodie Grisham with calm acceptance of the insult. Every shop on Honey Lane was open, and Goodie had customers standing right there, no less. He looked at Margaret and Rose, and his gaze made Rose's throat catch, as if there was something she should say but could not. She felt guilty for saying nothing. Something about the moment, the man, required a better response.

He bowed and exited, and Goodie Grisham grabbed the door to keep it open. The three women crowded into the frame to stare at the carriage before it started away. The curtains parted only a shy distance, so that the occupant could see the shop but not be seen.

Margaret spat on the ground and turned her back. Goodie pulled the pair back into the shop as she shut the door, her face cold and resolute. Henry had had his women, rumors said, but this one was a bold card, playing for the crown when the suffering queen was still wearing it.

"No righteous woman will stand this insult to our sex," Goodie Grisham said. "Old wives are still good wives. Anne thinks she can steal the crown just because she's young. She's young. Oh, but she'll get hers in the end. She'll be old like me, and let's see how she holds onto her man. Oh, yes, she'll get hers."

Margaret was nodding and smiling, and Rose smiled back to agree. She tried not to reflect on what she knew was true: That all over the city husbands with money looked for young girls in need, girls who walked the streets hoping to sell the only thing they owned. Whether the wives at home were good had nothing to do with it. Plagues, droughts, and unending death made the gentleness of youth a precious commodity, and the men paid well. Youth was a seasonal item, like a ripe fruit, that must be sold and for the highest dollar, before the cold winter of age.

"Your father, he's going to run these types out," Goodie continued. "I've heard she reads all the banned books, even Hutchins. Stirs the blood, it does. Stirs the blood. She has all the blessings of God and country and spits in the cup she shares with us all. Someone needs to teach her some true religion."

Margaret ended the conversation. "Goodie Grisham,

could you please show us the suitable fabrics so we may choose and be on our way? You know how my father is if I am not back before the sun quits the day."

The words sent Goodie Grisham spinning off in a whirlwind of smiles and commentary, unfolding fabrics all along the tables and calling up the tailors to wait upon them. Rose chose the fabric with the unicorns that had first caught her eye.

"Unicorns mean God's fortune and blessing."

Margaret chose another design, a swirling brocade.

"Very good, ladies. Now, I may need an extra week on these, as I've had a girl run off on me."

Agreeing to this, and saying their good-byes (hearing Goodie Grisham's twice), they were back in the litter and moving through the streets again.

⚜

"The heat was extraordinary, was it not?" Margaret was waiting for Rose to step down from the litter and enter the house with her. "A crock of cool wine will taste so good!"

Rose nodded, too tired to pretend to be excited about wine, or fabric, or anything else.

Still, Margaret persisted. "I know I'm going to drink my weight of it when we sit for supper."

Rose smiled and followed her into the house, so grateful to be home. The thought caught her, and she sighed with pleasure.

Margaret hurried off to change for supper and called for a servant to fetch a drink for them both, as the day had been hot. Something about the day set at an odd angle in Rose's heart. Perhaps it was the Yeoman, the goodness she perceived in him, although he had spoken not one word and she had done nothing but dishonour his master. Perhaps it was the fever that infected Margaret the longer that Goodwife Grisham prattled. Rose bit her lip, pondering, until she was interrupted by Margaret calling to her.

"Come, Rose! Let us be refreshed!"

The room was tar black when she awoke, disturbed again by some movement in the room she sensed rather than heard. She caught her breath and strained to detect what it might have been, but the room was silent.

Too quiet, in fact, and Rose lifted herself up off her mattress to peek at Margaret's bed. It was empty.

Rose jumped up and ran to the door. She still had her shoes on and grabbed the robe she had left by the door. She had been waiting for this moment for weeks.

Easing down the hall and through the house, she made light, quick steps to the door that led into the garden. As she stepped from the dark house into the night, she saw the moon above her shrouded in a cloud, like an old man's milky eye. She shuddered and turned to look round when she saw, far ahead on the path towards the gates, Margaret on horseback, her hair flying behind her, the horse making good time on the soft path.

Rose ran to the stables, her mind working through all the possibilities she had imagined, setting them in order before her as she saddled her horse with great speed. Margaret's secret was out there, and tonight Rose would know it.

❧

Her face went pale with long lines deepening on her forehead, like fingernails of fear scraping across her skin. When Rose rode closer, and Margaret recognised her, the fear turned into something else—a tired, cold anger … a fire with the heat gone out of it but unwilling to be swept away.

Rose pulled her horse alongside and said nothing. Margaret stared straight ahead.

"Did you think the wine would guarantee my sleep?" Rose asked. "Did you think you could slip away from under my watch?"

Margaret set her mouth and did not look at her.

"Since I am here," Rose continued, "you can tell me where we're going."

"Since you are here," Margaret spat back, "you can think for yourself. I'll not say another word to you."

Margaret slowed her horse at the edge of the woods. Tying him to a tree, she walked into the forest.

The trees towered like dark sentinels; something stirred the branches. Rose searched the darkness with her eyes but saw nothing. Whatever it was had moved out of her sight. Rose took a deep breath and followed Margaret farther in.

There was no path, so she was careful to mark Margaret's steps and place her own feet in the same places. She could hear animals scurrying away in the underbrush and tried not to think about what they

were, or how big. She had lived a rough life before Sir
Thomas's house, but it had still been a city life. It had
taken her years to understand its dangers, and here was
a whole new world with its own set of rules. Rose pulled
her skirts up and closer in to her body, praying nothing
touched her and she took no stupid steps.

A clearing was ahead. Rose saw a gathering of
women, one with a small torch that sputtered and
burped fat little sputums of glowing wax, hissing as it
worked. The women were all in plain nightclothes, some
with a shawl thrown over their shifts, some with wraps.
Rose could not tell who these women were, for they
had none of their day clothes on, the clothes that told
of rank and family by their colour and cut. Underneath
their robes, every woman wore a linen shift. Tonight,
every woman, young and old, looked alike. There was
no rank or class among them. Hair hung loosely at their
shoulders. Their faces were plain, not pinched or made
up. Rose thought she would like to see them painted;
their plain beauty would surpass that of the European
masterpieces.

"Come on! We must begin!" The woman with the
torch was impatient for Rose to finish navigating the steps
behind Margaret, who had already joined the group.

"Who is she?" someone demanded.

"She's mine. A maidservant," Margaret replied.

"She can be trusted?" someone else asked.

Margaret dismissed the question with a nod. "By
my troth."

The woman with the torch whispered something to
a short little woman on her left, whose pale face was
luminous in the torchlight. She removed a dagger from a

satchel at her feet and walked to meet Rose. Rose let her hand be taken, and the woman held a dagger over it.

"You will never regret this, sister," she whispered, and with a delicate, graceful stroke, pierced Rose's skin with a slash down her palm. The blood bubbled up, little beads that joined together in a red river. Rose clenched her teeth, trying not to scream, watching the women's eager faces as the blood glistened in the moonlight.

"Take the oath," the woman said. "By my blood I pledge my silence."

Rose repeated the words. "… and may the words of our Father be my light, the faithfulness of my sisters be my assurance."

The woman with the torch passed it to another and opened a book. It was not much bigger than Rose's hornbook for learning letters, but it had a wide roped spine, and Rose could see it had a thousand letters all running into one long page, page after page being nothing but these letters.

"We continue. My friends, we have read all the way from the history of the Master unto this, His apostle who carried the message far beyond the Master's home. We will read for an hour, then we have business to attend to before breaking."

She began to read, and Rose was utterly lost.

> "Because therefore that we are justi-
> fied by faith, we are at peace with God
> through our Lord Jesus Christ: by
> whom we have a way in through faith
> unto this grace wherein we stand and
> rejoice in hope of the praise that shall

be given of God. Neither do we so only:
but also we rejoice in tribulation. For we
know that tribulation bringeth patience,
patience bringeth experience, experience bringeth hope. And hope maketh
not ashamed, for the love of God is shed
abroad in our hearts, by the holy ghost,
which is given to us. For when we were
yet weak, according to the time: Christ
died for us which were ungodly. Yet
scarce will any man die for a righteous
man. Peradventure for a good man
durst a man die. But God setteth out his
love that he hath to us, seeing that while
we were yet sinners, Christ died for us.
Much more than now (seeing we are
justified in his blood) shall we be saved
from wrath, through him. For if when
we were enemies, we were reconciled
to God by the death of his son: much
more, seeing we are reconciled, we shall
be preserved by his life."

Her reading went on, but Rose could not bear the
words. Her mind was seeing the bleeding Christ hung
above the altar, the awful sight she had turned away
from in the church. She had condemned the Church
for letting Him hang, exposed and brutalized. *He chose
to die,* she realized. *He refused to come down.* His blood
would run until there were no more sinners.

The thoughts broke open in Rose's heart as she
stared at the leaping, dancing flames. The world, the

word, was suddenly alive to her, and she did not move as a great shadow rose from behind her, spreading itself out over the fire. It was the shape of a towering creature with wings, and his arms held a bowl, which he lifted above his head, tipping it out over her.

Some of the women saw it too and screamed, but Rose lifted her face in rapture as the blood washed over her, making her free, washing the darker stains away forever and making her skin as new and tender as an infant's. She covered her face in her hands to weep, the new life as sweet as honey under her tongue, the relief sweeping through her tired body like an indescribable ecstasy.

Someone put their arms around Rose, holding her as she wept, and she realized it was Margaret. Margaret wore a strange expression—one Rose had never seen anyone give her before. She stared at Margaret for a full minute until she could name it. It was envy. She pulled Margaret in, not letting her go, cradling her.

"His blood is meant for you, Margaret. Do not refuse Him. You can know peace."

A bird's cry startled them all. Margaret pushed away, smoothing her hair down, setting her jaw. Her cheeks were flushed red, but Rose could not decide their meaning.

"We must depart," the reader announced, "but we have business." She closed the book. "Spies are at every port. The apprentices are young and poor and fast to accept a bribe. The work grows harder."

"I can't steal any more money, or my master will surely notice," a woman protested.

"No, Hutchins and his men have enough money.

Wolsey wanted to stop the books, so he bought every edition they printed. They sold the lot at top price and when they heard it was Wolsey who was paying, they added a fee!"

The women grinned. Wolsey had stolen enough bread from their mouths to make his own misfortunes a delicious pleasure.

"Hutchins is using the money to finance a new edition, one with all new plates, none of the typesetter's errors to be repeated. It will be glorious."

"So what does he ask of us?" one girl asked.

The reader motioned for the women to lean in. "What he needs is your underwear."

The shock registered on everyone's face. Indeed, if everyone's mouths were to shut at once, Rose thought, there would be a great popping that would give them all away.

"I'm not wearing any," a woman ventured.

The leader continued, in a louder voice now because of the snickers. "Linen. He needs linen for the presses, to make the paper. He cannot buy it for the spies watching every shop. He needs our linen shifts and our husband's underwear. I'll get it through the ports and out to him."

She pulled a pair of men's underwear from under her skirt pocket and tossed it on the ground in the middle of the group. The women looked at each other. Margaret was the first to tug at her bodice, but everyone began moving. Some ran behind trees and pulled off their shifts, going bare beneath their robes. Everyone tossed their linen clothing into the pile, trying to contain their giggles.

"Every gathering of women like us is doing the

same tonight," the leader said. "And there is one other request."

One woman yanked her outer wrap tightly about, glaring at the leader.

"No, not your clothes, Goodwife Lewis." The leader laughed.

Goodie Lewis smiled uneasily but did not release her hold.

"We must try to live as we believe, yes?"

The women all nodded.

"We all serve fish on Fridays, do we not?"

They nodded again.

"And why?"

"Because," one woman answered, "because … it is what the Church commands."

"It's not in the Bible. God never said it. We're free to eat meat if we want. Any day. All day on Friday if we want."

No one looked comfortable. Rose wondered if this Bible would make it into their kitchens.

"On Friday the fifteenth no one is to prepare fish for the evening meal. Put on sausages, letting them cook all afternoon so that the tempting aromas conquer the entire home, making the men hungry. If anyone asks what you are doing, tell them you prepare it for the next day's breakfast, but if they want some, please go ahead. Unless, of course, they know of a Bible verse that prohibits it. After all, we are simple women who are not allowed to read the Bible for ourselves. They must teach us the verse, so that we, too, may be sure to follow every law of God. Let's let the men choose whether to follow tradition or truth."

"Aye, we know which side their stomachs will be on!" One woman said with a grin.

Rose guessed she was long married.

A lone woman raised her hand. "'Tis the Feast of Assumption, Mary's Holy Day."

"Don't quit," the leader urged, as an owl began calling in the darkness around them. "All the women on our side will do this."

No one spoke as they retreated into the trees, each woman heading in her own direction, each woman keeping to her own thoughts, none of them wearing underwear.

Chapter Fifteen

Annc held her breath and listened. Her Yeoman raised an eyebrow, but she paid no mind, pressing her body against the wall, leaning her upper body in, inch by inch, until she could catch a little glimpse.

Henry sat on a rather plain wooden chair, surrounded as usual by fanning, doting servants, including his Ward of the Chamber, always ready to follow Henry to the privy and dump the esteemed products with much solemnity. Anne thought her job here was not so different, receiving publicly the favour of Henry that amounted to nothing more in private than rank stench.

But before Henry knelt Sir Thomas More, easy enough to pick out for his hook nose and ermine collar, his red robes of the Star Chamber making him stand out in a room of servants in plainer livery. Wolsey stood, either having paid honour to Henry already or feeling no need to do it.

Anne missed some of what was said; with so many people in the room, the men's voices were muffled by the simplest movements or deep breaths of others. Anne held her breath more tightly and leaned in, pressing her whole side against the wall, straining her neck to get her ear as close to the door's opening as she could without being detected.

More spoke first. "I cannot reply to this."

Henry was not pleased with the answer. His hushed tone carried barbs.

More's tone did not change. "I do not know how he came into possession of the letters. The Pope is scattering them abroad, though, and by now every foreign power has read them. This is why they came to my attention first, from the diplomatic channels I maintain."

Henry screamed at him, and Anne heard a violent smashing, probably the chair meeting its unhappy fate. She jumped but did not cry out.

"Who is responsible for this?"

"Good king, this is why I have brought the matter to your attention. The people are angry with Mistress Boleyn. Everyone in the realm knows she desires the crown, though you are still married. They know she has brought the Hutchins book into the court, a court that will not let the public read it. The unrest grows by the hour. Corn prices have not resolved, and families are going hungry. August promises more of the drought's vengeance. And their fury is not directed at you alone. Wolsey is a target as well. No one in your house is safe from accusation. I am simply advising you how best to correct the course."

"Burning? It hasn't been done in a hundred years or more."

"It must be done. There is a plot stirring that will provoke the king's good patience with these people and this book."

"What of me?" Anne heard Wolsey's thin voice. It was a mistake to ask in front of Henry—even Anne recognized this. Sweat had broken out upon her upper lip from the mention of her name in there.

"The people are angry at paying the high taxes to the Church, Wolsey. They blame you for their poor state, for everything that they cannot trace back to the king, even the new bouts of sweating sickness plaguing the country. I have this week arrested a group of men in Rochester who were plotting your death."

"They were going to kill me?" His voice was not steady.

"No, this would be a great crime, which even they knew," More continued. "Your office is held in esteem although they are angry with the man. They were determined not to lay a hand on you, but they were going to drill holes in the bottom of a boat, and set you in it, far out at sea. They would leave it to God's good pleasure to determine what to do with you."

Anne could hear Henry's laughter. No one else joined in.

Wolsey spoke next, but his voice was better. Anne imagined him taking a deep breath as he looked round the room, sizing up how best to extinguish the threat. These men were but errant children to him, and he was going to roundly scold them back into place.

Henry spoke. "It is an English marriage, so it will be decided in an English court. We will convene at Blackfriars' Church and be done with this. Sir Thomas, see to it that

Catherine knows nothing in advance of this, though make sure she is appointed proctors to speak for her. And prevent any of her letters from leaving England. I do not want her playing to the Pope's sympathies, especially since the Pope is at the mercy of her nephew, King Charles. Can you keep my secrets?"

"Yes, your majesty," she heard More reply.

Anne was knocked off balance by the door slamming back. Wolsey, his billowing red robes riding unevenly across his bulging stomach, stood over her.

Anne struggled to her feet, assisted by her Yeoman, who had crossed the distance between them in less than a second, and faced Wolsey. "You stole my letters!"

Wolsey smiled, relishing some little moment. He leaned in, stroking her cheek with a finger, his lips wet and pursed. He leaned in, closer again, until he whispered in her ear, "I did not. How many hidden enemies you must have, Anne."

His breath on her ear, so like a tick's crawl, made her shudder.

"Oh, Anne, had I known you were to be this much trouble, I would have had you dealt with. I misjudged you. I am surprised a woman as dull as you can hold his attention thus. Your sister certainly didn't. If you had simply given Henry what he wanted, neither of us would be in this condition. It was your own stupid ideas about God that threaten us. Leave God in the church, Anne, and stick to what women know best."

Wolsey smirked at her Yeoman. She saw the guard's hand reach for his dagger, and the gesture alone sent Wolsey scampering.

Her heart began to race, and her neck felt tight,

as if a string was being pulled around it, tighter and tighter, until her throat burned and she was blinking back tears. She reached out for her Yeoman as she fell into darkness.

He cradled her in his arms, brushing the hair from her face. He was so gentle. She let her eyes focus on his red beard and remembered it on her cheek. Henry was over a foot taller than she was, and muscular, and she was like a toy held in his arms.

She knew she should be afraid, but he felt so good surrounding her, supporting her. She had no one to rest upon, no one to carry her burdens. She decided to let him hold her, and she would pretend it was safe.

Looking up, she saw she was in a new chamber. The bed was an enormous, perfect square, almost as big as her bedchamber at home. It was gilded and carved, and there were angels in the design: two sweet angels on the footboard holding a bowl. She guessed the design was repeated above her, on the headboard. It comforted her. The only other place she had seen angels was in the chapel Wolsey had built at Hampton Court.

He stroked her arm, smoothing her gown in places, watching her reactions. "It is my bedchamber," he said.

She started to rise up, grasping at her bodice to see if it was in place, but he caught her hand and kissed it.

"I would never have you that way, Anne. You have nothing to fear from me. Please rest, and let me be your servant today. I am so sorry for the trouble I have poured out upon you."

Anne remembered everything. "Our letters." She groaned.

"Sshh," he whispered. "No one can harm you." He moved her in his arms so that his mouth could reach hers, and her body rose to melt into his kiss. It was not enough.

"I cannot have this," Anne said, wanting to cry in frustration. She wanted to be lost forever in here, beneath his coverlet, entwined against him, sheltered. But God's law said it must not happen until there was a marriage. Why must she be cursed with a heart for God? She groaned again to herself. She wanted nothing more right now than his flesh upon hers, his back turned against the world, spreading himself out over her, so she could see nothing but his face and taste nothing but his lips.

Henry smiled and set his finger on her lips. "I said you would be safe here, and that is even from me." He grinned. "I will sleep elsewhere. But tell me, why were you listening as I spoke to More and Wolsey?"

"I do not know who betrayed me. I wanted to know my fate, if you were going to discard me."

"Because of the letters?" Henry laughed softly. "Anne, my first thought was that you had sent them."

"I would never allow myself to be exposed in this way!"

"I know. I have my spies too."

She did not know what this meant, but his tone was still kind, and he was still touching her with affection. Anne was confused. Her body craved his touch, was warmed by it. She longed to bury her face in his chest and release all her fears, yet her mind spun, weaving little worries and fears into something bigger, something that demanded she escape. He let his finger move from her arms to her shoulders and across her neck. He bent down for a kiss and she received it, darkening her mind to anything but the pleasure of him surrounding her, his lips on hers. She was greedy for affection; this court had turned so cold. She could not help herself.

It was Henry who pushed her away. "You want me. Why won't you have me in bed?"

Breathing hard, Anne struggled to awaken her thoughts again, to compose herself, to sit up. He helped her, lifting her off his lap and setting her back against the pillows.

"Don't you see it, Henry? I alone submit to God. No one else in this court does. They all practice a false religion."

"You've been reading the Hutchins book?" he said.

"Yes," she lied. She was afraid of the book, of what it might say of her, of what it might say of her brother.

"I set it out that my servants may see it, and even read it, Henry." This much was true.

"Are you so foolish, Anne? Your servants are educated and can make wise decisions. But it will encourage lawlessness among those who hear of it."

Anne reached for him, taking his hand. Maybe he lashed out because he was wounded. Maybe she could soften him, nurse the raw edges, and he would be tender to her always.

"I know your marriage is void in the eyes of God," Anne said, keeping her voice as soft and inviting as she knew how. "You tell me that is God's Word, and I accept it. But if you found such truth in one small verse in

Leviticus, why should you withhold this book from your people? Maybe they are in need of truth too. Something troubles me at night, Henry. I cannot describe it, but I do not think I will sleep well again until this book is free and among the people. I think it is God's will."

"What is the will of God?" Henry asked. His voice sounded tired and his eyes were not on her.

"Sons," she whispered, squeezing his hand.

Henry looked up and she read his face.

She had found her way into his heart.

The Thames was moving fast, and at this early hour, the stench of the city in summer had not risen. She sat, keeping her eyes ahead, past caring that her Yeoman never spoke. He was a shadow behind and before her, always, but he said nothing. They landed on the steps to lead into the church, and he helped her out of the barge. She was careful to keep her hood low so no one could see her face as servants escorted her in secret. Blackfriars hurt her eyes; the church had endless rows of glass that caught the morning sun, bouncing back bolts of every colour. She walked past window after window until she came to the back steps, where the poor begged. Earlier servants must have kicked the drunk and infirm away, because she was unhindered as she sneaked in, easing the plain wood door open.

Everyone knew where the trial would be. The servants had spoken of it freely enough, and there was much gossip about Catherine. Anne had heard them speaking with gristly satisfaction, the way the hungry picked at discarded bones after the meal, licking them to remember the taste of the flesh. This court feasted on the misery of its women.

Her eyes adjusted to the darkness as she felt the cool, still air at the foot of the stairs. The church was heavy with incense, and it made her head hurt. These close quarters were always pungent; she had been spoiled by the trip down the Thames in the fresh morning air. Anne had not thought until then of how drenched in odour the city was—how she had to brace herself before leaving a garden to go indoors, or kneel before the cross in a chapel. Wolsey's peculiar habit of carrying an orange before his nose as he walked through confined spaces, looking like a horse holding his own carrot, made sense. The city loomed above everyone, but the odours were the closest companions, crowding in unpleasantly and leaving one no air.

She began the ascent up the stairs, the air growing thicker and warmer. Her Yeoman had motioned for her to step aside and let him lead her, but she had declined. He followed as she sneaked into a private box. She kept her back to the wall so no one would see her, but it afforded her a good view. There was a semicircle of chairs at the end of the church, and all pews had been moved along the sides to provide seating for the court members. Henry's great throne sat at the top of the arch in the semicircle. It was the sun that all else radiated from, nestled just below the crucifix.

Anne saw that the court members were jostling for seats and there was much hushed conversation as the judges took their seats around Henry's throne. Campeggio, the cardinal Rome had sent, looked uneasy. Wolsey was there, his red cardinal's robes capped with fur, his face already red from the morning sun that found its way in through the stained glass. He would sweat himself to death by the end of the morning. She felt hot just looking at him and decided to remove her robe with the hood. No one would see her up here. The summer sun, the full court, and the lack of air promised to make this a difficult morning.

There was a stillness that began to grow as everyone waited for the king to appear. Anne studied the Christ resting over them all. His face looked so peaceful, and this gave Anne encouragement. Everything here was under His arms.

But blood ran hot here, a marked contrast to the men she had known in France. Every young man in England stood ready to defend the realm and destroy her enemies, grinding them into a fine dust that history herself would disdain and sweep away. The only enemy the English couldn't conquer was death. *Christ, save us,* she prayed. *Save us from ourselves.*

A trumpet startled her, making her heart leap as Henry entered the church in golden robes, layered over with a chain of stones as big as her fist set in thick claws of gold. The morning light came in from behind him, and he indeed looked like the sun. All bowed in reverence as he walked past to take his seat. As he did, he commanded them to rise and allow the proceedings to begin.

The queen entered, looking unwell, as if the weight of her robes was too much for her emaciated frame. She approached Henry's throne with small, weak steps, finally throwing herself down before him, her arms outstretched as if he would catch her. He didn't. Anne saw her back rise and fall, as if she was weeping, but no noise carried.

At last Catherine stood, and Anne saw no one bow. Catherine must have realized it, too, for she smiled sadly at the men circled around her. "You have no authority to read that book and make judgment on me. Death be on Hutchins' home! As for you, husband, I was a true maid. The marriage is lawful under God's eyes and the Pope's."

Henry called a witness.

"Aye, my king, on your brother Arthur's wedding night, when he had taken this Spanish princess as his bride, I was his attendant. Arthur emerged from his chamber in the early morning hours looking pale and tired. He said he had been traveling in Spain and it was hot work."

The court erupted into laughter, which most men corrected into fits of coughing.

Catherine glared at the witness. "This is not true! My marriage to Arthur was never consummated, as God is my witness. I put this to your conscience, Henry. The law of Leviticus does not apply to my marriage."

"If I have no authority to read and make judgment by it, how can you?" he replied.

Something about his gaze troubled Anne … the absence of emotion, though his wife of twenty years fought for her life before him.

Catherine pulled herself up to stand board straight and looked around the court. "I do not recognize your right to try me. As Queen, I am subject only to the Pope's laws, not yours. I have sent word to the Pope that he must try this case and render a just verdict. It is in his hands, God be praised."

As she turned to leave, Anne saw Henry grip Wolsey with an intensity as if to break his arm. Wolsey was trying to wrench free, keeping his back to the court so no one would see his dishonour. He whispered something to the king, and Henry smiled and released him, looking at the doors Catherine had just exited, followed by Wolsey. It took several minutes of deep, shuddering breaths before Henry was able to sit and formally adjourn the court. Anne fled down the back steps, her Yeoman once again behind her, unable to protect her should she meet an enemy suddenly. Anne's mind was racing—the Pope was no friend to Henry. The Pope catered to the Spanish for his own good reasons, to protect his own realm, and Catherine was unyieldingly Spanish. That she forced Henry to confront the Pope on this issue was a sign that she put more faith in Spanish power than in English law. Unless, of course, Catherine really believed the marriage was lawful in God's eyes and was fighting for faith, which Anne doubted. Anne had heard too many rumours about Catherine to think anything good of her.

Lost in her swirling thoughts, Anne took no caution as she fled and ran full into Wolsey just as her Yeoman's hand reached out and caught her. It was too late. Wolsey spun around, the cold smile of surprise on his face telling Anne that he had some reason to be glad she was here. It could not be a good one.

"Anne," he said.

She did not like her name on his lips.

"What's this I hear about you setting out a Hutchins book in your chambers for all to see? And you've been riddling Henry's mind about it, tempting him to create these grievous errors? Did the French send us a devil to cause mischief in the English court?"

The humiliation made her face red, though she already had a blush from the heat.

"When you stole into my library I knew why you were pursuing the king and seducing him at every turn. At least, this is what I tell the cardinals in Rome and those loyal to the church. You are either a treacherous reformer or a seducing witch, but your punishment will come regardless, and swiftly."

"Why do you poison my name?" Anne asked. "Nothing you say is true!"

"Ah, but this is: I have prepared a bedchamber at an estate where Catherine has been sent to recover from her exertion in court today. I have instructed her maids to care for her most gently and lavish all care on her that she may be pleasing to a man in every way. Henry should be arriving there. I have arranged for them to dine in her bedchamber, and Henry will make every effort to calm her outrage. Perhaps we need not involve the Pope in the king's great matter. Henry knows how to persuade a woman, does he not?"

Anne's stomach went sour, her throat closing around tears. "Henry will have the annulment because it is the law of God," she said, trying to speak without letting a tear escape. "As cardinal, this is your concern, yes? The law of God?"

"My concern as Chancellor of the Realm is Henry, and Henry needs an heir." Wolsey leaned in closer. There was rank decay on his breath as he whispered his next words. "I know you will not sleep with him, Anne, because you are not yet his wife. As long as Catherine still wears the title, why not give her one more chance to provide what you will not?"

I saw David bent over his work. There was a glass of whiskey on the table: I could smell it, the musky sweetness of grain and the sting of alcohol. I found I could move in this vision, as if I were in the room too. The Scribe stood behind me, his back to the door, so that it would not open. I didn't know if he was holding me in or something else out.

I craned over David's shoulders to see the papers scattered all over his desk. They were letters. I craned my neck to read one. They were all addressed to me.

> *Dear Bridget,*
>
> *All I ever wanted was to make you smile. I failed you, and when you were diagnosed, I tried to save you. I bribed every doctor I ever met at your cocktail parties until one of them came through. I got you into the best research study going for ovarian cancer. But it fell through because you can't stop making enemies of everyone you meet.*
>
> *But I never stopped loving you.*
>
> *And if there's an afterlife, I never will.*
>
> *Yours, David*

I gasped and David sat up, flicking something off his shoulders. Frowning, he looked around the room, looking through me. He must have felt my breath over his shoulder.

He reached into a desk drawer and pulled out a gun.

"Stop him!" I screamed to the Scribe.

"No," he replied.

I saw it, the most unlikely of books in the most unlikely of places. It was the Hutchins book and I knew it at once. It sat on his desk, a great thick black leather edition. He must have grabbed it for solace when he prepared for this moment. I shoved against it with all my might, trying to push it into his lap, startle him, stop him, but I couldn't move it.

"Please!" I begged the Scribe.

David was checking the chamber one last time, snapping it back into place as he released the safety.

The Scribe nodded, and the book scooted to the edge of the desk. It tumbled to the floor with a resounding thud. The noise frightened David, who screamed just as he pulled the trigger.

Chapter Sixteen

Rose stared at the coat of arms, rising red above her, the great lion and the unicorn frozen forever in flight around a Tudor rose. There were dragons on the fence posts, and inside farther down the lane she could see busts of famous healers from centuries past. This, at least, was whom she assumed the lifeless cold heads to be. She had only heard praise of them from the other desperate women who had brought their dying here. All of them fled before morning, so the boys would be presumed abandoned to the king's mercy.

Rose strained her head to see inside one of the windows, which were all firmly shut to prevent foul humours from the street to enter the hospital. The patients inside were sick enough without the dread diseases of her world being carried in on some chance breeze.

When she wondered which room her brothers had died in, drops on her eyelashes escaped down her cheeks. But they were disguised by the morning rain and Margaret's grabbing of her hand in fear. Rose's secret was kept another day.

Wolsey stood on the platform set in the field before St. Bartholomew's. A crowd pressed in on them from all sides. The vulgar cheers and jostling made the morning unpleasant. But Rose knew the late August sun would reveal itself soon enough from behind the clouds and they would all suffer. The mood would turn. She hoped the prisoners died before that happened. Margaret was trembling like one about to die herself, and Rose lifted her own clammy hand to place it over Margaret's. She held Margaret's jerking hand sandwiched between both of hers and took a deep breath.

It had been so long since Rose had experienced the spirits of the street, the meanness that lived here, the desperation. From the carriages and litters, the early morning London streets were beautiful, the grey stones wrapped round with white fog, the spires rising far above them into the heavens, the dragons and unicorns that appointed every post from a child's happy dream. But when humanity stirred and awoke, the fog became suffering and the dream was far away.

Sir Thomas sat to Wolsey's left, looking regal in his chancellor's robes and fur, watching his daughter and her servant with pleasure. Rose knew he expected this to be a great lesson for them. Seeing sin purged violently from another was the surest defence against allowing it to creep into one's own life. The public burnings, he said, were not only good for the condemned's soul but for the soul of England herself. Much mischief would be cut short here today.

Wolsey did not wait long for the crowd to silence so he could speak. Rose heard the murmurings around her; this waxy, fat cardinal lived in great luxury while they suffered to pay his men. Wolsey traveled through their streets upon a white horse, with two men carrying gilded crosses before him, lest anyone forget whose business Wolsey arrived on. The crosses, Rose thought, were a wise touch, as they were all that checked the wagging tongues around her. But it had always been this way, she knew. Nothing contented the people of the streets except money, and money was never enough. Poverty infected the blood with a painful hunger that nothing would ever fill. Justice herself was consumed and spat out in little shards; there were always rumours of a great Judge to set all things right someday. The rumours had not enough meat to sustain a child on, but they kept the half-truths with them always.

Wolsey held up a copy of a book, only slightly bigger than his own hand. "I have here a book of heresy!" he proclaimed.

The crowd listened.

"A man named Hutchins has translated the Holy Scriptures into the English language. This is his New Book, the words of Christ torn from their beautiful perch of Latin and discarded at your feet in a base language."

Not many spoke or moved. Rose knew most did not read anyway—what was a book to them?

"I offer a cash reward—five silver groats—to anyone who turns in this book today, or gives information about those who read it or sell it. It contains grievous, poisonous errors, great heresies against the Church, and it must be destroyed! If you want truth, come into the

churches, good brethren! Do not be tempted to destruc
tion by reading the Scriptures alone, without aid and
instruction. Indeed, to our shame, even women and
simple idiots gobble this book up, as if it were the fount
of all truth!"

The crowd laughed and Margaret tried to jerk her
hand away, growing so nervous she was shaking all over.
Rose held her hand with more force, turning to catch her
eye and steady her with a cold gaze. Margaret stopped
fluttering and rested against Rose, like a stunned animal.

Wolsey continued, waving the book over them all.
"It is a door to hell, leading these prisoners to a most
pitiful death, which by God's infinite mercy may purge
them of His wrath before they encounter Him face-to-
face today!"

Guards parted the crowd, leading a woman covered
in blood and feces through. She stank, her greasy hair
hung like ribbons around her face, and her body was
broken in so many hidden places that the guards had to
drag her, supporting her under her arms. The woman
lifted her head to catch the drizzling rain on her tongue,
and Rose cried out. It was Anne Askew. The crowd began
taunting her, pelting her with soiled rags and withered
apples. As the crowd parted before the guards, Rose saw
that a stake had been set at Wolsey's feet, not far from
the pulpit, with iron chains attached and bundles of
wood laid all around it, several feet high.

Sir Thomas stood. "Anne Askew, you are guilty of
reading the Scriptures in English to other women. Do
ye name them?"

Rose gripped Margaret's hand for strength.

Anne's head hung limp, and Rose did not knew if

she was still alive. "Oh, God save us, she's been racked!" Margaret whispered.

"Anne Askew, profess to the truth and receive God's mercy. Do you believe in the sacraments of the Holy Church?"

Anne lifted her head and the crowd gasped.

"The Bible speaks only of baptism and the Lord's supper, my lord. I cannot find the others there."

A few giggled under their breath. It meant nothing to them to see this; they wouldn't burn when the fires were lit. Rose began praying under her breath. It was all she could think of to do, but the prayers she knew were in Latin and she did not know what they meant. She whispered them anyway, the words in her mouth like a talisman, gone over and over again. She hoped God accepted them.

"What say ye about the sacrament of the host? Do ye receive the very body, bone, and blood of Christ when ye take communion?"

"I receive the spirit of His sacrifice. It is a great sin to push me to say more." Anne shook her head at More, and droplets of blood flung out, landing on her guards. They grimaced, and she drew a deep breath.

"I will ask you a question, Sir Thomas," she said. "If a mouse steals a bit of the bread, does he in fact nibble away the very body of Christ? Is it the bread or the spirit at work in communion?"

Many in the crowd laughed. Sir Thomas's lips set in a thin line and he shook a finger at her. "Saint Paul commanded that women must ever be silent, never to speak or talk about the Word of God!"

"Nay, this is not what Paul said," Anne replied,

"for I have read the passage. Women are not to speak in church to disrupt the teaching of Christ's words. I have not hindered the words of Christ! Have you read the Bible, sir? I do not think you understand the charges, so how can you prove my guilt?"

Sir Thomas grabbed the book from Wolsey and slammed it to the ground. No one moved.

"God's mercy upon me for my weakness!" he screamed. "If I was about my own business, I would see you burnt slowly today. But I am God's man, and I will offer you your life if you name the women of your sect."

Rose's blood rushed through her heartbeat, the violent beating rocking her off her feet. She clung to Margaret, who was staring at her father in a trance.

Anne's head dropped back down. She said nothing.

"I sentence you to burning!" Sir Thomas screamed again.

Anne's head lifted, and Rose saw white trails on her face, where a river of tears had washed away black filth. "I have read the Scriptures," Anne said. "Christ and His apostles ne'er put one soul to death."

Sir Thomas did not reply. He swept his hand to the back of the crowd. "Bring out Bilney!"

A man was dragged through the center of the crowd, but this man Rose did not know. She was relieved, as if his death would be less terrible to her, and was ashamed. Bilney was a tall, emaciated creature with a shaved head and burn marks evident all over his arms. Some were white and blistered, some red and oozing. He was draped in a thin linen shift that barely covered him down to his thighs.

"He's been practicing," a woman whispered near Rose. "Practicing over a candle, willing himself to be strong when he is burnt whole."

Wolsey stood and took over the prosecution as More collected himself.

"Thomas Bilney, you are charged with reading the work of heretics, this foul book in English. You have read this work and given it to others, including women. Will you repent?"

Bilney did not answer. Rose saw a thin treadle of spit hitting the grass at his feet as his head hung. Whatever tortures had been spared Anne for being a woman were surely visited on this man.

"Do you believe the church has authority to forgive sins?" Wolsey asked. The people strained to hear if there was an answer. Attending a bear-baiting was not nearly such sport. These matches provided great wit. Rose did not know how many in the crowd were swallowing back tears.

"No man, no thing, takes away sin but the blood of Christ."

The crowd gasped to hear Bilney's strong reply. There was no strength left in his weak frame for this.

"It is a sin for you to sell forgiveness."

"You are a heretic. I alone judge all matters of religion in this realm," Wolsey replied easily, as if he was brushing away a fly. "I am the Pope to you, and I say that the church offers cleansing through repentance and taking of the sacraments."

"What is the Pope to me? I do not find him in the Scriptures. I only find Jesus," Bilney answered, holding his head steady as his guards held him up under his arms.

"Oh, we have a true apostle!" Wolsey cried out, and the crowd snickered. "What say ye about Masses for the dead? Do they minister to those departed?"

"Nay! I must consider but one death, and that is Christ's. No one can help those who are already gone."

This was the reply Wolsey had hoped for. An angry spirit swept over the people, those who had lost children and lovers and sold everything they had to provide release for them from purgatory.

Rose threw her hand over her mouth, trying to stop herself from being sick. She did not know what Bilney was talking about, and prayed he was not right, and prayed he was not wrong. She had spent her money on a baptism for her baby and not medicine. She had spent what little she had to secure God's welcome for him into eternity. If Bilney was right, she had let him die, and would God forgive her that? Would the child, or her heart?

The crowd's faces swirled, and Rose's knees gave way. She heard Bilney yell out that Wolsey was the wolf who would not feed the flock but instead would eat them. As a man caught Rose and cradled her in his arms, she saw Sir Thomas trying to catch a glimpse of her over the crowd. She was dizzy and sick, but his kind eyes kept finding her, and she tried to focus on them, to give herself a center to steady the spinning world.

Anne and Bilney were led to separate iron stakes and secured to them by chains, a pile of wood all around them up to their thighs. No one in the crowd talked. The sheriff stepped forward and lit the fire, his back to the wind to give the flames a good start. Neither of the condemned spoke, their pale faces looking white against the blackened chains pinning them to the stake.

The flames snaked through the wood, scorching their feet. Anne screamed. The wind gusted past the sheriff, extinguishing the flames. Rose looked to the sky, to see if a strange deliverance was at hand, but the clouds were gone. There would be no rain, and the wind would not hold.

The sheriff tried to light the fire again, but the wind snuffed out his bundle of wood. Again he dipped his faggot in a torch burning on the lawn of the hospital, and this time the flames roared ahead of the wind, consuming the dry wood, the flames going as high as their thighs. Anne's shift, being longer, caught fire, and she was lost behind a veil of flames. Rose tried to stop herself from hearing her screams, but the effort of putting her hands to her ears swept her off balance again, and her rescuer pulled her from the crowd to Sir Thomas's carriage.

The stallions ran with great speed. The bumps and dips clacked her teeth together. Margaret sat, her eyes too bright, a doll's smile on her mouth.

"Why such haste, Father?"

More was looking at Rose but turned his attention to Margaret. "I learned today how deep the heresy is rooting here. Hutchins has been delayed finishing his translation of the Old Book into English, because the plague is moving again through Europe this summer. I must finish my public reply to his poisonous book and get it to the people to read."

Margaret's eyes were brimming, Rose saw.

"It's only a book, Father—little words on a page! Why did they have to be burnt?" she asked. "Perhaps Anne thought she was doing the right thing, letting women hear the words in English, so they could more correctly live by them."

"There are priests to teach women how to live, Margaret. Women cannot understand the whole of the gospel and render just opinions on its meaning. The Bible is law, and laws are administered by those with training. If every man tried to judge the meaning of the law for himself, would not chaos be the result?"

"But you taught us to search for truth!"

"Oh, Margaret, did I not teach you first to trust?"

Margaret wept, burying her face in her hands. Sir Thomas leaned across his seat and took her in his arms, patting her back. Rose cast her glance away, ashamed to witness this. It was her curse, wasn't it, to condemn those people who were to her the blessings of God, even as she fumbled in service to Him? She looked away from the pair and did not look back, even when Margaret spoke.

"I am sorry I doubted you, Father. I pray that book will be destroyed, and all who read it will fall under your just and merciful hand."

Chapter Seventeen

The first burning was in the city today; she had heard news from the servants. Closing her eyes, Anne saw the Pope's reedy, grim fingers encircling the city, choking believers, weighing purses and loyalties. Reformers wanted nothing but God's law taught plainly; the Church taught that this would lead only to chaos, if every man judged the law for himself.

Anne looked out over the Thames and knew she was the only woman with such a close view of this truth. She watched Henry, day by day, choosing whom to believe and when. He kept the Church close, despising its passions and coveting its power. He gave free reign to Sir Thomas to scourge and burn believers who presented inconvenient arguments of reason. More and Wolsey, who mocked grace and mercy, were destroying the city. She had heard such rumours about Sir Thomas that they set her teeth on edge. He persecuted heretics and scooped beggars and lost souls from the streets, forcing them to work in terrible conditions, living as slaves in his house. His wife had died under mysterious conditions, she had heard, no doubt driven to her death by his violent manner. Any man who was so cruel to heretics in public could only be a monster in private. Anne was sorry for his children and their certain suffering.

Henry would give him free reign to murder as it pleased the Pope, until the Pope gave him the annulment so he could marry Anne. She shuddered and was glad she had only peeked at the Hutchins book in her rooms, never submerging herself completely in the pages. She would not be drawn further in.

She inhaled and caught a whiff of fire. Probably a fire from the kitchens behind her in Greenwich Castle, but the smell of the roasting spits turned her stomach. She had business with the cook, however. She needed to speak to him.

As she walked from the kitchens, back through the portico shaped like a sun, the warm stones under her feet, she heard the hooves of horses and saw a servant running to raise the royal flag. Henry was back in residence. Anne rushed to find a place to hide. She was ashamed and betrayed, having trusted in him. She had thought he was becoming a man of comfort and righteousness. But he had spent all his good intentions in Catherine's bed, hadn't he? Anne looked the fool. Whether queen or concubine, forever she would be giving her heart and losing her dignity, in a dance that returned her again and again to this cowering moment. Shame burned in her stomach, branding her cheeks with red blotches. How could she have been stirred to love him? How could he have slept with Catherine if he professed to love Anne? She had not slept with Henry, but this was in obedience to God's law. How would God let her be humiliated for it?

A whiff of the fires caught her again, turning her stomach. God was on no one's side in this. Anne frowned.

A hand on her shoulder made her jump. Her Yeoman had found her, huddled in a dark hallway, unsure of where to run. It was a gesture that could cost him his life, but neither moved. His grip flooded her with peace. She closed her eyes, letting it wash down her body and work into every knotted muscle. She remembered being a child, when her father would cradle her or her brother would take her hand as they walked. There was still goodness in the world, she thought. There was still hope.

He dropped his hand and led her back into the portico. Henry was just entering and saw her. The Yeoman stepped into the shadows. Anne reached for him, but he was gone.

Henry took the distance between them in four strides. He towered over her, taking her hands in his own and lifting them to his lips. She was pulled into his embrace. His hands circling around her waist, she was tempted to believe she was wrong. Henry stroked the hair back from Anne's face, tucking it behind her ear, her jeweled crescent hairpiece letting too much hair spring loose. Henry ran his fingers over her face, setting little curls back into place.

She looked at him as he loomed over her. Her doubts were too weak to stand in his presence. He bent to kiss her, but she pulled back.

"What is it, Anne? Am I not to have even this?" His voice had an edge.

"I thought you would have had your fill," Anne replied, her heart pounding. She couldn't believe she had the sudden strength to test him. It was strange to her that he could make her so weak and so enraged in the same breath.

"And if I had, what business is it of yours?" He could turn in the same breath too.

She saw the courtiers all frozen, some from fear at witnessing an intimate moment, others in great hunger for more detail. This would make the gossips favoured seating partners at tonight's dinner.

"Leave off!" he shouted. Everyone fled like scurrying mice.

Now Anne was completely alone, drifting in the center of the portico. Henry circled around her, his anger setting itself in his jaw, flashing in his eyes. She looked down at her feet. The hairs along her arms prickled and rose. She could sense Henry behind her.

His arm shot out, grabbing her around the waist, and she screamed as he dragged her into the shadows.

They were alone in a stairwell, the cool air tainted with the scent of mould and leaching moss.

"I'll not be made sport of in public," he said.

"You come from Catherine's bed and accuse me of making sport with you?" she asked.

"Anne, she sent her case to the Pope, refusing to acknowledge me as her authority. I went there to convince her to step aside with grace, to save what little dignity she has left."

"And what of me, Henry, what of me? What of my dignity? Am I nothing but the king's whore?"

He slapped her. Anne placed her hand over her stinging cheek, turning to run from him. He caught her, pulling her in tightly. "Anne, Anne …"

She shoved back from him, fighting against his tightening grasp, jerking her arms, trying to stab him with her elbows.

He gave her a little freedom, releasing her only enough that she could look at him, keeping her arms pinned against her body.

"You have ruined me!" she cried. "If you let me go, what good would I be? My sister only received an offer of marriage after you ordered it. Who would dare love me?"

"You think I am going to discard you?" he asked.

Anne stumbled for a second over his sudden shift in humour. She took a deep breath, exhaling before she met his gaze.

"I am trapped," she said, his grip on her arms remaining firm. She laughed once, the irony lost on him. "You will not let me leave your court. Outside, my name is dragged through the streets. Inside I am betrayed by courtiers who hope to steal a little nibble of my soul, a moment of my distress, to make good conversation at their tables. This is a court of madness."

Henry stepped back from her, shaking his head. He turned to walk back into the light of the portico.

She sank down on the steps, her legs feeling like they were made of water.

"God help me," she whispered.

If Henry was violent in professing love for her, she did not know how he would behave when he was angry with her tonight.

Jane put her knee on Anne's back, leaning back and tightening the laces on her bodice until Anne cried out. Another girl was below her, fluffing out her skirts and strapping pattens to her shoes. Anne couldn't see her.

Jane came round and attended to Anne's hair, combing it carefully, making little ringlets set off from her face. She set the hairpiece on next and draped the veil across Anne's shoulders. Next came the cosmetics, a little powder with rouge for her cheeks and lips. Jane always was a little overzealous in applying powder to Anne's darker skin, and Anne reached out to steady her hand.

Tucking a pomander of perfume—her favourite, roses—into her bosom, Anne followed Jane to the dining hall. Anne forced herself to breathe in little measured doses.

Henry and Wolsey were already there. Anne took her place next to Henry, and her servants moved to another table, stealing glances back. It was a small dinner tonight, with only ten or so tables, mainly for all the body servants and a few special courtiers, the men who never did much beyond gossip and spy. But, Anne thought, Henry was a king who didn't mind intimacy with an enemy.

When the servers pushed open the wooden doors,

Anne knew what was cooking in the kitchens. Henry and Wolsey must have caught the aroma, too, for they glanced at the servers with questioning looks. Henry conferred quietly with Wolsey, who nodded. Anne's heart began beating faster, and she fiddled with a piece of bread she had no interest in eating.

The aroma was overpowering. The servers were running up and down the halls, staging their trays in a little room just outside the doors. Every time the doors opened, a stronger whiff of the meal came in with them. Everyone began to murmur. Some tried to eat the bread, keeping their eyes on a tapestry across the room or making meaningless chatter with their neighbour. But the scent grew, the warm summer air making it unbearably delicious.

Finally, they came in with it: great heaping platters of sausages, sizzling and steaming.

Henry jerked to his feet. "What is the meaning of this?" he screamed.

The youngest of the servers dropped his platter in fright.

Wolsey stood, outrage on his face. "Do you not know what day it is?"

Anne rose next. Jaws were flopping open all across the room.

"My king, do not be angry," Anne said. "Perhaps this is a most fortunate mistake."

Henry turned to her, his eyes blazing. The servant boy stooped, trying not to draw attention as he scooped the sausages back on his platter.

Anne turned to Wolsey. "My friend, we have a custom of not eating meat on Friday, and this is from the Church. Could you please remind us of the passage from Scripture that commands this practice? We would all be edified to know it, and the cooks will not make this same mistake again."

Wolsey's eyes narrowed. She would not be safe again around him. He smiled and addressed the room. "I see you have persisted in reading Hutchins. The Church teaches—"

"Forgive me, Cardinal Wolsey! I did not ask what the church teaches, for we all know that quite well. I am but a woman, and the Church will not allow me to read the Scriptures. So you must tell us where in the Bible it says we are not to eat meat on Fridays."

Wolsey took a sip of his wine, looking at Henry and the hungry courtiers, clearing his throat before speaking. "We honour …," he began.

This time Henry cut him off. "The passage?"

"I will retire to my room and find it, my king." Wolsey excused himself from Henry with a bow, not looking at Anne again, and left.

Anne whispered to Henry, "He will not be back. The passage does not exist. It is one more way the Church has controlled your life, your realm."

She smiled innocently at everyone in the room. "I have heard a delightful story today! Shall I tell it?"

Henry was still looking at the doors where Wolsey had departed. He muttered his "yes" to Anne and sat.

Anne spoke to him but with enough volume that others could hear. "A priest was wandering among the poor, selling indulgences. Salvation was to be purchased for a silver groat, and release from purgatory for the dead cost a half-angel. Forgiveness of all sins was included when you purchased salvation. One rough-looking boy approached the priest and asked, 'Sir, does forgiveness of sins cover only my past, or will I be forgiven for those acts I have yet to commit?' The priest was delighted to save such a rough-looking fellow, and he replied, 'Aye, purchase salvation and all sins are forgiven, even those sins not yet committed. God is wondrous to forgive us all our debts!'

"So the rough-looking chap paid a silver groat and listened as it fell into a purse weighted down with coins. The villagers all came round, marveling that the boy had been saved. The poor gave the priest their money, securing eternal rest for their dead and salvation from their sins. It was a happy day in the village, and as the sun went down, many people feasted and drank what little they had left, while the priest went on his way. But he had not gone two miles out of town when the boy leapt from behind a boulder, beating the priest mercilessly and stealing his coin purse. He ran all the way back to town, giving everyone back double and triple what they had given the priest, because the boy had paid in advance for this great sin, and it was no sin at all."

With that, Anne speared a great sausage and commenced eating. If there were whispers of protest, she didn't hear them, for her heart was beating too loudly.

Chapter Eighteen

"Destroy it!"

Margaret stood above her, with a finger jabbed in her face. Rose closed the book and stood, clutching it to her chest, shaking her head. They were in Margaret's bedroom. No one else was near; all the others were taking their exercise. Rose had begged off, saying her head hurt, but Margaret knew why she sought time alone.

"Listen to what I read today, Margaret:

> "And behold, a woman in that city, which was a sinner, as soon as she knew that Jesus sat at meat in the Pharisee's house, she brought an alabaster box of ointment, and she stood at his feet behind him weeping, and began to wash his feet with tears, and did wipe them with the hairs of her

head, and kissed his feet, and anointed them with ointment.

"When the Pharisee which bade him, saw that, he spake within himself, saying: If this man were a prophet, he would surely have known who and what manner woman this is which toucheth him, for she is a sinner. And Jesus answered … There was a certain lender which had two debtors, the one ought five hundred pence, and the other fifty. When they had nothing to pay, he forgave them both. Which of them tell me, will love him most?… I entered into thy house, and thou gavest me no water to my feet: but she hath washed my feet with tears, and wiped them with the hairs of her head. Thou gavest me no kiss: but she, since the time I came in, hath not ceased to kiss my feet. Mine head with oil thou didst not anoint: but she hath anointed my feet with ointment. Wherefore I say unto thee: many sins are forgiven her, for she loved much.…

"And he said unto her, thy sins are forgiven thee.… Thy faith hath saved thee, Go in peace."

"Shut the book." Margaret's voice was cold. Nothing had reached her.

"Margaret, the priests are wrong! They are teaching error! You must trust me: This is life or death to the simple! You did not know me before I came here. I trusted the priests and it wrought death! Here is the truth! Please, Margaret, open your eyes. It is the Church that must be destroyed!"

Margaret slapped her with such force that Rose fell back against the bed.

"The Church is my father!" she shouted at Rose. "The Church is law and orderly lives, and these things my father has given his life to. I will not see it undone by a *servant*." She spit that last word out of her mouth as if it were sour to her.

A great shouting out in the hall startled them both. The boys were whooping and running about, and Margaret went to the door to peer out. She turned back to Rose, her face still hard.

"Wipe the tears from your face, Rose. The king's messenger is here."

Margaret swept from the room. Rose started to replace the book under her mattress, but she knew Margaret would look for it there. There were not many other hiding places in the room. There was a washstand and little desk, plus Margaret's bed. Rose slipped the book under Margaret's mattress and wiped her palms across her face to clear it before she ran out.

"What is the meaning of this?" Sir Thomas looked horrified to be holding a red velvet pouch.

"Cardinal Wolsey has been fired. He surrenders the

Great Seal and the king ordered it delivered to you. You are to replace him."

"On what grounds was Wolsey fired? What has happened?" More asked. He still held the pouch out and away from his body.

"His many failures are known to the king, chief among them his failure to obtain the annulment from his master the Pope. The Bible says one cannot serve two masters, so Henry has freed him from his burden."

Sir Thomas opened the bag, as if he was uncertain whether the messenger spoke true. He emptied it into his palm, and Rose saw a wide silver medallion, catching the light enough to make the figure of a king on horseback visible even from her distance.

Sir Thomas, looking pale, sat on a couch. "Is it my job, that I secure the king's annulment? So he may marry the Boleyn girl?"

"Aye, sir, the king holds great respect for the universities of England, of which you are a brilliant example. He is satisfied you will bring speedy justice to the matter."

A household servant walked, unawares, into the room. He looked frightened to see all gathered around More, who did not look well. He studied the livery the messenger wore and fell to his knees. "Long live the king!" he cried out.

More looked up, the spell broken. He laughed, a small, unmerry snort. "There is no reason to fear. What do you need?"

The boy focused his glazed stare on Sir Thomas. "Bainham, sir. He will not abjure."

Sir Thomas sighed. Rose thought he looked heavier around the face and midsection. Perhaps it was just the angle he sat at. She wondered if the burnings and persecutions worked upon his appetite, making him ever more hungry. Could he feast on the deaths? She wondered how a kind face could hide such secrets.

He caught her staring at him and she blushed, her stomach tightening with nervous pinches.

Sir Thomas addressed the messenger. "A heretic," he explained. "I had him whipped at my Tree of Truth, but to no avail. This madness runs deep. I cannot dig the whip in far enough to scourge it out." He turned to the servant. "Have him sent to the Tower for racking."

The servant bowed and left.

More turned to the king's messenger.

"I will accept this charge, with my most humble obedience to the king. God preserve Henry and England!"

The messenger left, and Sir Thomas put his head in his hands. "I have heard such rumours, always rumours, trailing the king like body servants. There was a rumour that Anne served sausage on a Friday just to taunt the faithful. All these whispers, but the truth is as black as the stain of rumour. She is a witch, despising the things of God, consorting with the devil to cause England to fall."

He rose and walked round the room, biting his lips in thought. "Witches can be saved only through burning, but I cannot get to her." More didn't speak this to anyone but the air.

"I cannot understand Henry's mind in dispensing with Wolsey, save that she has cursed him," he said. "Wolsey was his link to the Church. How can Henry take the law into his own hands and dispense with the Church?"

He was becoming agitated, speaking. "I heard Anne gave him a copy of the Hutchins book. Filth! I have sent my own treatise on the subject to the king but received no word back. Perhaps the Boleyn witch got to it before he did and destroyed it. Dear God, save me! This evil woman may desire my death! I will fall under her curse unless You save me, unless I work against her. As long as she is near him, he cannot be made to see truth, for he is bewitched. She has to burn, or he will not be released."

He stopped and looked up, past the girls, not seeing them, his eyes wild before they closed in prayer. "Oh, God, may this cup pass from me!"

⚜

Margaret heaved Rose's mattress up on one side, peering beneath. Scowling, Margaret dropped the mattress back to the floor and walked to the door as Rose watched.

"Do not leave this room tonight. I will attend my father and return later."

Rose sat on her mattress when Margaret was gone, not sure what to do, not even sure what to think. Sir Thomas said Anne had served sausage on Friday. Was Anne truly a reformer, or was she just provoking the faithful? Who could be trusted? A king with two women or a chancellor with two lives? Sir Thomas had as many secrets as any man she had met, yet he had a veneer of honour. Yes, he was honourable, was deeply good, and this is what comforted him as he did the bloody work. He was willing to educate girls but burned those who read the wrong book. He loved his queen, Catherine, and served the king who betrayed her. And the last secret, Rose knew, was what he kept in his heart for her—the thing that pushed him to punish himself each night with a whip and scourge.

The birds were loud tonight in the garden. One called above the others, a single voice piercing through the twitterings and wisps of songs. She listened to him, waiting for each new call, wondering what made him sing. A cool breeze caught her from the window and refreshed her. She had not realized how tired she was, how flushed and sweaty. She had needed this air.

Her gown was too hot and she couldn't bear it touching her skin. The linen shift beneath it was damp and sticky, the bodice too tight for a good deep breath. Rose got up and fled the closed hot room. She would find comfort tonight in the garden, the buds and blooms that stayed constant whether storm or sun.

It was a child's rain, soft and toying, tapping gently, unseen on her shoulders and the top of her head. Only a spider's web caught the shimmering, winking little droplets, pinning them against the deep green leaves. The birds sang, but she couldn't see them nestled in the trees and among the roses. There were no other noises, save for her footsteps as she moved between forgetful blossoms that gave no care to the wind's sharp reminders. She stopped and sat on a bench, pinching and picking off the green lichen that grew and reminded her faintly of turnips.

She stayed until her damp shift was cold and a chill crept into her bones. The summer was almost past.

Though flowers remained, and jasmine surrounded her as it crept over the walls, she knew the winter was creeping nearer. She didn't want it to come. She didn't trust it.

No lights were flickering in the windows above her. The children and servants must be in bed, she realized with a start. She had stayed too long. Margaret would be furious. Margaret was ready to throw her from the house, Rose knew, except that Rose could spill her secrets and bring shame to the family. Margaret wanted to keep a tight leash on her.

She crept past the torch at the garden gate and to the torch dancing in the breeze near the house door. She slipped off her pattens from her shoes so she would make no noise as she crept to her room. She entered the silent home and kept a hand along one wall as she moved, not waiting for her eyes to adjust to the darkness. Voices caught her attention and she slowed.

It was Sir Thomas; she could tell by his inflection and the deep bass of his voice. The servants had all been so nervous due to the whippings of prisoners at the gatehouse that their voices had grown higher lately. The other voice was softer, a woman's voice.

Rose crept down the hall to his study and listened. Yes, it was Sir Thomas, and she thought the second voice was Margaret's. To be sure, she crept closer and peered in through the door left cracked open for a breeze from the garden gate.

Margaret was lifting off a hair shirt from her father—a bristled, thick garment. Rose saw that Sir Thomas's broad back was red with scratches and wounds. Margaret dabbed on an ointment from an amber-coloured glass jar. Sir Thomas groaned under his breath. The medicine

smelled like lavender to Rose; its sharp scent flowed out
to find her.

"Let me take this away," Margaret said softly.

Sir Thomas shook his head.

"It has done its work," she protested.

Sir Thomas shook his head.

Margaret picked up the shirt, lowering it over Sir
Thomas's head as he moved to put his arms through it.
Rose could hear him suck wind through clenched teeth
as it touched his skin. Next, Margaret lowered a linen
shirt over his head and helped him into this.

"The Church teaches our suffering catches the eye of
God," Sir Thomas said. "Suffering makes Him inclined
to answer our prayers."

Rose shook her head. She suspected suffering caught
the devil's eye just as fast. Those who suffered were the
first to drown in whiskey and live abused. They always
tried first to purge their pain with evils; it was the only
thing they knew intimately. They were all children,
afraid that grace burned at first like medicine on a cut.

"But why must you suffer?" Margaret asked. "Is it
punishment that you weren't a priest? Do you regret
having us?

Sir Thomas turned and took her hand. "Regret you?
No. Suffering keeps my thoughts pure. I must be a good
father, a holy example. You are the reason I wear the hair
shirt, yes, but only that I may bear the punishment for
sin in my body and spare you from it."

"But I have sinned, Father," Margaret said. Rose
saw her chin trembling. "The book you seek, the man
Hutchins? I ..." She paused for a steadying breath. "I
read it."

"I know," he replied. "A servant found it under your mattress and brought it to me. You are young, Margaret," he comforted her, "and illicit ideas will sometimes sway the young. I have taken vengeance for your name, my dear. I have arrested the women who were responsible for spreading the books, encouraging you to folly. They will be racked, and perhaps burned if they cannot ask forgiveness. I will make sure the idea has no appeal to any other youth, and no other father will suffer the grief I felt."

Rose was sick. The darkness forced itself down her throat, making her retch. She clasped a hand over her mouth.

"Are the dresses you have ordered ready?" Sir Thomas asked.

"Yes, Father," Margaret replied. She did not look well, either.

"Most excellent. King Henry has invited us to a banquet. He has seized Hampton Court from Wolsey and will hold the banquet there. Anne Boleyn will be in attendance, I suppose, but you must not speak to her. I will not have you infected with her pratter. Stay with Rose and follow her good example, for she loves you."

Rose clucked her teeth in sorrow, an involuntary tic that escaped without her willing it. Sir Thomas and Margaret glanced towards the door.

Rose crept quietly back, pressing into the wall so that the darkness hid her well. As soon as she was farther down the hall in safety, she turned and fled to her room.

❊ ❊ ❊ ❊ ❊

I couldn't stop laughing through my tears. David was still shaking from the accidental firing; he had blown a hole through his elderly neighbor's ceiling three inches wide. She was cursing him in between puffs of oxygen.

"You're nothing but a *scribbler!*" She wheezed the word like it was the very definition of filth. "I raised my sons to earn their bread! Not like your kind!"

He sat, the book in his lap. When his own breathing returned to a steady cadence, he noticed what was written. He read the words. And read them again. Looking around the room, he knew someone was with him.

I bent to kiss him but was swept away.

Chapter Nineteen

She walked slowly towards him. Her stomach was lurching and cramping; she had not held on to her breakfast that morning.

Last night she had dreamed again of a black crow, eyes cold and dead, flying to her. The bird alighted on the parched dry grass and craned its neck to peer at her. Anne stumbled back in her dream and fell far, far away, until she awoke sweating and sick. Her Yeoman replaced the dying torch outside her chamber, and she slept closer to the light after that.

Henry sat on a tall wooden chair, its back rising a few inches above his head, emphasizing his height over all the men in the room. They all were nervous around him and cast their glances down and away when she entered.

He wore a crested golden doublet with a golden embroidered robe over his shoulders. His legs were crossed and he sat at an angle, showing them to their advantage.

Anne bowed before him. Obedience came easily to her. It was not godliness. It was her weakness. It was her fear and her secret.

Henry rested his chin in his hands, one finger stroking his lips. His eyes were hungry and hard as he snapped his fingers. Anne heard a commotion behind her as a man's hands wrapped around her neck. She met Henry's eyes and sank, her knees giving way. The man behind her moved his hands to her waist, holding her up. Henry's eyes went up at the corners; he might be laughing at her.

She found her knees could support her and stood, and the man behind her released his grip, returning to his assignment. His hands went round her neck again and cold metal was fastened, pulled tight across her neck. Next he came round and took her hand, slipping a fat egg of a ring on her finger. Her hand was so weighted that she raised it several times without thinking, testing the strange feeling. The man continued until the jewels rested on her body like pikes, driving her further in, making her smaller, pinning her in this body. Her splendour complete, the courtiers raised their eyes to see her, and all bowed.

Henry stood, offering his own hand, weighted with jewels, veined and warm. She took it. Her stomach came alive again, flipping and burning, her body responding with its own language at his touch. His skin was reassuring on hers; no one touched her here except by accident, she thought, or when she was being dressed or fed. He touched her with clear intention, and her body came alive. She clutched his hand tightly, wanting more, wishing it would find her in this dress, under these jewels, and release her from this bright, smothering world. Surely there was a man under those robes, those jewels. She had never known him. If only they could slip free.

"Your rival is gone."

She did not understand his meaning. "My king, please tell me, who is my rival?"

Henry laughed, looking back at his servants and courtiers, who all laughed, too. They knew, Anne realized. How much happened in these walls—a universe that spun and changed while she was not present.

Henry rose and kissed her on the forehead. His doublet was scented with the thick spiciness of his clove perfume, and she sensed the warm flesh under the heavy robes, the strong beating heart just beyond the gold crest.

"To please you, Catherine has been banished to an old, forgotten estate where she will trouble you no more. She has surrendered the crown jewels to you, as the rightful queen."

Anne opened her mouth to say something, pushing back from his embrace, and he caught her open mouth with a kiss.

He spoke. "Tonight there will be a banquet in your honour, where I will bestow not one, but two, earldoms upon your father. His name will be secure, and your brother will be the heir. Many will attend tonight to see the new queen and discover what justice God has wrought."

He leaned to whisper in her ear, and his breath was

hot on her neck. Her stomach flipped at the sensation. "See how I love you."

She was hungry. That was the shame of it. There would be elderberry syrup, as the elderberries were at last ripe for picking. Those fall fruits encapsulated a perfect spring rain and lingering summer days and let you remember them both in one satisfying bite. She remembered picking them with her brother ... how the juices stained her chin and made his teeth black. They had howled with laughter, careless in their joy.

The other fall fruit, hawthorns, would be turning orange, and the songbirds would eat those before flying away for the winter. Anne, too deep inside the palace to hear them, was suddenly sad because they would take something of herself with them and only leave the dread of winter. She closed her eyes and stopped, as if she could hear the beating of their wings. *God,* she prayed, *how I long to fly away with them. How different this would all look from a distance.*

She opened her eyes in the cold air and realized she was crying. Her Yeoman stood at her side and nodded, once. Perhaps it was just as terrible to be a Yeoman, or any other servant in this palace—all of them witnessing events, none of them able to step outside of who they were, none of them able to act. Everyone's livery served to announce their moves in advance—how far each may go, and what each may say. Only Henry was free.

Except for this: The Pope would not grant the annulment, and Anne would not grant her body. Both claimed to serve God's interest, but Anne suspected, from His distance, there was no real interest at all. This was the growing fear in her heart, the reason she dreaded winter. She had once thought all things were under His control, and He would allow the bitter weather to claim only so much ground but no more. Maybe in the past, winter had claimed only what it had appetite for. Maybe it was hungrier now. Maybe many more would die.

She pushed the Hutchins book under her mattress, afraid to even touch it. She wanted any reason to never read it, but it called to her each day. If she listened, she could hear of sword striking sword, of metal shields and boots marching through darkness, the great iron heart of war, beating between its pages. It terrified her.

She was led to her table and seated. She searched the room and saw, with much relief, her father and brother seated at the table near Henry's seat. The room had been arranged so that Henry's table was at the top of the room, nearest the doors the servers used, which served two purposes. First, his food was the hottest and fresh, and second, that every other table could be turned to look upon him as they ate. The other tables were lined up, perpendicular to his, all in a row, with about sixteen people at each table, and eight tables all in a row across the room.

George and their father looked well. Anne bit her cheek as she smiled and nodded. She would not let them see her distress. She would not spoil tonight for them.

All rose when Henry entered and took the seat

above her, just on her right. The jewels of the queen dug into her green silk dress, and she waited as the guests murmured their comments on her placement, her dress, her jewels, and her demeanour. What stories they would weave out of the thinnest material, the way she reached for the butter dish, the way she ate with pleasure or disinterest, the way she held a fork or smiled at a server.

Henry lifted his goblet, and it commenced.

As they ate, Henry singled one man out. "Anne, you have heard stories of the man, but have not met him. This is Sir Thomas More, and his daughter is seated at the table just beyond us."

Henry pointed to the table facing hers on the left. A girl who looked to be no more than sixteen stood, her eyes not meeting Anne's, her body rigid as she bowed. It was not so hard, between women, to understand that the girl hated her. It would be lost on Henry, of course, and impossible to explain. The daughter had a servant, though, and this girl smiled and met Anne's eyes for a second before she bowed her head in respect. Anne tried to keep her face still and composed. There was no sense giving the servant away and causing her a beating later tonight.

Sir Thomas was asking a question, and Anne returned her attention to him.

"How do you find the English court? Do you mark it well as compared to the French?"

"Aye."

Anne would not follow a snake back into its den. She would stay here, in the plain sun of easy conversation. It was curious, though, how unremarkable his face was. Perhaps another woman could find it compelling and wish to kiss those lips, but Anne could not imagine how a woman would blind herself to the evil he did, and allow herself to be swept into his bed. While they dined, were not a dozen or more poor souls in the Tower? She had the book herself, in her bedroom not far from here. The servants rushing in and out of the doors at the end of the hall—they had stolen glances at it. Some had even read a page or so … those who had learned to read in their time here. Anne looked over the room and wondered how many of them More would like killed tonight.

She raised her goblet to her lips, keeping her face turned from him, and drank. More's daughter gasped. Anne froze, Catherine's ring before her face as she held the pewter goblet.

Henry continued eating.

"Forgive my poor mind, for I do not know what has happened at court today," Sir Thomas said. "You wear the queen's ring. Are you made queen?"

Henry dug his spoon into a terrine set before him. "She will be queen soon enough," he commented, and the dish was passed to Anne. "The marriage is a formality."

It was her favourite, brawn, and she had no appetite.

Henry followed her to her bedroom. He was brushing her hair away from her shoulders, and his hands were moving along her back, finding the buttons on her bodice. He was pleased with the evening. Anne saw her hand and knew she had what she had asked for. She had honour and a secured good name.

She grabbed his hand and kissed it, praying if she held it so, it would not strike her when she spoke. "Henry, we are not free yet. I thank you for the earldoms of my father. You have given me what I asked."

He pulled his hands back, but she would not release them.

"You have her jewels and her bed. Why are you not content?" he asked.

"You have not given me God's blessing of marriage."

Henry sighed, and Anne released his hands. He walked a pace away, turned back to her, coming and wrapping his arms around her waist, brushing his face against her hair.

"Anne, you are too new to court to see this well. There are two questions here, are there not? What is the will of God? And what is the will of man? The will of God has been made plain. Catherine is cast off, and you will bear a son. This I have done, and this you will do, but you must silence your inexperienced mind and let me be king in all matters."

The pleasure that swept over her at his touch was the rush of fools. Her mind was opposed to her desire.

"And for the will of man?" he continued. "The will of man is power. The Pope wants power over my realm, my enemies want power over me, and I want the power of a great name."

"Aye," she replied. It was safe to agree to this much.

"But, Anne, who must you please: God or man?"

"Henry, I am but a woman. It is you I must please."

"Why will you not have me?"

"Because you are a man who is king. Once there was a woman who found what was pleasing to the eye and good to her taste, and when she offered it to the man, death entered the world. I will not make her mistake."

"Let this sin be on the man. Let me taste first."

"Have you not thought that perhaps the will of God is bound up in the will of men? I fear your desire for me is God's judgment on the Church. That to have me, you must free the people to read the Scriptures for themselves. Let the Hutchins book go out. Call off Wolsey and More. I am afraid there is a coming war."

"Is what they say true? Are you a witch, sent by the reformers?"

She took his hand and pushed it into her bodice, between her breasts, to the hot, flushed place where, beneath, her heart was beating too fast.

She wanted to kiss him, to let him feel her willingness beneath his touch.

Henry's face turned stern as he moved his hands to pull her in close, his eyes lingering on the place his hand had been. He pulled her in tight, too tight, so that his strong hands were bending and snapping the bones of her bodice, digging them in to her side. She bit her lip to keep from crying out.

He whispered in her ear. "If I am driven from the garden for this, I will not go alone."

He released her and called to a servant who ran and listened to a quiet message. The boy returned, the court scribe close behind, trying not to spill ink from the black glazed inkwell, the feather dancing in his hand over the flapping papers. A boy behind him carried a candle and dish and was sweating profusely as he tried to keep the flame alive despite his fast pace.

The scribe, clearing a place on a table near them, set down the goods and prepared to write. The servant ran and fetched a little stool from the kitchen and the scribe thanked him, then cleared his throat and looked in Henry's direction.

"Write for me two warrants," Henry said.

The scribe picked up the feather quill, dipping it in ink and tapping.

"Write for me an arrest warrant for Cardinal Wolsey. He is to be tried for praemanuire, challenging the king's authority by exercising too much of his own. He will be tried in Leicester at my first convenience. Write a warrant for Cardinal Fisher, too, the priest who botched Catherine's trial and sent the case to the Pope. The Pope finds great delight in this man's clever thinking. We will send the Pope his head, with our best wishes for a speedy conclusion to my great matter."

The scribe made a noise like he was choking as he tried to swallow. Anne's skin grew hot and prickly, her breath shallow as she met Henry's eyes. He was smiling. The scribe worked quite fast, no doubt having written many such warrants for Henry in his time here. His was, in fact, the only safe job in the castle, as Henry's wrath was always narrowly focused on another when his work was being done.

The scribe stood, the documents finished. He held a dish over the candle and nodded in Henry's direction. Henry took off his ring and handed it to Anne.

"Seal the warrants," he said.

Anne held the heavy gold ring with his seal.

The scribe poured the melted red wax onto the paper, and Anne watched the thick red pool as it reflected the candlelight. All waited. She felt them all tensing, all except Henry, who pursed his lips in pleasure, as if watching a cockfight. She held the ring a moment more, and wished it were a dagger that she could drive into her stomach. She heard a heavy coarse breathing, and realized it was her own. The wax was cooling on Wolsey's warrant. She tried to summon an image of the man at his worst but instead saw his watery eyes, looking at her with pity on her first visit to his office. He had not wanted her here, and he had been right.

"I will send men to investigate Sir Thomas," Henry promised. "Perhaps there is something out of order in his estate."

She plunged the seal into the wax, scalding her fingers where she held the ring too close. Wolsey had not saved her, and he was damned. Maybe they both were.

Next was Cardinal Fisher's warrant. The scribe poured the wax and stepped back. Anne turned and looked at Henry. He looked alive with pleasure. He saw her faltering and stepped to her side.

"Anne, Anne," he whispered, stroking her hair. "Finish it and we will be together."

Anne began to say something but Henry whispered again.

"If it proves too difficult for you, I will finish. But I will write more. Your brother, for instance. He is guilty of an unspeakable crime, isn't he? One deserving a wretched, public death."

Anne clenched her jaw and forced the seal into the wax. The servants slipped the papers from under her hands and fled.

Anne turned and looked at Henry, her stomach sickened. She thought she was going to faint and reached out to him to catch herself. He caught her and dragged her into his embrace.

"That was," he said, "delicious."

Chapter Twenty

Rose shoved the coins into the leather drawstring. She looked around the room for anything else of value that might fit. She spied a ring with a nice thick pearl. Margaret never wore it. It would not be missed. She was slipping it into the bag when she was aware of someone watching her.

Spinning around, she saw Sir Thomas in the doorway.

"You're stealing from Margaret," he said and sat on her bed with a sigh.

Rose held the bag in plain sight, being too late to hide it.

"She's gone to the kitchen to ask for milk," he said. "We're alone."

Rose did not like him sitting on the bed or his casual manner. It frightened her.

"What have you done, Rose? What have you infected my children with?"

"I do not know what you mean," she replied.

"They were obedient children until you came here. Margaret is reading this snake they call Hutchins; her mind is poisoned by sick rhetoric. Who are you, Rose? A spy sent by him to destroy me? To get at me through my children?"

"I was no one before I came here. I never heard of Hutchins."

"That's a lie. The day I questioned you in my study, you told Cardinal Wolsey and me that he was preached in your parish."

"I just wanted to give you the answer you wanted. I was afraid you might throw me out if I didn't please you."

"I'm going to throw you out now."

"No, you're not. Margaret needs me."

"Margaret needs a steady hand. I won't have her infected by the world. Not their lies and not yours. I will keep her in this house, and in the Church, and you will not taint her!"

Rose bowed her head. "Everyone is tainted, Sir Thomas. We are all scarred, we all have secrets, and not one of us is clean. This is the truth you hide from the people, and from your daughter."

"More lies! More heresy! The Church is holy! Her saints are holy! Never speak a word against them, or I will throw you out, girl." He rose to his feet, his face pinched and flushed with blood."

She didn't want to argue. She didn't want to break him. But some truths could turn to poison in your veins if they're not spoken.

"I was Wolsey's mistress. He abandoned me to the

street when he found I had slept with another priest. I had a son."

"Another man has known you?" he whispered. Something like hope fell away from his face.

She looked at him plainly. "No man has known me. Many have had me." She paused to let her words find him. "We are all stained," she said quietly.

Margaret walked in, the door swinging in its arc and startling Rose and Sir Thomas. Margaret, seeing their faces, grabbed the door to stop it and retreat.

"I am finished with her," Sir Thomas said to Margaret, with a light voice that strained to sound carefree. He left without looking back.

Margaret looked so tired, Rose thought. She had aged these last few months, and when she turned her head, the candlelight showed the woman she was becoming. There was so little of the child left in her. Rose tried to pretend it was only childhood passing away, not innocence. She could not live with the guilt if Margaret became hardened.

Rose was stupidly holding the bag, her secret plainly between them. But she did not set it down.

Margaret looked up at her. "I do not wish him to die, Rose. I love him, did you know that? He was once one of us, seeking patronage among the rich, among Father's friends. A good-looking boy, with red cheeks and dark hair. He was so earnest, so impassioned. I believed in him deeply, though I met him only a handful of times, often as he was leaving a house, dejected that no one was interested in his ideas. He wanted to translate the Scriptures—not from the older translations, but go back, he said, to the original texts. He would master Greek and Aramaic and translate from these. Everyone thought he was a fool. The Vulgate was hard enough to understand for the priests. Why did we need a boy's interpretation of the original text?"

Her voice was far off, and she stroked her skirt as she smiled. "But I believed in him, though I had no idea what he was really talking about. I gave him a coin I had stolen from my father's purse, and he kissed me on the mouth, sweetly. It was my first kiss." She sighed. "It has been my only kiss."

She pressed her palm against her mouth, closing her eyes. "I want that life, Rose. I want to know a man and be kissed every night. I want to be in a home where books do not matter as much as love."

"Margaret," Rose began.

"We do not wish him to die, do we? Let us take the money we can gather and send it to him for secure passage. There is a safe house in Antwerp where the law will protect him. If he can make it to this house, no one can arrest him as long as he dwells in it. We will pay for his safe arrival and board. "

Rose did not move or reply.

"Everything will be all right, Rose. You'll see."

Margaret took off her shoes and lay on top of her bed in her clothes. She closed her eyes for sleep and shared her last thoughts of the day. "Sentiment is turning in Henry's court. Hutchins is gaining favour. Anne promotes him freely. My father will have to accept Hutchins. The differences of theology will be mended, and he'll see how I have changed from that girl to a woman, how I have aided him in secret here, how I have read his works as no other woman has, with great intensity and clarity of mind. He will be entirely captivated."

Rose held the bag and looked at her. Margaret's face had settled into peaceful lines. Rose set the bag on the night table between them and blew out the candle.

Rose heard the rain, a thousand little drummers against the roof. The room had a chill, and she pulled her blankets up, tucking them under her chin. This season was the most accursed on the streets. The autumn rains were heavy and often, and the wind came behind them to freeze your skin to the bone. The sun slunk away, defeated earlier every day, so that by the time you found something to eat at noon, you had to worry about the night. Sir Thomas had rescued her from that life, and he had not thrown her back to it, not yet.

Margaret was up and dressing herself, so Rose heaved herself out of the warm bed to help her. The room was dark; the sun had not broken through the dark clouds. Margaret laughed at Rose's fumbled attempts on the buttons of her bodice. She had been so sweet these past few weeks; no more had been spoken of the leather purse, or Hutchins, or his book. Rose was uneasy about this new peace. It was not from God—that much she could tell. Something had passed between father and daughter that Rose did not know and could not understand, having no father herself.

A servant holding a brass candleholder knocked and eased the door open. "Come, come! Sir Thomas has a visitor. He wants to see you."

They followed her into the family room lit by candles, though the curtains were drawn back. The windows showed the sky being a dour grey colour, tinged with modest blue.

Sir Thomas sat on the couch, a low piece of furniture with a soft yellow covering. Around him were bits of grass and herbs, dried flowers, and a thick blanket sweet smoke. Rose inhaled, trying to place the odour. When she realized it was frankincense, the scent of the Church, her stomach sickened. A woman dressed in a nun's robes stood in the corner not looking at any of them. She held her arms at her sides and spoke in whispers to herself.

Sir Thomas must have decided to let most of the household sleep, for there were only Rose, Margaret, the oldest boy, and a few of the servants. Sir Thomas did not look well and perhaps had not slept. His eyes had puffed, loose bags beneath them, and his mouth was drawn tight with exhaustion.

He looked at Rose, studying her slowly as if she were appearing in his dream. He sighed, shook his head, and began.

"God has heard my prayers. This is a praise to Him, and it is my fear." He was standing, walking to look out the dark window. "All of my life, have I not exhorted that He was close? The wickedness of man would bring Christ to earth in vengeance. What I did not understand, my children, is that many would be caught in His net."

He addressed the nun. "Do you still wish to speak to the children?"

"Darkness falls on the land in the ninth hour!" she crooned, her voice waving and rolling in crescendo. Rose wanted to slap her. It was a cheap way to earn a living. What Rose had done had no honour, but it was still better than this.

"The faithful must endure many sufferings," the nun cried, "but blessed is he who remains faithful to the end!" She wrapped her arms tightly around her chest and spoke in whispers to no one.

Rose listened but heard only rain. Not even a bird sang in this storm.

Sir Thomas addressed Margaret, keeping his eyes averted from Rose. "Cardinal Wolsey has been arrested. Henry accused him of praemanuire, of taking too much authority, depriving the king of influence."

He dropped the curtain's edge that he was holding back, and it fell. He sighed, twisting his lips. "But Wolsey died yesterday, on his way to the trial. He just dropped dead. It was grief that killed him. He was the only father Henry truly ever had, and Henry tossed him aside for the pleasure of a fleeting kiss. There is no one near Henry who loves him. He killed the only friend he had."

Rose sat still, every muscle tensed, wondering what Margaret might say or do.

Sir Thomas smiled at them, a faraway look in his eyes that told her he did not really see them. "But God is good. He fights on for us. The sweats are striking the city of London again, and there are rumours that the plague has returned, too. The king has fled to the country and his courts are on hold. All the good people are locked up in their homes. The rest, those filthy reformists carrying about Martin Luther's works or the heresy from that man Hutchins. My men have had an easy time these last few days, picking these pestilent fleas off the streets and disposing of them." More squished his thumb and forefinger together as he said it.

Margaret interrupted. "You wish us to remain at home?"

"You are to remain loyal!" he snapped at her. "All fell away from Christ at His hour of crucifixion. Things will happen, things that make you sore afraid. Do not lose hope. Do not abandon Christ."

"I had only thought to bring comfort to Catherine," Margaret answered. Rose could see she was holding onto tears. "She has been forgotten."

Sir Thomas considered it, chewing his lips. "This would please God. She has friends, powerful men, in Europe, who can still affect our will. Yes, you may go. Only straight there and return. She is at an estate of Wolsey's, not in the city. You will not encounter any sickness."

Margaret and Rose stood.

More turned his back, looking out again over his garden, clipped and hedged to perfection. "Ask Catherine to pray for me. You must pray for me too, as dear children. My enemies are many and time is short. I am racing the devil for the soul of England."

The carriage made fast work of the deserted streets, lurching wildly when the driver took a hard curve, unused to having the entire lane to navigate. Yellow sunlight fighting through the clouds burnt against the orange leaves of autumn. To Rose, it looked as if all of England was on fire. The leaves would be dropping soon in great numbers. These, and the winter rains, would make these streets slick and treacherous.

When the carriage slowed to its familiar crawl, Margaret lifted the curtain concealing them and protecting them from the debris and dirt flying up from the street. A group of men and women, stripped to rags, bearing unlit torches on their backs, walked slowly through the streets, their eyes on the ground. In front of them a soldier carried a sign that identified them as heretics. The few on the streets were spitting and cursing them.

One woman stumbled and could not catch herself. Her arm hung oddly at her side. She cried out and tried to stand again, but her limbs gave her difficulty; she only rose after heaving herself up against her thigh. A soldier behind the group hit her with the broad side of his sword, a fast, thick smack that sent her reeling again.

Margaret let the curtain fall back into place. "It won't do any good, you know."

"What?" Rose asked.

"They'll persist in their sin. It's the only thing they've truly ever owned."

The estate was abandoned; only a dog ran out to greet the carriage. A few leaves, early fallen, swirled around the wood door framed by a white stone archway. Margaret and Rose alighted and pushed open the door.

Inside the main room was a bed, with candles burning on a night table and sun-bleached linens piled high around a shrunken figure. A servant, saying her beads over the bed, was startled by Rose and Margaret's arrival. The figure in bed turned her head and looked at the women.

"Praise be to God," she said, her voice high and thin.

"My queen," Margaret said, not moving.

Rose breathed through her fear, the secret horror of seeing death eating away at a woman. She would not let Margaret run from this. *This* was the end of life, of passion and first kisses. She grabbed Margaret's hand and forced her to the bed.

"What happened?" Margaret asked.

Rose winced at the girl's cold fingers digging into her own for courage.

Catherine smiled. Her face was nothing but hollows and caverns, deep etchings of sorrow. Tiny popped veins were evident around her nose and eyes, from tears that had not ceased. Every bone on her face could be plainly made out.

"I am dying, child. It started when I was at court. I knew the signs, but Henry would not permit me treatment. He wanted a son."

Margaret nodded as if she understood.

"But young girls do not go visiting without their fathers. These are remarkable times." The queen exhaled and started to close her eyes. "I know why you're here." Her eyes snapped open. "Has the Hutchins book called you, Margaret?"

Margaret went red as Catherine's eyes narrowed.

"It has. Margaret, mark my dying frame. Look what has become of me! I refused it, and it swept me from my home." She turned as if to look out the window, but her face fell back against the pillow, eyes closed.

The servant stood to escort them from the room but Margaret came alive.

"My queen!" she said loudly.

Catherine opened her eyes.

Margaret reached into her robes and set a leather purse on the table before she leaned in and said something to Catherine. A shadow passed over the queen's face.

"Your father approves?" Catherine asked.

"This is what he wants," she answered.

Margaret laid her head on the queen's chest, but Catherine had already slipped under, into one last dream.

❈ ❈ ❈ ❈ ❈

"You didn't save her."

The Scribe shook his head. "I don't save. What writer ever could?"

"Why are you telling me this story?"

"You could have sent me away. You wanted to write these words. I wanted to tell them."

"But that's it? I'm going to write the story down and die. I don't get a second chance?"

"Second chances aren't your forte, are they?"

"I have unfinished business!"

"More than you know."

"What was David talking about? Why didn't I get into the research study?"

"I do not have permission to tell you this story."

"But there is a story."

"Yes."

"Is there anyone else who would tell it to me?"

I hated myself for asking, fearing another angel would appear. I suspected none of them would look like the imaginary angels I saw in gift shops, skinny women with flowing hair and harps. Real angels would terrify.

Crazy Betty started screaming—it was time for her vitals check. She always screamed when the nurses woke her in the dead of night. Sometimes Mariskka screamed back.

The Scribe nodded and I understood.

Chapter Twenty-one

In winter, London was a feast for the senses: the smoky fragrances of burning coals, roasting hazelnuts, and the last of the young venison, the ringing of horses with bells on their harnesses, the sight of the vendors' stalls lined with hanging birds of every variety for the cooks—woodcocks, thrushes, robins, hens, wrens, quail, hawks, pheasant, partridge—though the palace cooks insisted that from now until Lent, hens were the only proper bird to be eaten. The rag dealers would be doing a fine business, selling the castoffs from the shearers and weavers.

Anne spied a group of heretics being led and kicked down a side street. A small crowd followed them, mainly children who were glad to be entertained by a suffering worse than their own. The poor souls looked ill used, and Anne had no doubt they had been tortured, either for information or pleasure. Henry had never liked the reformists; their kind had caused such unrest in

Germany that they threatened to unseat the authorities. And he had once loved the Church. Now he set about destroying it, breaking her back until she swayed easily in his embrace.

Many more people had read the Hutchins book and the blame fell partly to Anne. They thought they were safe, that she had much influence, that the crown was becoming fond of their secret passion. She did not want to suffer; how could she have led these people to it?

Anne fingered the dress that sat next to her. It had looked lovely when Goodie Grisham had presented it to her, but the woman had been so tight-lipped that Anne decided against trying it on for one last fitting. She would make do with it. She touched the design at the neck.

La Plus Heureuse, it said in a thousand delicate stitches. "*The most happy.*"

Anne burst into tears.

Henry was at his prayers when she arrived at Hampton Court. He had gone there upon learning of Wolsey's death. Wolsey had built Hampton Court for himself. Every sign of submission to Henry's throne came across as an afterthought, a thin scrape of plaster over the heart of stone and wood.

The chapel was a fortress of oiled wood and strong sunshine. The stained-glass windows running on each side cast a rainbow of light across the dark pews, and above the altar were angels. It was the only chapel she had been in that had these angels, fat children reaching to each other above the repentant. These angels seemed no more than God's children, and He could not get them to sit still during church either.

She sighed and waited for some sign that Henry would be through soon. He was bent over, alone, kneeling in prayer before an empty altar.

Anne wanted to pray, too, but all her prayers were memorized as a girl, and none worked for this moment. She considered the Lord's Prayer and decided it was close enough. She bowed her head and repeated it to herself. "Thine is the kingdom," she whispered at the end, "and the glory, and the power, forever and ever. Amen." The final words were like bread in her mouth. There was a sweet, satisfying taste of peace, an easement of fear, and she let the words sink deeper, nourishing her weak heart. Yes, she repeated the prayer, wanting more strength, wanting the peace to linger, afraid that if she moved it would fly away again.

Henry's shoulders heaved up and back. He was crying. Anne made her way to him and knelt at his side.

Then Anne saw he was laughing. He had trails of tears on his face. Rising, he took her by the hand and kissed her full on the mouth. With the brush of his lips and the tickle of his beard, she felt the warmth of his body and for a moment—just a fleeting, shy moment—she liked the warmth. Confused, she cursed herself under her breath.

Henry led her from the room, past guards who would not meet her eye, men whose rumours and insinuations would work their way through the court until they ruined her name even as she slept alone night after night. There was no one to comfort her, no one to see her long, lonely vigil. She was the faithful virgin, waiting with a full lamp of oil for the bridegroom to invite her into the feast, but the nights had grown so long with no stirring at her door. She held out in obedience, and honour still fled from her. She saw the stone angels overhead, closing her eyes as she took the step from their world into the court of bitter tongues. She had waited for God to save her, as a sign of His favour for her faithful deeds. She stepped out into the world of the court and opened her eyes.

Anne could hear the low rush of breath, in and out, like small waves breaking on a shore far away. Her servants were asleep. They had plaited her hair into a long braid to keep it out of her face as she slept and set a new piece of fur on her pillow. The lice she had collected at court would find her smooth skin unpalatable and seek this fur out while she slept. The servants would discard it in the morning, and so had fallen asleep, their work done.

She swung her legs off the bed, landing them gently on the floor, holding her shift bunched up in both fists so it wouldn't swing out and tickle anyone in their sleep on their trundles on the floor. She raised one hand, still trying to grasp her shift, and pulled open the door.

Her Yeoman was there, wide awake, standing and staring. She let out a cry as he turned to her, his face changing in the shadows, a rippling as he came into the light. Her stomach knotted up in fear. No one stirred inside her chamber. He moved to block her path. She

saw he had been staring at the tapestry of Sarah and
Abraham, and a tear wet his cheek.

He had always had a gentle way about him, escorting her as though his position was not a way of earning
bread but of saving her. She had walked behind him all
her days since that early May morning when she had
been thrust into this new world, watching his broad
muscular back, seeing courtiers step aside as he moved
confidently through the dimly lit passages, escorting her
past every petty dowager, every seducing virgin intent
on winning Henry away. He never left her side, never
accused, never grasped.

Perhaps she had imagined his goodness. She did not
deserve it. Not when she was about to destroy everything
precious to her. If God had made His plan clear to her,
perhaps she would not be doing this. Time was so short.
She could wait no more.

He stood in her path and did not move. Anne
looked back at her chamber, the peaceful quiet calling
her to return. Her Yeoman shifted his weight on his feet,
and the torchlight sent a reflection into the room. She
caught sight of the book on her bedside table.

"I will wait for His blessing no more," she said, grit-
ting her teeth and pushing past her Yeoman.

The hallways were quiet, the flickering yellow torches
against the stone walls giving only enough light but no
heat. The floors were so cold under her feet that she
wished she had slipped on her shoes, but her servants
had taken those after they put her to bed. Her skin

raised in little gooseflesh bumps, the cold air biting her through the thin shift, drafts of winter finding her again and again. She paused before the great twin doors, the carving of the Tudor rose on them. His guards bristled and shook themselves awake, though both were standing, not expecting to receive a visitor at this hour. Anne thought she saw a smirk on one's face as he peered at her before settling back into the darkness against the wall. She turned and looked at her Yeoman. He had walked behind her. He did not lead, not down this path.

"Do not wait for me," she whispered, and with one last breath for strength, pushed against the doors.

There was a flickering candle on a little stand near the doors, and then the great ocean of night. She could hear no one stirring, indeed no one breathing, so her entrance had not disturbed the chamber as she feared. She reached for the candle and held it before her with both hands. It was slick and heavy, and she walked slowly to keep the flame high. She saw a wooden leg of the bed and searched to find the other one. It was a distance away, at least ten or eleven feet, and Anne did not know which end she had found first. She could see bed linens, and she strained to see beyond the shadow into the bed, but could see nothing. She reached out with one hand, touching the edge, and followed it round the leg to the other side. The other leg was just as far away, a good ten feet and some. She crept along the edge, disoriented, her heart beating faster, not expecting to be confused by such a simple thing.

She had waited for this moment since she was a girl, but never had she imagined she'd be groping blindly in the dark for her bridegroom. Never had she imagined she would have neither Church nor husband when it came.

She saw him sleeping. She set the candle on a stand next to him, and he stirred, blinking in the new light. His eyes met hers, and he watched without speaking as she untied the ribbon at her neck, loosening her shift, letting it fall at her feet. His face was impassive. He did not move as she lifted the linens and lay at his side, her hands shaking so hard that the linens made little waves around him.

"Why now?" he asked.

A servant built the fire up in the room. Anne gagged at the pinching smoke of burning wood, her stomach swimming as she woke up. Jane had brought some dry bread, salted twice to settle her stomach, and set it on the table next to the bed. She sat quietly while Anne tried to wake up without getting sick again.

"What must I do today?" Anne asked.

"The cook wants you to approve the menu for Christmas. There are two parties before the day, besides. He's getting impatient with your delays. Says there won't be any good meats to choose from."

Anne groaned. "I can't."

She retched over the side of the bed. Jane caught her, patting her back, whispering to another servant. "Bring me some lemons for Anne."

Anne sat back up, tears in her eyes. "I can't do this."

"Shh, shh. Of course ye can. You've already made two months. Not much longer till you're past it. With your permission, I'll look over the cook's menu and make recommendations, in your name, of course."

Anne nodded.

"And we should get ye dressed, for Henry is awake and about, asking for you. You must tell him."

Anne stood, grasping the table to help steady herself as she rose from the bed. She tried not to breathe as Jane lifted her shift and lowered in its place a new shift, and on top of this, a dress. Every night, the dress she wore would be aired out, and in the morning, it would be perfumed to mask any odours that remained. The result was a dress with thick, violent layers of perfume. Anne had never noticed it before, but it made her stomach churn.

Jane, seeing her gasping like a fish, trying to breathe in fresh air, fetched a new pomander and ran it around her waist. It was a silver ball that snapped open in the center and could be filled with dry herbs and perfumed linens. Anne's usual infusion of roses did not set well with her lately, so Jane had poured in cloves and orange peels. It was a moderate success, Anne thought. It did nothing for her sickness, but it did not provoke it either.

Dressed, with a bite of bread to coat her stomach and a bite of a lemon to keep it down, Anne was led down the hall towards the garden nearest the Thames. She prayed the cold currents would have swept all the trash well away overnight, and the air would be clean.

Henry was sitting on a swing that hung down from a heavy beech tree. He had a blanket with him, which he spread around her shoulders as she lowered herself to his side. The swing's motion upset her stomach and she asked him to stop it. He did, before wrapping his arms around her and holding her. He did not speak, and she used the time to beg her stomach to keep its peace too.

Greenwich had always been his favourite residence, and his preferred home for Christmas. She did today too. The Thames, a most perfect courtier, swept all the rubbish away. She listened for the birds; a few still sang in the trees above them, especially the song thrushes. They were small and timid but sang louder than any bird she had ever heard, their song never the same, always changing through seasons and moods. A few were singing this morning, and Anne knew they would sing loudest tonight, just before darkness was complete and they fled to a deep, hidden life within the trees. The blackbirds were out this morning too, those rude, oafish creatures, pecking at the ground, searching for any crumbs from the court kitchens.

Henry waved them away with a wave and a hiss, and Anne was glad.

He bent his face down, nuzzling her neck, kissing it once. "I missed you last night."

"I fell asleep quite early. Jane did not want to wake me. She said you returned from hunting late."

Henry sat up and cleared his throat. "Yes."

Anne placed her hand on his thigh, and he turned to her, relaxing.

"I'm with child."

He was still, the muscles in his face losing their taut play, his expression going soft and loose. Stunned, he couldn't coordinate a smile, let alone a verbal reply. He burst from the swing, lifting her off it with him in one motion, holding her too roughly so that she was gasping for breath, crushed between his robes and her stiff bodice. Her skirt billowed out so far he had to hold her all the more tightly to crush it flat.

Laughing, he was kissing her over and over on the mouth, and she had to push against him with all her strength to get a breath. He tilted his head back and shouted, pointing at the sky.

He looked like a maniac when he turned to her, his finger still shaking at the clouds above. "I am vindicated! A son will be born to me. My dynasty will be greater than any king England has ever known. All generations will know my name."

He was doing a little dance, which Anne could scarcely believe. Knowing he was to be a father had turned him into a child.

"Henry, do you love me?"

He stepped to her and bowed. "There was never a queen loved like you. How may I prove it to you? Haven't I already broken the Church, rearranged the governing of England, and generally set the world's course around pleasing you?" He was grinning. "What more should be done, my good queen? Speak it and it will be done!"

"Call off Sir Thomas. Do not let him persecute those who want to read the Scriptures, for these people, in their way, are only trying to get closer to the God who blesses you. They should not die for this crime. And bring

Hutchins back to England safely. Do not provoke this war of words."

Anne remembered the words of her brother: *"Only two people dare speak for God: the optimist and the fool."* Anne looked at Henry's joy, his face radiant as he extended his hand and took hers, gentle as a lamb, leading her back into the palace. Servants and courtiers alike parted without speaking, staring at the king who was still grinning wildly. He led Anne to his chamber, where he spent the day stroking her hair and turning her smallest whispered request into a loud barked command. Anne was every inch the queen. Marriage was a formality they could attend to later, Henry said. After all, God's will had been done, evident in her womb.

The force of life in this man was so great, his own will roaring above the others around him, that Anne had no more troubling humours. Henry was her strong tower, and she turned to him in the quiet of the chamber, thankful at last to be forever free of the storm. Christmas was fast approaching.

Chapter Twenty-two

"I would like time to read this well, my friends. It is a large document, as you have said yourselves. The best minds in England have produced it; how could I, then, understand it in one brief glance?"

"No. Henry requests your assent. Today."

Sir Thomas sighed and stood. Rose and Margaret were watching from the hallway, peering into the family room where several officials from court were circling around Sir Thomas, including a man they had only just seen, Cranmer. Oh, but he was a sour-looking man, the line of his mouth always drawing down, the heavy flesh above his eyes hooding them so that he looked to be always squinting. He had a tremendous shadow along his jowls and above his lips, where coarse hairs defied the morning's razor and sprang up. Sir Thomas had often spoken of him with disdain. He was the worst sort of cleric, More said: an ordained priest who was secretly married and carried his wife about in a trunk so they would not be discovered. They compared the disdain More had for him with the very man himself standing before them and judged More to be right.

"He's a greasy weasel," Margaret whispered.

"A pock-faced bit of trash," Rose replied. They tried not to giggle. Margaret held her hand, and Rose patted it, grateful for the assurance. Sir Thomas had disagreed with men before, even men of the court. He would shake these men off.

Cranmer folded his hands across his ample stomach. He wore a billowing white shift, with black robes over it, and a long black sash around his neck. The effect was that he looked like a great white sausage bursting out from its narrow black casings.

"Sir Thomas," he said, "it is my belief that the marriage between Henry and Catherine was unlawful, by God's law and the laws of this land. Will you join me in correcting this grievance?"

More smiled and raised his eyebrows. "Tell me what you know of God's laws, my friend. Do kings dispense with barren wives and clerics marry big-breasted girls who come to confession?"

Cranmer lunged at More, but a low table blocked his way, which he did not see because of his stomach and the robes. He stumbled and caught himself, smoothing down his black vestments, clearing his throat. "I will make my report to the king."

"You say that as if it were a threat," More replied. "All I have done is request time to read the document."

"Time is not on your side, More," Cranmer replied. "And neither is Henry. You haven't been at court since

the sweats broke out, but Henry has been busy."
Cranmer started laughing. "Oh, he's been busy! What
news!"

More stared at him, not asking for details. This sent
Cranmer into more rage, and he ground his teeth as he
exited, pushing past Margaret and Rose roughly, the
other men following behind him without a word.

Sir Thomas saw the girls when the doors swung
open. He sighed and sat on the couch.

"How much of that did you hear?" he asked.

Margaret rushed to sit with him, and Rose stood.

"Are you going to sign it, Father?" Margaret asked.

Sir Thomas picked up the stack of papers left by
Cranmer, the letter requiring his signature laying on
top. He walked to the fireplace and threw them in. The
flames fed upon the papers with lust, snapping and
growling. Rose saw the ashes collecting. A few flew up
the chimney. It was strange to her mind that some would
do that. All she understood was that none of them could
be pieced together again.

"But what was he saying about news from court?"
Margaret asked. "If the sickness has passed, let me go to
the Christmas revelry there. I can find out what is going
on."

"I'll not have you involved!" More shouted at her.
"You have done too much already!"

Margaret looked at Rose and back at her father,
her eyes wide in alarm. Rose saw her biting her lip to
keep composure. Tears were pooling in her eyes, but she
spoke sternly to her father.

"You are not safe. Cranmer said that himself," she
said.

Sir Thomas smiled, a serene look washing over his countenance. "I am not safe. Perhaps. But you, my daughter, you are safe. I am willing to sacrifice everything so that you may live."

He was looking at Margaret as he spoke, and Rose wondered why there was mixed in his expression such tenderness, with such cold recognition of something ahead she could not see.

The household came alive with activities; the darkening afternoons and stinging winds told Rose that Christmas was almost upon them, and Dame Alice would return with packages and complaints. The rushes on the floors were freshened, and the kitchen was a combustion of servants stirring, basting, and kneading. Freshly dressed birds hung from the rafters, a continual fire burned for the preparation of different savouries and breads, and Rose heard much familiar foul language as the servants prepared to celebrate the birth of their Saviour. Sir Thomas pushed everyone to matins each week, but he had yet to tame their tongues, especially when they knew he was absent.

The youngest children were rehearsing each day for a pageant they planned to present at the Christmas feast. Little John was playing Saint George, dressed in a light suit of armour but carrying a sword as tall as himself. When he swung it, he stumbled after its arc, making the actual slaying of a dragon a true miracle. The dragon was Cicely and Elizabeth, in a costume that both fit in but neither could control. The dragon walked as if having fits, none of its limbs in unison, his great serpent head lolling from side to side like a sleeping dog shaking a flea from its ear.

There was the matter of presents, too, which distressed Rose. The household would exchange presents on New Year's Day, and Sir Thomas was so busy attending to the present he would send to the king that he paid little mind to the household. Rose had no money of her own to buy anything, and Sir Thomas would not allow her to town anyway. Margaret told her not to worry; her father had presents to give to everyone. There would be no need for anything else.

And so the days passed, and More was often absent, attending to matters in town. When he was at home, he stayed in his study, the door closed. Messengers came and went at odd hours, and letters bearing More's seal went with them.

On Christmas Eve, More emerged from his study looking worn but triumphant. Rose was tempted to peer into the room, to see what unknown adversary he had defeated, but she knew it was empty. Whatever More had faced was battled and won with paper and ink, dispatched through ruddy-faced boys glad for a half-angel coin just before Christmas.

Rose set out her best dress and Margaret's too. They had been beaten and aired out, with fresh pomanders hung round the waists. Rose inhaled lavender from More's garden. It was too sharp and sweet to have come from anywhere else. When they emerged from their chambers, they saw the family gathered in the family room. Everyone looked cleaned and fluffed.

The family ate the first feast that night, More giving a long prayer in Latin that all understood except Rose. It was marvelous to her just to learn to read English; the language of angels was too far beyond her. The roast capons were greasy, with blackened crisp skins that snapped under her fingers when she took hold of her portion. She slit the top off her beef pie and set it aside, letting the steam roil up. Everyone was doing the same; they looked to be dining under a cloud, so great was the steam the pies gave off. The illusion disappeared, and the children giggled in awe and returned to their plates. They had sausage, mottled red and brown with a thick waxy-looking casing, but Rose did not have an appetite for this.

Sir Thomas poured everyone's first cup of wassail. Rose held out her cup, which was a low, wide bowl with a bit of a stand beneath it, so that it held as much wassail as discreetly possible in one serving. She studied it as he continued down the table, pouring generously, receiving fresh decanters from the kitchen as needed. It was a deep nutty brown colour, and from the piercing fragrance assaulting her nostrils, the cook had used a mighty amount of ale and rum to temper the innocent apple cider. Lamb's wool clung around the edges, the foam of the apples that were mashed for the cider. On top of this, a toasted slice of bread floated, absorbing some of the liquor, she hoped, or the children would not make it through the meal.

More returned to his seat and lifted his own cup. "I propose we toast!" he commanded, and everyone replied by lifting their cups and toasting to him.

"Mary's travails this night were great, but by morning, she had birthed a Saviour for all nations. Let us not grow afraid when we face our own trials, for God can still work miracles out of our suffering, for the salvation of many!"

The younger children shouted in affirmation before anyone else and gulped at their drinks. Everyone else raised their cups and blessed Sir Thomas and his health before drinking.

After dinner, the children presented the pageant of Saint George killing the dragon. Saint George wielded his sword more steadily, having learned through his practices that a jab would not dislodge him from the ground like a swing. The dragon, however, having no way to see through the costume, and no means of controlling both ends in unison, ended up presenting its hindquarters to Saint George. Little John, in the confusion caused by stage fright, took his fatal stab anyway, and so the dragon was slayed by a might blow to his rear. This was met with hearty applause and calls for more wassail

After the pageant, the family and servants went outside to stand over a roaring fire built in a clearing of the garden. Far away they could see lights in the spire windows of London churches, torches that would stay through the night as the world awaited the Saviour. The night above them was as black as an inkwell, dotted by brilliant, glimmering stars. This was how the shepherds had spent the last sad day of the age that had never known salvation, More reminded them. He kept staring at the lights of London, walking away from the fire, and Rose was afraid he would catch a chill. She took a blanket from a pile set out earlier for the evening and brought it to him. She offered it without a word, her head turned away, so that the household gossips would not be aroused.

He spoke so they would not hear. "A heretic named Barnes is burning tonight. It may be my last." He looked with grief at the city.

Rose wondered in horror which flames lit church courtyards, and which were set around a stake.

"Jerusalem, Jerusalem," he said, a tear staining his cheek. "My time is upon me." He smirked and brushed past her into the house, leaving her with the dread and fear.

The wassail and the marvelously disrespectful death of the dragon still had everyone around the fire in good spirits. The children, as Rose predicted, had drunk much more than they should have of the wassail, and she excused herself to help see them off to bed. She wished she had drunk none of the wassail, for the fear of his words had no restraints, growing and leaping in her mind, creating such dread that she prayed Christmas would not come.

As she carried the sleeping Cicely, the other servants warned her not to remove their clothes or shoes, but to let them sleep on top of their beds, which Rose did, before falling asleep herself in a similar fashion. Her dreams were blessedly dark.

His hands found her in this dark ocean, pulling her back through the night until she blinked in confusion, a candle only inches from her face.

Sir Thomas was in her chamber. Margaret was not in her bed.

"She's asleep with the others. They stayed up through

the night telling ghost stories," he said. Rose nodded, trying to sit up.

"I have an early New Year's gift for you," he whispered. He held out a small parcel, and by its weight, she judged it held coins.

"There is a parchment in it. Do not open it or read it until my time has come. You must give it to the sheriff. It is for my salvation. And yours."

"What do you mean?" she began to ask, but he grasped her around her shoulders, forcing her back onto the bed, his mouth on hers, the taste of rum making his kisses sour and slick. She tried to turn her head and cry out, but his weight was too much. She tore her fingernails down his back, down the scourged field he broke open every night, and though he jerked against her hands, he pressed down on her with more force. His hand was clawing at her bodice.

His violence broke open the sour secrets of her past. Awful flashes of guilt convulsed her. This was what she was when she came here—how could she have thought she would become something now? She closed her eyes to submit, letting her body go limp.

She sensed a presence, something she remembered from a night long ago, a night of blood and tears, and opened her eyes. Standing at the foot of the bed was a monstrous thing, a man with a wild mane of gold and burning cat's-eyes, his muscles straining as he wielded a sword over his head. She screamed as a servant rang a bell somewhere far back in the house, alerting them that the barge had arrived to carry them to church.

More scrambled from her bed, running from the room.

Chapter Twenty-three

Christmas still hung about Greenwich palace; the scent of fires burning through the night in stone hearths, pomanders of cinnamon and oranges set about every room, roasted hen and dark baked breads, and the crisp clean winter air sweeping past outside, piercing the still chambers that had arrow-slit windows.

Anne clapped and a servant presented another gift. It was a fine gold cup, and Anne considered its weight and design before nodding her approval to the record keeper. A note of her thanks would be dispatched to the earl who had sent it.

Another servant stepped forward with a book, her name and seal etched in leather on it. Anne opened it and read the note it bore her.

To Anne Boleyn,
from William Hutchins.

*Presenting you with the New
Book, translated from original
texts, free of error.*

She couldn't resist cracking open the stiff spine;
the woodcuts were new and interesting. Perhaps later,
she would read. There was no reason why she should
not master this book. She was safe, her future secured.
Nothing from these pages could find her here. There was
so much time.

She set the book aside.

It was a lovely tradition, Anne always said, this
opening of presents to celebrate the New Year and the
gift of another Christmas just past. Anne had never
received so many gifts of such value; her chamber was
a hive of activity, each servant carrying a heavy purse
or parcel.

"Is Henry coming soon?" Anne asked, turning
her head to the left a bit so Jane would know she was
addressed.

No one answered.

Anne, with much effort because the scarlet pillows
were stacked high all around her tender midsection,
turned and saw Jane was not in her place.

"Where the devil is she?" Anne yelled, slapping the
red coverlet.

The servants stopped, their eyes on the floor. Anne
saw she would not get an answer and summoned the
next girl forward with her gift.

Jane burst through the door, all apologies, bowing
to her mistress. "Forgive me, my queen, I was checking
the wait line outside. More presents are arriving."

"But not Henry?" Anne snapped. "Am I to have no comfort?"

"You know he loves you," Jane answered. "And you know why he cannot be your companion here. He says to content yourself until the blessed hour."

Anne looked at the bed, made of dark oak, with a heavy wooden canopy and urns carved into the posts at the foot of the bed. On her worst nights, it was like a coffin. And she was having worse nights more often since she had been moved back into her own private chamber, where Henry would not visit, for fear of harming his unborn heir.

But he had ordered that all would be done to make her comfortable. There were scarlet pillows and a coverlet in scarlet with gold embroidery. There was a separate chamber pot for retching, which was kept at the side of the bed so she never had to ask for it.

Even her dress was extraordinary proof of his affections: He had fabric sent to her as a gift and crafted into a dress of such luxury that no other woman in England could claim to be adorned like her. It had a bodice of gold, with gold embroidery and a marvelous ruby brooch in the center, with a row of rubies sewn along a scarlet velvet ribbon. Her puffed sleeves had slashes at the wrists so white silk could pop through, and a long velvet braid with a swinging tassel down the center of the dress, with a dozen tiny pomanders of gold hanging down it. Her fingers were heavy with rings.

But in truth, Anne sighed to herself, the bodice caused much pain, pressing her swollen and sore breasts up tightly so that she winced whenever she turned. Her fingers were swollen, too, and the rings dug deeply in.

She couldn't bear the bodice against her stomach, and kept trying to push against it by hooking her thumbs under the seam along her ribs and pulling it out and away. Yes, she looked splendid, and it was splendid proof of his esteem, but she wanted only to be in a simple shift and sleep for days.

"I am sorry, Jane," Anne said. "You must forgive me. I am not myself these days."

"My mistress is tired, is she not?" Jane called for the attention of the other servants. "Our mistress needs rest! We will resume presenting gifts tomorrow."

Everyone filed out, and Jane moved to leave, but Anne caught her hand.

"Please, Jane, help me take this dress off." Her voice was thin and pitiful, she knew, but she wanted only to be free of this weight and sleep deeply again.

The room was cool and she slept on top of the ruby coverlet, but still her neck was damp and she pulled her hair away from it. Rolling to her other side, facing the door, Anne tried again to find a moment's relief from this sweaty nausea of pregnancy, and sleep. The shadows grew darker in the room; it must be getting close to late afternoon, Anne realized.

"Why can't I sleep?" she moaned. Never had she been so tired, and never had sleep proved to be so fickle.

One shadow at the door shifted, and Anne saw it was the shadow of her Yeoman on duty outside. He was the only man in England never to sleep, she thought. He was always there.

"Dear God, please just let me sleep!" she whimpered. She must be going crazy with this nausea—that was not a prayer she had ever learned at matins. Her eyelids grew heavy, and she hoped this was it. But still a hand seemed to hold her back as she stood at the edge of a deep cold river, one she desperately wanted to be lost in.

A wild thought came. She had only to cry out and the Yeoman would save her. He could steal her away and she could sleep in her own bed, in her father's house, where the rooms were quiet and her mother made ginger tea to cure a roiling stomach. George would be there too. He would stay at her bedside, telling outrageous lies to amuse her, until she slept at last.

Anne looked about the room. There was much gold. And in her womb, an heir.

She did not cry out. She turned over, once again, resolute, and cursed the sleepless minutes that passed.

⚜

"My lady, wake up!" Jane was at her side, shaking her gently. Anne groaned and tried to slap at the hands pressing on her. It had been a full month since the presenting of gifts, and sleep still came late in the night, and morning still brought this sickness.

Her stomach pushed up into her throat, and Anne reached for the chamber pot, retching violently. Jane held her hair out of the way. Anne collapsed back onto the pillows, and Jane handed her a leather cup with some warm liquid in it.

"From Dr. Butts. A tincture for your stomach. Today should not be ruint, he says."

Anne swallowed a bit of the tincture. It had a sour taste to it, like grapes before their season. She could take in only a little, but Jane pressed it to her lips again.

"Look, Anne!" Jane wanted her to see something, and Anne blinked heavily, watching a chorus of girls enter the room bearing a large box. It resembled a coffin, and Anne's hands trembled, spilling the tincture so that Jane grabbed it away from her.

The girls opened the box, lifting out the contents for display.

It was her wedding dress.

After a gentle washing, and rinsing her mouth well with mint, the women set to work dressing Anne. She stood shivering in her undergarments while the women steadied her and helped her step into a petticoat. A corset was next, and Anne winced as they tightened it, though Jane scolded them to use a light hand. A farthingale made her silhouette complete, and the sweeping skirt came next, with a forepart panel of gold and layers of white silk. A velvet bodice with sweeping strands of pearls, pearl buttons, and sleeves ending with lace cuffs—all were finished with fine silk thread. Anne held out her arms to inspect the sleeves, which blossomed beautifully and had buttons made of diamonds at the cuff. Over these was draped a white fur.

While the girls busied themselves with the final touches—her headpiece, jewelry, braiding and setting her hair—Anne smiled, despite the dress and despite the nausea. She would see Henry today. It would all be finished: her work to establish a good name for herself and her family. Her brother's station in life would be secure; her parents would be provided for by the crown. God had been so good to her, blessing her with an heir, paving the way for this marriage, disposing of the false queen.

She was led, in secret, through the castle and to a barge that took her to York Place. A few on the shore saw her and stopped, but the cold winds and grey skies demanded their attention elsewhere. She met Henry in a turret on the west side, which afforded them a view of London, from Charing Cross to Westminster. Anne stood, sick and weighted, under the shadow of the Tower rising above them as the marriage was conducted. Her family was not there. This was to have been a day for music and dancing, but instead she heard the iron heart beating closer, and she held to Henry for her life.

Three days later, the world wore silver and scarlet and every beggar and thief lined the streets to steal a glimpse of her glory. Warships in the river made her bones as cold and loose as the water. Guns firing from their sides and the Tower made beads of sweat pop out with every explosion.

All monks of St. Peter's Abbey greeted her wearing their golden robes, with the Duke of Suffolk carrying the queen's crown in front of her. Two earls carried her two sceptres as she was carried under a canopy of gold, wearing a kirtle of red velvet, an ermine sleeve capelet, a robe of purple velvet with ermine trimming, and a headpiece of pearls and rubies. An older woman, the Duchess of Norfolk, carried her train.

Jane followed in a scarlet robe trimmed with white fur.

She was brought to St. Peter's at Westminster, set in

a high platform before the altar, anointed and crowned Queen of England by the Archbishop of Canterbury.

She did not breathe until the Mass was done and the feast laid out in the hall.

Her brother and father fell at her feet as she entered. She had not foreseen that her father and brother would bow to her; she had only coveted the crown for what it might lay at their feet. She was alarmed to see them fall and motioned for them to rise.

Anne caught George's smile, an ear-to-ear grin from her childhood, his eyes twinkling. Anne ran her jeweled hand along her skirt for her brother to admire, a sly grin on her face too. He nodded just slightly, tilting his chin to her. *Well done,* it said.

Anne burst into a laugh and the court around her applauded, which made her laugh harder. She held out her hands, allowing her brother and father to escort her to her dining seat. *Well done, indeed,* she thought. It had been a bumpy, harsh road, but she had arrived in splendour and the gates were thrown open to her.

She would never again doubt God's will, for her halting obedience in matters too great for her to comprehend had still brought her to the pinnacle of this empire. The heir within stirred, and Anne realized she hadn't eaten in hours. She was famished.

Anne counted the hours off with the church bells that sung every hour for seven hours as they feasted. The platters were in constant motion, courses being set and removed at great efficiency at every table, with every meat

Anne had ever tasted in England served in every possible configuration, even little pastries shaped like swans.

There was momentary confusion when Anne stood the first time. Everyone stopped eating, surely thinking she had some remark. Anne blanched at the silence and motioned for her Lady of the Chamber, shuffling away in her billowing skirts to use the chamber pot in privacy. As the hours, and the wine, wore on, Anne did this with such frequency that the diners did not look up anymore but simply set their knives down and continued talking until she returned.

Only one seat remained empty.

"Where is Sir Thomas More?" she asked.

Archbishop Cranmer replied. "He declined to attend, my queen."

Anne's head was drooping. Seven hours of sitting had made her sore, and seven hours of feasting had made her sleepy. A man and woman were brought in shackles to the table. A guard kicked the woman to make her bow when she hesitated, seeing Anne.

"It's the Mad Nun, and a merchant known as Bloody Christopher. He is unkind," Cranmer told her. "My queen, it is your honour to release a prisoner as you wish."

"What are they accused of?" Anne asked.

"The man beat another servant to death for stealing," Cranmer replied. "The other is one they call the Mad Nun. She is accused of prophecy, my queen, proclaiming evil tidings of dark days ahead for the king and his queen. She claims great love for you but tells the people you will die with that crown upon your head."

"What say you? Does this man speak truth?" Anne asked her.

"I speak only what I see, my queen," the woman said. "I have naught but love in my heart for ye. God save me, God save us all!"

"Well, God is not making this decision," Anne replied. Her tongue was getting away from her. The wine was sitting heavy in her stomach, and the crown was heavy on her head.

"I can offer proofs, my queen! Proofs of my affection! For I have been to the home of the Morus, the great fool, and I have heard his whispers. He has no love for you!"

The Mad Nun turned her head to acknowledge those who giggled beneath their breath at her joke. She meant Sir Thomas, of course, but Morus was the proper name of fools, and it drew a laugh even now.

But not from Anne. The nun had been in Sir Thomas's home, as well as Anne's own bedroom at her father's home. The nun had heard secrets at both houses.

"Interrogate this woman. See what she knows," Anne said. "Release the merchant."

The nun cried out for mercy as Anne stood and emerged onto the street to a crowd wild with joy. She did not know if this was for her or the coins she began to scatter among them, but she believed it made no difference. She threw coins to everyone, many dressed in masks and mummery, all of them with dirty palms clutching the air for what she might cast to them.

God's triumph was complete. He had delivered her enemy, given her the crown and an heir, and now she dispensed this same mercy to the poor. She felt the power, and the glory, of being the hand of God in England.

Chapter Twenty-four

Rose heard the heavy footsteps of marching men, the rhythmic beating of metal upon metal, the iron heart of war. And it was here. The men came through the gate, past the gatehouse where another heretic was suffering in the darkness. Sir Thomas was dressed and clean-shaven, ready to meet them. He had ordered the children to their studies and glared at them when they peeked through the windows, as if they spied on him in some private, shaming matter.

Margaret had gone to the city for shopping. Sir Thomas had sent her with an exorbitant sum, and she was not expected to return today. Rose realized with grim admiration that Sir Thomas set everything in motion around her for this moment. He would have this just as he wanted. He was the only man she had ever met who could control the fates. The thought stabbed her heart. He had done nothing for her, save given her a letter to deliver. In the end, she despaired, that was all she was to him: a servant to be used. He cared nothing, really, of her fate.

Rose went out in the garden and watched as the men read Sir Thomas the charges. She had seen men arrested, men who fought and wanted to die on the open street rather than see the inside of the Tower. More only pursed his lip and nodded when they finished. She could tell he was impatient with their long list of accusations.

He called to her as they took hold of his arms on either side. "The letter, Rose! Do not tarry. It is my salvation."

"And mine," she replied, repeating what he had earlier told her. It lingered in the air like a question between them.

He stared at her, a tenderness in his eyes that shocked her. Sharp pains shot through her stomach, pains of fear, pains not so different from desire. She blushed to have such strange thoughts at this moment.

He shook his head, answering some question she had not asked. "I am sorry," he said as they pushed him away, forcing him to begin the walk to the gate.

He turned at the gate, saying something to the guards, so that they allowed him this pause. He turned and surveyed his utopia. Rose saw him weep.

The children were murmuring, and nothing could bring them to concentrate on their studies. Rose tried to steady their rising fears, and she was afraid that she sounded as patently bad as the pageant actors on the streets.

"Everything will be all right," she crooned.

It set their teeth on edge.

Her words were meaningless. She did not have answers.

"I must go; I cannot stay," she said to Candice. "If Margaret returns before me, tell her I have gone on an errand for her father. I will return."

Going by barge would be faster than horse, for the tide was in her favour at the moment. She could go on foot when she arrived in the city.

She sat on the barge, the sole customer. The cold wind skimmed the top of the Thames, stinging her cheeks with little pecks of ice.

She thought on everything that passed between her and More, and the strange vision on Christmas Eve that caused her to scream, the bell that rang from the kitchen, making everyone spring from their sleep, so that all complained later of the bell and no one made mention of having heard her scream. The others had stayed up late that night telling ghost stories. *Could she have seen one herself?* she wondered. But ghosts are vengeful spirits, and this one, though more terrifying than any tale told round the hearth, had saved her in her hour of rebuke.

That misfortune was what she had deserved. She was not pure of heart, and perhaps she had tempted him beyond what he could bear, but the apparition saved her from it. How could the unseen judge her so differently? And how could this tale ever be told, for who would judge her worthy of such salvation? Who would believe More, the great purger of the church, the man who laboured to present the church as the faultless bride, the man who above all else wanted law to reign in the land, who would believe he would do such a thing? He was purging evil and error from the hearts of men. How could his own be so unclean?

She thought of him scourging himself. He had done more to be pure than anyone she had ever known. Who else tormented their flesh nightly so that he may live clean in the day? If this was not enough to purge himself of evil desires, there was no hope for purging the church. Not even Hutchins could do this. She had never heard of Hutchins scourging himself. If More, a master of learning and obedience, could not cleanse himself, there was no hope for the common man or the greater church.

Perhaps Hutchins was a fool.

Rose got out at the Wharf. A woman was busy picking lice from a blanket, sitting on the corner of a street, quite near the channel cut out to carry urine from the city. The sun was strongest in that spot, even if the odour was too. The woman did not mind.

"What's in the bag?" the woman snapped, looking up from her work with hatred as she took in Rose's black and red dress, the white lace peeking out from her sleeves and the pomander at her waist. The woman snagged a louse that had given her particular trouble and pinched it with a grimacing smile between her fingernails.

"I have not opened it," Rose replied.

"It's coins. Ye got one f'me?" The woman's voice had a strangled sound to it.

"No, I—"

"Be gone!" the crone shouted.

"I need to find the sheriff!"

"Ye'll be robbed soon enough on this street. Then he'll find you!" She laughed out loud, throwing her head back, and Rose saw layers of dirt in the lines of her throat, like the rings of a tree trunk. The woman's great mouth yawned open as she guffawed, and Rose witnessed her complete lack of teeth.

A man approached her and did not make her afraid. He kept his eyes down but pointed her to a door.

Knocking, she waited for an answer. She turned back to thank the man, but he had vanished.

"Go away!" a voice scraped from inside.

"I am sent by Sir Thomas More!" Rose called, pressing her face close enough to the wood to get a splinter in her nose.

The door swung open so fast that Rose stumbled inside. A man grabbed her and dragged her across the threshold before slamming the door.

"Why did you yell that name? Do you want to die today?"

His face was badly pocked. Rose wondered how sick he had been; he was lucky to have survived, but no one with these scars ever seemed grateful. His hair was longer than most men's and a dirty orange colour. It clung to his damp neck even though winter braced the house on all sides. His eyes looked hung, not set, in his face, with watery bags drooping below. She handed him the bag and waited.

His home was not well lit, she noticed, with a few tallow rushlights out and a fire that made the room thick with smoke. The room she was in merely had a table and a simple hearth. A short flight of stairs was on her left, to a visible larger room above, and above that, an even larger dwelling. It was an odd feeling to be at the small center below the home. Above must be where he and his family slept. No one was stirring.

On the wall next to the table, hanging, were the implements of his job: a heavy club, shackles, and one good pair of boots. On the table covered with green bazik cloth was a heavy book, laid open so that as she sat, she could see it contained names and sums—probably a tax record. The sheriff always collected these, which was why he often got into scrapes and took folks off to the jails. He was in charge of law and order, and the law of the land was gold.

He had opened the bag and removed the letter, breaking the seal with a long thumbnail.

"There's a lot of money in here," he said at last.

Rose nodded, not sure what to say. His words were an accusation.

"Do you know what this says?" he asked, waving the letter at her.

"No."

He grunted. "Go home before night falls. The heretics and fools of the new learning have unleashed hell here. A fine thing like you will not last a minute on the street."

❊ ❊ ❊ ❊ ❊

I raced down the hall, the darkness of night real and alive, peering in at me through the windows. An overhead bulb popped and burned out, letting the shadows in, stealing closer to me as I ran. I tried to outrun them, but bulbs were popping and burning out, little showers of sparks chasing me down the hall. The shadows closed in from behind, cold and pulsing, pushed by a wind that growled with pleasure. I could hear Mariskka cursing and calling out for a night guard to bring her a flashlight so she could check on the patients.

Crazy Betty was sleeping when I burst through her door. She grunted and rolled over as I ran to her side, shaking her awake.

She sat up and slapped me. Fluffing her pillow, she tried to return to her sleep.

"Cr—, Betty," I stammered, "I need your help."

"Do I know you?" she asked, smushing her face into the pillow.

"Not exactly. I'm Bridget, from the hospice wing."

She lifted her head a bit to look at me. "You're dying?"

"Yes," I answered.

"Bad day for you," she said. "I can't sell you crazy and that's all I got, honey."

"No, Betty, I was going to get into a research study, but I didn't, and a man said you knew the story."

She bolted up. "What did this man look like?"

"Uh, big, a black man, wears an earring in his ear, and sunglasses, even inside."

"Looks like you're already ate up with crazy. I never seen the guy."

"Betty!" I gave her a look to scald her awake.

"All right, I'll tell, on one condition. I want to be free of pills and booze. I never want to crave them again. Never want to have even the slightest need for them. You do that for me, and I'll tell what I saw."

"How could I promise that? I can't fix you."

"I already knowed that. I wasn't even talking to you." She rolled her eyes at an empty corner of the room. "You had a boyfriend. He knew you couldn't help being what you are, any more than I can help what I am. He enrolled you in a study, and they were having real good success curing your kind of cancer. But someone stopped him from taking you outta here. Someone who craves, like us. You were so proud of who you were, and what you had, that you couldn't smell your own greed anymore, and when it rolled off her breath, you couldn't smell hers, either. So Mariskka made sure you was gonna die. And she's gonna get really rich. But it won't stop the craving."

She slapped me again. "Mariskka still had a chance for a better life! You poisoned her good now."

I took a breath, trying to process what she was saying, but she cut me off.

"Don't forget: we have a bargain."

Mariskka's flashlight swept the room. Betty's window was larger, and there was enough light from the lamps outside that we could see her face contort with anger to see us together.

"Back to bed, ladies. We need our beauty rest."

Chapter Twenty-five

England slept, the white fugue of winter descending on the wisteria gardens and narrow paths. London's own streets were drunk with fog and mist. At night a halo could be seen around the moon. The rains gathered for each new morning, unleashing such torrents that none were in the streets but the army of raindrops, stealing away into cracks and crannies and uneven doorways. The rains washed away the previous year, scouring the smells off and out, rinsing clean debris and stains of memory.

Anne took to her lying in, claiming a chamber inside Greenwich palace—the same one, Henry said with pride, that his mother had used. Swept clean and laid with fresh plaited rushes, dried mint, roses, and vervain, he had ordered it decorated with the finest white silk fabrics embroidered with gold and pearls. Artisans had been commissioned to create special dishware for her, because she would take all her meals in bed. Every dish, done in a wonderfully heavy crockery that did not spill, featured a secret—an underside painted with good omens like healthy male infants and happy fathers. Anne of course had to finish each meal before she could safely turn over the crock to see her good wish for the moment. It was one more little amusement that kept her full and happy.

Gifts had been arriving with regularity. Anne's favourite was a hanging from her brother, George. It was the colour that made Anne grin. It was green, the colour of spring leaves. In France, where she had spent so many hours longing for home and writing George letters of her dreams, dreams of a quiet life away from court, green was the colour reserved for royal births. Anne watched it hung near her white bed, and saw the contrast displayed so well between her dreams and her future.

There were clothes for the boy, a dress for her churching from Henry, too, elaborate as usual—and, Anne thought, too small through the waist. But Henry was impossibly optimistic. There was also the birth announcement, done in advance and sent for her approval. Everyone in England would celebrate when they heard the guns being fired again from the Tower.

Henry visited in the afternoon before he went out hunting. He supplied himself with a special stock of stags and deer and blessed the quiet that had stolen over the country. With so much rain keeping everyone inside, there was less mischief and less law to write.

Today Henry brought her a mass of yellow primroses, which were in winter bloom, along with Candlemas bells. He rested his head against her belly and listened.

Anne reached down and stroked his hair, noticing that Jane blushed and turned away.

Anne made a note to speak with her. Jane had been in service to her for too long to still be nervous when the king entered the room. Anne gave her an encouraging smile so she would not be afraid.

Henry lifted his head and leaned to Anne, kissing her lips and her forehead. "How precious you are to me."

"I am sorry," Anne whispered, trying to keep him close as she said it. "I know it cannot be easy."

"What?" Henry asked.

"Waiting like this. Waiting for the birth … waiting until I can be back in your bed," Anne replied.

Henry stammered something, backing away. "There are too many in here," Henry said, looking at the number of people attending Anne and his own servants following him. A fire kept at a constant crackling height caught his attention too, but it would be needed for warm water when the birth occurred. "The room grows too hot for the mother. I must go."

"No, Henry!" Anne protested. "Stay but a minute more! What news? Tell me a tale and keep me company."

Henry looked uneasy but returned to her bedside. He did not want to upset her, this was plain enough to her, but the baby kicked so wildly in her womb, knocking about between her ribs, that Anne had no fear its life was too delicate for his amusements.

Henry looked at his folded hands, pursing his lips.

Anne burst out laughing. She reached over and took his hands in hers. "It's all right, Henry, really it is. Give me news."

"I have done more to assure your place," he answered.

"Yes?"

"Three more acts have I passed. The Act of Succession, so that the throne will pass through your son, not the girl Catherine gave me."

Anne was uneasy at the way he spat the word *girl*.

"The Act of Supremacy," he continued, "to be assured that I retain the power to govern in my own country, and not some puppet Pope in another realm." He paused. "And lastly …"

Anne squeezed his hand.

"Lastly, the Act of Treason. To be assured of loyalties."

"And all have been sent out? All have been signed?" she asked.

"All have seen the future and will follow," Henry said. "The people, I am told, the people are relieved to be free of unjust clergy stealing bread from their mouths. They see me as their great defender."

"It is a title the Pope gave you."

Henry was the only man she had ever known who could look so utterly alone in a room crowded with people clamouring for his attention, ready to spring up and do his will. Anne saw the realm in his face—the cries for relief, the bitter scrambles for position and power, the burdens that Henry would let no one else carry. It was arrogance to her, once. She began praying under her breath, asking for wisdom for Henry, for comfort and aid. He was alone in this battle, alone on a front where the soldiers behind him could be a danger as much as the enemies in front of him. All she had ever had to offer him was herself, and now this comfort too was denied. All she could do was pray.

He stood, knocking her bedside table. The Hutchins book hit the floor with a great whump. Henry bent to pick it up, studying it before he replaced it and left.

The pains began as a dull ache in her midsection. She had her girls remove her bodice and skirts. Her midwife began rubbing a stinking ointment on her belly to ease the pain.

The baby was still not delivered in twenty contractions. Midwives sent the alarm downstairs, but Anne ignored it. She would not fail in this. Yet she knew that, all below her in the palace, doors were being thrown open, cabinets propped open, every lock released, every knot pried free and loose. The palace was working desperate magic below her to assure her body would open and release the child. If she failed, next they would have soldiers from here to the Tower shooting arrows in the air.

She pushed again, bearing down, mad with pain, not caring about crown or reputation. Nothing mattered, nothing existed, except these awful contractions and the animal urge to push.

"I see the head!" the midwife yelled. "Push harder!"

Anne heard the midwife christening the baby as the head emerged. It was a secret gesture between the women in this sacred chamber, so that the child would be baptized before birth. In this way, no child would be born unbaptized and risk purgatory.

"In the name of the Father, Son, and Holy Ghost, I

christen thee Henry, Prince of England." The assurance was all Anne needed for strength, and she gave one last mighty push.

The immediate crowd at her feet told her the baby was delivered. Anne screamed in relief and collapsed back into the arms of another girl. The air of the room was thick, and she thought she saw the air shimmer.

There was much whispering, and Anne watched, dumb from exhaustion, as the midwife, cradling the heir in her arms, tied off the cord and cut it with her scissors. The babe was washed with wine, and a little salt rubbed on its tongue. Anne had heard that some midwives recommended washing the tongue in hot water, to make for smooth speech later in life, but Anne had forbidden this. It was too harsh.

The midwives wrapped the baby snugly in strips of clean linen and carried him to Anne, nestling the tiny bundle in her arms. Anne beheld the face of her future and wept. The baby was beautiful, exceeding any miracle the church had ever proclaimed, any relic they had ever offered the people for viewing. She caught her Yeoman stealing a glance in, smiling.

"Who will bring him to Henry?" Anne whispered, not taking her eyes from the beautiful face.

"Anne," her midwife began, "there is something we must tell you. We rejoice in a safe birth, we rejoice in a healthy baby."

"What is it?" Anne interrupted her.

The midwife was crying.

⚜

Anne could hear Henry's scream, and she winced.

When he entered the room, he was carrying the baby. His courtiers trailed closely behind him, their eyes down, but he turned, glaring at them, glaring at the women in the chamber. Everyone fled from the room, leaving him with Anne alone. He laid the baby in the cradle, tucked in the darkest corner of the chamber. He stayed in the darkness.

"She is beautiful," he said finally.

"We should call her Elizabeth. It would have made your mother happy," Anne said. She didn't have the strength to get out of the bed and walk to him, to try to persuade him to comfort or happiness. She could only lie there, exhausted. Her best offering had been in his arms, and it was not enough. It defined her relationship to him.

"Why, Anne?" he whispered.

She could not answer.

He came out of the shadows and laid his head on her empty womb. "Why? Why was it a girl?"

He was crying. He was shaking under Anne's hands.

She cursed herself under her breath … a stupid little fool, she said. Where had she gone wrong? She felt naked, her faults all exposed in this tiny bundled baby.

"I have done all this for you!" he screamed at her. "I dismantled the Church! Two cardinals are dead because of you, Anne, and many men are in the Tower tonight, suffering, because you promised me an heir!"

"No, Henry," she tried to say. "I tried. I did everything you asked."

"Where is my son?" he screamed.

"I don't know!" she screamed back. "I obeyed God in everything! I never prompted you to do those things! I only said love God and honour His Word!"

"But do you, Anne? Jane tells me you flirt with the Hutchins book but have never read it, not all the way through. You are not who you seem."

"What does Jane know?" Anne said.

"She knows how to please a king, I tell you. Her body is ripe with heirs. I knew it every time I caressed her in my chamber, while you were in here gulping down dainties, cataloguing my treasures, instead of doing your duty as my wife!"

Anne felt her chin trembling. She was terrified to break in front of him. She didn't trust him now, as a husband or a king. "I alone am loyal to you. It is God who has betrayed us!"

"You do not even know Him," he said with disgust.

The baby cried, breaking their locked stares.

Henry grunted and left.

Anne called for a nursemaid. "Nurse her, and leave her here with me to sleep. She must never be left alone. Perhaps she will not be king, but she will be loved."

Jane did not attend her again. She was moved to private chambers, a pleasant little apartment where she was kept under guard, with fresh flowers brought to her bedside. She could spend the time in warm, sweet walks with Henry through the sleeping winter garden. This was what Anne learned from the servants still attending her, though it took days to pry each piece from them.

Anne devoted herself to being ready for her churching. All of Henry's accusations would be upturned in a single day. Except perhaps for the reading of the entire book Hutchins had sent; it was a thick book with so many words. She could not simply choke through it in one afternoon. She would set this task aside for another month in which she had more leisure. This was a time for alarm and strategy, she reasoned, not leisurely reading.

A thrill shot through her limbs and heart; she had not left this chamber for a month. Today she would join the palace again and the world. She wore white, with a long white veil, so that no one would see her in her shame before the priest declared her clean. The women were reminding her of the instructions:

"Do not look at sky or earth until the priest places the host upon your tongue."

"Do not lift your veil! It will protect you from all charms and spells, and from demons who wish to needle you."

"The king will remove it as a sign that he has accepted you back into his bed."

Her Yeoman opened the door, and Anne saw there were other men with him. They walked to either side of her, lifting her in the air and carrying her to the litter outside waiting to take her to the church. Her feet would not be allowed to curse the ground, unclean as she was, until she had partaken of communion again.

The sun was strong and warm and Anne lifted her face to it, wishing she could be free of this shroud with the sun on her skin. The church was within sight. Anne's heart was pounding. Everyone would be inside. She would only be permitted to kneel at the church's back door, like a beggar, until the priest bade her clean to enter.

The guards lifted her from the litter and carried her to the steps, rapping loudly upon the door.

Anne saw shards of broken glass at the far end of the church. She had heard the gossip, rumours that those immersed in Hutchins's book were striking out at the church, desecrating the images and relics that had coloured their lives. Anne felt a stab of sadness, seeing the bits of brilliantly coloured glass still reflecting the sun, though lying in dirt. There was so much beauty in the church. She did not want that destroyed. She had only wanted more of it, more of what made God so beautiful to her, His very words. But they could touch nothing of human hands without upending it.

And here she was: a new mother, with a husband who may not want her back in his bed, with nothing to show for her striving in faith but a girl. Had she not prayed? Was there a Mass she had not said, if only in her heart? Why had His words done so little for her?

The door opened, and a priest tipped his head to acknowledge her.

Her hands were shaking as she lifted the white cloth

to him. The cloth had been draped over baby Elizabeth at her baptism; giving it to the priest would protect the anointing on Elizabeth's life.

He stared at it, not moving to accept it, and Anne's heart raced. Henry had passed a law that protected Anne's offspring, but the law did not change the heart. The priest could throw her out, leaving them both to the witches and angry crowds.

He swallowed and took it, his warm hand touching her own. It did not stop the sweat beading along her forehead and bodice.

The priest handed the cloth to another priest behind him, and Anne saw he was attended to by two such servants, one carrying candles and one a bowl of holy water.

He read the 121st Psalm in Latin. Anne closed her eyes in ecstasy, the words being balm to her body, wounded by birth, and her soul, wounded by things she had yet to name clearly. She felt so poor, so lost, that to lie here receiving the words of God was strengthening her very bones.

A stirring behind her reminded Anne she was not alone. She was attended to by servants, and behind her servants were the guards, including her own Yeoman.

She held up a hand and stopped the priest. "In English," she commanded.

The priest reddened and did not speak.

"For the sake of my servants, who wish to hear the Word of God."

"They do." His voice was thin and sharply edged. "They cannot understand it."

The priest fumbled with his robe, tucking his lips

into his teeth. He turned to the two priests behind him, who were careful not to look him in the eye.

He cleared his throat and began.

> "Forasmuch as it hath pleased Almighty God of His goodness to give you safe deliverance, and hath preserved you in the great danger of childbirth; you shall therefore give hearty thanks unto God, and say,

> "I am well pleased: that the Lord hath heard the voice of my prayer; that He hath inclined His ear unto me: therefore will I call upon Him as long as I live. The snares of death compassed me round about: and the pains of hell gat hold upon me. I found trouble and heaviness, and I called upon the Name of the Lord: O Lord, I beseech Thee, deliver my soul."

Anne repeated his words.

"Let us pray," he said. "Christ, have mercy upon us."

Anne, and her servants, repeated his words.

"O Lord, save this woman Thy servant," he said, "who putteth her trust in Thee."

They all replied. "Christ, have mercy upon us."

"Be Thou to her a strong tower," he said, not sprinkling her with holy water, "from the face of her enemy."

They all replied. "Christ, have mercy upon us."

He finished without passion:

> "O Almighty God, we give Thee humble
> thanks for that Thou hast vouchsafed
> to deliver this woman Thy servant
> from the great pain and peril of child-
> birth; grant, we beseech thee, that she
> may faithfully live, in this life present,
> and also may be partaker of everlasting
> glory in the life to come: through Jesus
> Christ our Lord. Amen."

Anne rose to enter the church, but he did not move aside. Hate filled his face, something evil swimming just below the surface of his features. Anne heard metal scrape against metal, and his eyes darted past her, behind her in the crowd. Anne closed her eyes in relief. Her Yeoman must have stepped forward. It was enough to frighten the priest into remembering his place.

He stepped aside.

Anne entered the church and inhaled sharply. She had not seen this many people for weeks. They all stared without blush or modesty, eager to see if her figure had been retained and her countenance proud. She had had a girl, after all.

Henry was kneeling at the altar, ready for Mass. Anne walked and knelt at his side. She was grateful to be forbidden to speak here, for she doubted she could say anything at all.

He looked just as she had kept him in her heart: regal, with ermine and scarlet and chains of gold hanging from his wide shoulders.

There was a commotion off to the side, the priests consulting one another. Anne knew the source of the disturbance. The priest conducting the service kept glancing from Anne to Henry to the room crowded with nobles and courtiers.

He approached Henry and whispered to him.

"You ask permission to conduct the service in Latin?" Henry asked. "Why?"

The priest waved his hands in an empty explanation. "I do not know it in English."

Henry's brow furrowed. Anne saw his appetite for mystery was awake.

"Do you not know what it means?" Henry asked.

"It is the tongue of angels, my king. It is sufficient that He alone understands."

"It is sufficient for whom?" Henry asked.

"The words themselves have such meaning, such great power, that merely to hear them will produce the desired effect."

"My words accomplish much the same effect," Henry said. "Merely to hear them sets the world in motion around me. And I have a word for you, my priest."

Henry waved his finger and the priest bent to hear the quiet command. "When you speak to me, you will speak in English, for this is the language of the realm. Latin is the tongue of the Pope and he speaks for Spain and France, not God."

The priest stood and cleared his throat, again. He would be hoarse by nightfall, Anne thought. He faltered for words, and the hour-long Mass was reduced to a few simple prayers.

"Christ's body!" he declared, lifting the veil to place the host on Anne's tongue, as the church bells tolled. He placed the host on Henry's tongue and gave them the wine to drink.

"Christ's blood!"

They drank, and Henry leaned toward Anne, lifting the veil away from her face, kissing her on the mouth. Anne caressed his cheek before he pulled away.

Later that night, back in his bed, their bed, Henry loved her with the tenderness of a new husband.

Tucked into the shelter of his frame, rejoicing at his solid arms supporting her, he pulled her closer in.

"The next will be a boy," she promised.

She shifted her neck to press more of his rough face against her skin, but he propped himself up.

"Anne, I asked you a question!"

"Yes! Yes!" Anne replied, disoriented, trying to pull herself back awake and focus on his form in the dark chamber. She reached out and stroked his hair.

"I asked if you were faithful in prayer," he repeated.

"I pray, morning and night, that God would grant us a son."

Henry lowered himself back down, saying nothing. Anne draped herself across him, and waited until at last his arm lifted and went round her again. As she listened to his heart, she remembered that she had left the Hutchins book in her lying-in chamber. She would get rid of it tomorrow; it had caused nothing but turmoil for her. She was ready for peace, and blessings, and sons. Sir Thomas was under arrest, proof that God was working on her behalf. She did not need this book any longer to assure her of His will.

"It can offer me no more than this." She smiled to herself, feeling Henry's gentle breaths, and drifted to sleep. A wind kicked up in the gardens below, and she heard animals scampering back into their dens before the storm.

Chapter Twenty-six

Margaret was vomiting, her head hanging over a brown hedge at the edge of the steps. The tutor, Candice, claimed to be suffering from vapors and fled inside, leaving Rose alone and trembling.

She handed the boy a silver groat and he fairly skipped back down to the steps at the bottom of the garden, back on the barge to return to the city. He had been thrilled to deliver the papers because it lined his pocket. His mother might eat well tonight, or his sister. Sir Thomas's impending death was feeding the world, Rose thought bitterly. They were feasting upon him already.

The papers, signed with a seal from the Star Chamber of King Henry, read:

> That he should be carried back to the
> Tower of London and from thence

drawn on a hurdle through the City
of London to Tyburn, there to be
hanged till he should be half dead;
that he should be cut down alive, his
privy parts cut off, his belly ripped,
his bowels burnt, his four quarters set
up over four gates of the City, and his
head upon London Bridge.

Rose braced herself and went inside.

"They will be coming! We must save what we
can." Candice was in the room, ghostlike, lifting a
silver candlestick and setting it inside a pillowcase.
She was taking the silver, leaving the portrait Holbein
had done of the family, looking with an ashen face
round the room.

"Who will be coming? Who will be coming?"
Margaret demanded.

Candice didn't respond.

Margaret grabbed her, shaking her until Candice's
face settled on hers.

"The king's men. When your father is dead, all his
property is forfeit. You will be turned out," Candice
said.

"But he is not dead yet! There is still hope!" Rose
cried.

"Children, go through the house. Bring me everything Father has written to you. All our books too."
Margaret commanded.

Margaret herself ran into his office, bringing out
papers and banned books he had hunted. She threw
them into a pile in the garden and set it on fire. She

grabbed a Hutchins book to throw in, but Rose stopped her.

"What else do we have left to cling to but these words?"

"Look what they have done, Rose! Everything my father did was to prevent these words from being in the hands of little fools like you! And look what mischief they have done! Laws overturned, churches desecrated, priests treated like criminals!"

"But I have read this book, Margaret. It says none of those things. It gives life to those who read it, not death!"

Margaret began to laugh.

"What is amusing?" Rose asked, confused.

Margaret refused to answer. Instead she turned to the children gathered around her, their chins trembling, fingers in their mouths. "I will encourage Father to sign the Act of Supremacy. He was once Henry's favoured servant, and his life will be spared if he agrees to this. Do not give up hope!"

Rose waited at the edge of the garden. Everything was lifeless. Winter's rains and winds had stripped the leaves from every plant. Those that remained were curled and brown. She pulled her shawl around her shoulders, waiting for her mistress.

Margaret was looking out over the black water, watching the barge move away into the grey fog. She had received a letter, written in coarse charcoal, from her father. As Margaret read it aloud, Rose came to understood its content in just a few sentences.

He was unwell, dying from the imprisonment. He did not know if he would be well enough to walk to his own execution. They had beheaded Cardinal Fisher this week. The letter said that cannons were fired to alert the king his enemy was dead. That was how Sir Thomas knew his own time was close. At least these were the words that Margaret shared aloud.

Weeks had passed since he had arrived in the Tower, each cold winter week falling upon the next, a stinking pile of frustrations. Margaret was at the end of her third month of helplessness. Sir Thomas still refused to sign the Act. He refused to comment at all on Henry's marriage to Anne Boleyn or the break with the church. He found death preferable to a life with his children—this was how Margaret put it to Rose.

Margaret had not yet sent Rose away. Rose did not know why. Rose preferred life on the street, the freedom she had once known, to this prison. There were other women, she knew, women who had lost sons and husbands, who read these same words. Many were in the Tower themselves, dying slow, shameful deaths. If their families had no money, they would not be able to pay the guards for food, or a shawl to keep warm, or even clean straw for a toilet. Rose could help them. She knew how to earn money. Anything could be forgiven to save these martyrs. She would not let these people die the same lonely, unloved, uncertain deaths of her brothers.

Margaret refused to release her. She only smiled, seeing something in Rose's future that was secret and delicious, wanting to wait for it to spring up.

Rose had kept the Bible, seared at the edges. She

read it alone, at night, seeing Margaret's sneer through the dim candlelight as she glided past.

Now Margaret broke the silence. "There is other news, the boy bringing the letter told me. Servants are falling ill at the palace all around Anne. It begins with a red spotted rash, red eyes, and spots even inside their mouths. It's from the devil, they say, the stinking pits of hell. They're afraid of the light, say it hurts their eyes. My only comfort is that Anne Boleyn can no longer hide who or what she is. She is a witch. She has no more victims in the court, so she turns on her servants. She's already gotten rid of the men who opposed her: Are they not all dead? Cardinal Fisher is dead, Cardinal Wolsey is dead, my father in the Tower, a condemned man. Can you not see her whole and only goal has been to exterminate the church? Father is a good man, a strong man, to resist her to the end."

Margaret had that faraway sound in her voice, but a new pride in her father was seeping into it.

"What news of the king?" Rose asked. "Has he received your petition for your father's life?"

"I do not know. Henry has fled to Hampton Court. He wants no part of this new sickness."

"Margaret, you must release me! I can do no good here! Let me return to the city, where at least I can tend to my people!"

"Your people?" Margaret laughed. "The only family you have are those pock-faced wenches, selling their bodies for a bowl of soup. Your brothers are dead, your son is dead—there is no one left who loves you, Rose."

"How did you know?"

"Father knew everything about you when you came here. You were his little experiment in social justice, to show those at court that even the basest person could be elevated through education. He used you to gain acceptance for his ideas, his methods. The more nobles paraded through our living room and saw you at your embroidery, or reading your horn-book, the higher father moved through the ranks of court. You served him well, Rose. Or didn't you?"

Rose slapped her.

"It doesn't matter. You've done more for him than you know." She was smiling. "But if you want to run away, I will take you to the city myself. We have an engagement."

She shoved the letter to Rose and walked away. Rose read it for herself, stopping with a sharp breath at the end.

The execution date was set.

Chapter Twenty-seven

Anne looked away as her servants emptied the bowl. She could not stop retching. The river winds rocking the boat were a curse to her.

Her servants fanned her religiously though it was cold. Anne should have been shivering, but she was hot. Nothing comforted her or calmed her stomach. When they pulled into the dock of Hampton Court and the guards rushed to help the women out, Anne exhaled her sigh of relief.

She was out of the barge before the men could open the door to her litter. She slipped on the wet grass, but another boy caught her, blushing with shame. Anne wondered if it was modesty or if he, too, had heard the rumours.

Anne would not allow these thoughts. They would be treason, punishable by death. To accuse Anne of infidelity put Henry's line of succession in question. It could unseat him and plunge the realm into civil war. Anne kept a close ear to the rumours, trying to ferret out the source, but she could not. It was as if the devil himself were at court whispering in people's ears.

The sun broke through the heavy clouds, touching her face. Anne stopped and inhaled, letting the breath go deep within, like a draught of crisp spring water. All would be well yet.

The litter whisked her through the entrance into base court, shielding her from the awful odours that could waft up from the Great Hall of Easement. Anne stepped out, her mind and stomach swimming as she was assaulted by the vast number of turrets, windows, and chimneys all around. The faces of dead Roman emperors glared at her from high above as the water clock struck the hour, telling her the tide was turning. Anne was glad to be done with the trip.

The cobbled courtyard made her unsteady on her feet; her pattens dug into her soft soles and she minced her steps, reaching out for her Yeoman. His arm was like an iron bar, and she clung to it.

From a dark staircase a throng of people burst forth, Henry and Jane in the center.

Anne tried to smile, but the skin was stretched thin across her lips.

The two groups stopped, and neither side of courtiers knew the protocol for the moment. It was Henry who moved first. He dropped the hand of Jane, who receded into the shadows, fleeing with soft giggles among her maids.

"Anne. Are you well? I heard rumours of measles at the palace."

"I couldn't stay there."

He circled, cocking his head as he studied her. "Why? Why would you follow me here?"

"Come and kiss your wife, Henry." She extended her arms to him.

"How does Elizabeth fare?" he asked. "Is she well?"

"Her nursemaid says she's grown with great vigor!" she replied, waiting.

Henry took her arms, pulling her in, kissing her on the mouth in full view of her court and the women who giggled in the windows above. Anne could see their white faces, set on either side of Wolsey's coat of arms, little fat cherubs hoisting his name above her. She turned her body a bit to the side so none of them would miss what she did next.

She moved Henry's hand to her belly, just beginning to swell. She tried a bright smile, hoping it would distract her from being sick. Jane's perfume was nauseating.

⚜

The sky in winter could be so impossibly blue that she was sure England was the only jewel in Christ's crown. The sun was high, warming her cold arms and face, and her heart.

"Winter is ending—can you feel it?" she asked, reaching out and touching the barren twigs of the garden. "There is life within."

Henry cast a glance behind them, up at the windows.

"I want that girl gone, and any like her, Henry."

"Which girl?"

"It makes me unwell to see all these bosoms and

pursed lips around you. We must be more careful this time. And you must join me, my good king, at night. We can read to each other and play cards. Your company is good medicine."

"I have things to tend to."

"What greater matter is there than your heir?" She slipped her arm through his. "It will be a glorious spring."

The nausea began to stop. The baby was kicking every hour, and she loved the first swishes of its limbs in her womb. Her maids slept well but she did not, exhausting herself in her prayers, praying for the movements to tell her if the child was a boy.

Henry often slipped from the bed early in the evening. She did not ask where he went, for she had rid the court of the seducing women that plagued her. Instead she would steal his pillow, inhaling his scent, and return to sleep.

In the early hours of dawn, just before the turtle-doves returned to the garden, she dreamed.

She was floating in the Thames, trying desperately to reach an empty barge. Others were in the water, and she heard their cries, but she cared only about the barge, about securing herself in it. Ahead of her was London Bridge, black and monstrous, its limbs plunging deep into the swirling water, lording its might over those in the river. It would not raise to let the ships through, and they scraped its belly as they crumpled under it, with sparks and groans littering the air ahead.

She grasped the barge, heaving herself in, and saw that Elizabeth was holding onto its edge. She reached to save her, but Elizabeth slipped away, under the black waters, and was lost to her.

"Oh, God!" she cried out, awakened. Her heart was beating too fast. She tried to steady herself, lest she harm the baby, and began to cry.

"I do not know what it means!" she said to the dark room.

Nothing stirred.

"Do not show me this, and give me no hope! Tell me what it means!"

Something stirred in the darkness beside her bed, and as an enormous hand passed over her face, Anne fell into a deep sleep.

He spoke. *It is a dream of Noah, Anne. Have you not read? 'By faith Noah honoured God, after that he was warned of things which were not seen, and prepared the ark to the saving of his household, through which ark, he condemned the world, and became heir of the righteousness which cometh by faith.'*

She knew his voice, and it comforted her. He continued.

"'Wherefore let us also (seeing that we are compassed with so great a multitude of witnesses) lay away all that presseth down, and the sin that hangeth on, and let us run with patience unto the battle that is set before us, looking unto Jesus, the author and finisher of our faith, which for the joy that was set before him, abode the cross, and despised its shame, and is set down on the right hand of the throne of God. Consider therefore how that he endured such speaking against him of sinners, lest ye should be wearied and faint

in your minds. For ye have not resisted unto blood-shedding, striving against sin.'"

He said nothing more, and Anne remained in her sleep until morning, the words replaying in her mind, with no dreams to interrupt them.

When she awoke, she refused breakfast until her servants had found and delivered the book. She began reading, determined to unlock its secrets. She had flirted around it for too long, embraced the fashion and form of the new learning and the men of the book, without becoming one of them herself.

She had not gotten deep into the book when her Yeoman opened the door to her chamber, and Henry entered. His face told her the news was not good, and her hand instinctively went to her belly. That was silly, she knew, for if anything had happened to the child, she would have known first. But she feared he had heard an omen or dreamed vividly, as she had.

He stopped when he saw she was reading the Hutchins book and exhaled.

"What is it, Henry?"

"It is nothing. Matters of state."

"Why don't we take a walk in the gardens?"

"It is not warm enough yet. Perhaps later in the day. Would you like for me to read to you?"

"No, no," she said.

He rose to leave but Anne caught his hand. "Henry."

"Let me be!" He left with a hurried stride.

She walked to her window, pausing to let a bit of sickness sweep over her and pass. There were men outside in the courtyard, and she could not decide who they

were. By their livery, they served Henry, but she did not
recognize their voices.

"It happened last week. Every petition of Henry's
failed."

"They will declare war on us."

"No, no, they won't. They did this to spite him. And
her."

"They say an Englishman paid for it. Henry will be
looking for him."

"Nay. Henry knows exactly where this man is. He
just doesn't know how he did it."

Something or someone must have alerted the men
and they stopped talking. When Anne leaned out further, to hear any last bit, they looked up and saw her.
One man crossed himself and fled. The others froze,
staring in horror at her pale face in the window.

A servant came in, carrying a tray of breakfast. He
saw the book laying on Anne's bed, and the tray shook in
his hands, the crockery bumping against each other. A bit
of wine spilled from her pewter cup and onto her linens.

He looked up at Anne in fear. "Begging your par-
don, my queen! Forgive me!"

Anne saw her chance. "You've ruined my linens."

"I'm so very sorry, my queen!"

"What's your name?"

"John, and it please you."

"Well, John, I can have you thrown in the Tower
or cast outside naked, depending on my mood. Which
would you prefer?"

His answer stuck in his throat.

"Or you can tell me a little news, to amuse your
queen after disturbing her so greatly."

"I, I could tell news! Um, the cooks have ordered new pewter goblets for Hampton Court that—"

She cut him off. "No. What has happened that has the court talking in whispers? Last week, something was done that made Henry mad. It was done in another country. Some say it was to spite me."

He shook his head, but Anne could see it was from fear, not because he had no reply.

"I have always been a merciful queen. You have nothing to fear by telling me the truth."

He looked at his feet, and Anne could see the colour rising in his face. She waited.

With a quick glance at the door and back to her, he confessed it.

Chapter Twenty-eight

The early spring air was chilly, but beads of sweat dotted Rose's upper lip. No one stirring in the house had the stomach for breakfast. The servants had set the table anyway, and bowls of porridge steamed, their vapors dispersing into the air above them. Rose could not look at them.

No one had slept; this was plain on their pinched, tear-stained faces. But a noise from the back bedroom caught her ear. Dame Alice, back from her travels, was snoring loudly. She must have drunk much wine and exhausted herself from packing. Rose did not expect the woman to be there when she returned today.

Sir Thomas had been held at Lambeth palace. Rose heard much news of him through the messengers that ran con-

tinually up and down the river below the gardens. All of
London was picking and piecing together the story of
their favoured scholar being treated as a criminal. Some
told it differently. The fiend of London, who scourged
the innocent and broke the weak, was at last suffering
too.

Rose closed her mind to their interpretations; what
did they know of him? Indeed, what did she know of
him? His secrets clung too closely about him, and she had
never been able to draw near. But she knew some facts
of these recent weeks: Henry had given him space and
reason to reconsider his rejection of Henry's supremacy
over the church. Sir Thomas did not have to reject the
church or reject Henry as monarch; he could have both,
if only he would admit that Henry had the right to reign
unfettered in the realm. The law of the land would begin
and end in the king, not priests.

Rose could not understand the refusal. Sir Thomas
could still have his church, so why deny the king his
realm? More believed the Scriptures were the only
ultimate law, yet he forbade people to read them. He
believed harmony was the essential element of utopia,
yet he rejected offers to reconcile. He educated his
daughters and showed mercy to the orphan, yet drew his
own blood every night and tortured those who sought
a new world. Rose was sick in her stomach. More had
made everyone, and everything, to conform to his own
image, but he had never seen himself clearly.

She had seen a glimpse of the man and he had
stirred her heart. His passion and appetite was tempered
severely by his mind and will. If only he had allowed
himself to love, Rose thought, a new man would have

emerged. But appetite and passion were lawlessness to him, so he struggled to scourge them from his heart.

He loved law above all else. Henry wanted law and order kept too, and kept under one rule. Why did it matter who administered the Scripture? Would it not be the same? Why did More predict such death if the Book that gives life was given to the people? Rose shook her head to clear herself of the questions without answers. The only answer was that this story of free salvation had condemned More to his imprisonment and death.

Last night a boy had run up the steps from the dock, shouting that he had news of good report. He made sure he was paid before he gave them the news, eyeing the half-angel, glancing back to see if there would be more. Rose still knew how to frighten a greedy urchin, and she drew herself up, pushing her face into his with a glare. He dispensed the news and fled.

"In recognition of his good service, Sir Thomas will be beheaded. What great mercy from the king! He is spared the death of lesser men! It will happen tomorrow; he will be brought to the Tower by barge. His family is not allowed to attend."

And so this morning had come, with the children sitting in the parlour looking like ghosts, and Dame Alice stinking drunk and snoring.

Margaret did not speak to Rose but dressed quietly. When Rose went down the steps to the dock, Margaret was behind her. There was nothing Rose could say. She had learned her letters, and even learned to form words from them, but there were none in her learning that could comfort. What word had she missed? What should she have been taught, or what lesson did she miss? It was wrong to sit in the barge in this freezing silence. There must be words for this. But none came.

It was raining, an annoying drizzle that pelted her cheeks despite the covering over the barge. The drops found their way in, swatted by the winds, landing on her face and hands, soaking through her cloak little by little. She drew her legs in and tucked her hands under her arms. The sky was a brilliant grey that made the winter limbs of the trees, budding in green, glow against its palette. Birds circled over the river, pecking among the floating debris for their breakfast. She tried not to imagine it, but she knew by lunch his blood would be washed away into this same river. Guards would be washing their boots of him, stones would be covered with fresh straw, and Sir Thomas—the man who had lived for a vision of the future—would fade into London's past.

Now the Tower was ahead, its white stones looking like the weathered bones of a giant stacked neatly one upon the other. It looked immense to her as she sat perched in a tiny barge, and her stomach began to flip. She couldn't keep her balance easily as she stepped off onto the slippery dock. The world seemed to be turning too fast under her, her legs unable to hold onto firm ground. Margaret was behind her and accepted Rose's hand with a hard grip as she stepped onto shore.

Rose held it for a moment longer than she needed to. She held onto Margaret's hand, wanting to hold her here, before the day made her coarse. Margaret would not return to these steps as she was. She would return as an orphan, fury being her constant companion. The bile of bitterness would constantly rise in her throat, giving her a frozen, mean look. Rose knew. She had seen these women. She had been one when More found her.

They pushed their way from the Old Swan Stairs to a platform above which they could watch for More to be brought here. A crowd was already gathered, mainly boys who shifted from odd jobs and found themselves with leisure when they cared for it. Today would be too juicy to miss. How many of them had been clapped into irons by More when they stole bread or robbed an old mother? He lectured in the courts about the need for law and justice, and today he would get a good taste of its blade.

More's barge came into view, and the boys went wild, catcalling and hurling insults. Other people came, hearing the noise, waiting for a sign that More had at last come to the Tower. Sir Thomas held his head high, looking them all in the eye, one by one, until his gaze fell onto Margaret and Rose. Rose saw his chin tremble and he looked away.

The constable of the Tower led More off the barge. Rose saw More had not faired well in his captivity. His frame was much thinner, and he walked with great effort. His shift was thin and a cheap-looking wool, not thick enough for the cold nights he had spent sleeping on soiled straw.

The constable led him through Old Swan Lane to Thames Street, the crowd growing with every step. One man brandished an unlit torch, his face contorted in hatred. She drew in a sharp breath. The man's other arm hung limp at his side. He was surely one of the heretics who had walked this path himself, scorned and carrying the torch More threatened to light under his feet someday.

The entrance to the Tower was upon them. Margaret broke through guards and knelt at her father's feet. The crowd was pushing and screaming, and Rose fought to get near to hear his words. He placed his hand on Margaret's head as if to pronounce a blessing over her. She rose and kissed him on the cheek.

"Be off! No family is permitted to watch!" the constable ordered.

"This woman," More said, "this woman is not family. Pray allow her to attend me in my final moments." He was pointing to Rose. The constable looked between More and Rose, chewing his lip. He grunted and nodded an agreement.

More motioned for Rose to draw near. Trembling, she started to kneel before him as well, but he grasped her, hard, and drew her face to his—he stank of rot and sour decay—and put his mouth over her ear.

"My Rose." His voice was breaking.

Rose threw her arms around him, supporting him as he leaned further in, his thin frame rattled by a wet, bubbling cough. There was still something of the old man there, the man always at the edge of revealing himself, the one whose hunger for life was not restrained by order. It was this man she held.

He took another breath and spoke in her ear again. "Hutchins is dead, Rose. You paid for his betrayal and burning. It was my last wish, for I could not leave this world to meet God if this man were still alive. Everyone knows it was you, Rose. You will never be safe among the heretics. I saved you from yourself."

She tried to push him off her, her mouth open for a scream, but his bony hands dug into her skin, forcing her to hear every last word, forcing them to resonate in her ear.

The constable, seeing More falling onto Rose, and Rose unable to bear the weight, pulled More up and off her, and began the final procession to the scaffold.

"Pray for me in this world, good men," More called out, his words taking what life he had left. "I will pray for you in the next. I die the king's good servant, and God's first."

He knelt at the stained block and began murmuring in Latin. If he was repeating Scripture, he alone knew what it meant.

The executioner was receiving final instruction from the constable, and More stood on his feet, rising fast. The crowd screamed, thinking he would run. The constable lurched and grabbed him, but More spoke something that calmed him, and he released More, who kissed the executioner on his cheek.

The executioner was wearing a red robe, spattered and stained. He was a local man, rumoured to be a barber in his other hours, who did not waste his fees on washing. Henry despised More in this, that he would give a common man the task of taking off his head.

"Be not afraid to do thine office," More said to the man.

He knelt again, laying his head on the block, looking at Rose. She froze, her heart stopping its rhythm, everything in her perched to watch the end of his days.

With one swing, More's head was off and in a basket.

A wind swept over the crowd, like the beating of the wings of a great bird, and a wave of peace rippled over them all, who did not know its taste. All were dumb-founded at that moment.

The executioner above them looked confused but grabbed the head to finish his job and get home. "Here be a traitor!" he pronounced.

This shook free the crowd from their pause. Their bloody appetites awakened, they forgot the sudden, fleeting taste of grace.

Chapter Twenty-nine

"I have read it, twice over—the entire book!"

Anne was awed with the secret message, searing in indictments, scandalous in generosity. Why had she waited to read it? If it undid the world, so be it. The book belonged in the hands of the people, no matter what chaos it loosed.

Something did trouble her, deep within. Something lodged in her spirit that she couldn't dismiss. She didn't know what to do with it, this thing that thrilled to hear the secret words, but felt fear when she considered her new happiness. She had it all—the blessing of an heir in her womb, the gift of the crown for her family and name. Why did she not rejoice in these blessings? Why was there no ease?

Henry grunted and sat on the edge of her bed, looking out the window. Hampton Court was so quiet these past few weeks with so many of the women gone and Wolsey dead.

"What is it, Henry?"

"Do you not wonder, Anne?"

"What?"

"Do you not wonder why things happen as they do? If they are not signs from God, indications of His pleasure or fury, what are they? How are we to read our days?"

Anne set the book aside.

"I do not know. But I am learning," she said, taking her time with these next words. "I am learning to think less of my days and trust more in God's purpose."

Leaning over to kiss her belly, he pressed his hands deep into the bed to steady himself.

He recoiled in horror.

Charging from the room, he began shouting. Anne could hear much yelling in the halls. She threw back the coverlet to rise and go after him and saw she had been lying in a pool of blood.

⚜

The cramps were constant. She found it hard to breathe. The pain stabbed and stabbed without stopping. She was panting, writhing to find a position that eased the muscles and kept the baby inside.

Dr. Butts was helpless, standing at the side of the bed with a look that she had seen only once before. It had been in the French Court, when the king had sentenced a thief to hanging. His family had stood motionless and without expression, as he was dragged away. If they ever cried, no one knew.

The pressure came, the force that crushed all reason

and objection. She had to push. She grabbed for Dr. Butts' hand to save her, as her muscles contracted, pushing.

"Dear God, make it stop!" she screamed, pushing again.

"Mercy! Mercy!" she cried out, to anyone who would listen, anyone who might help.

With one more push, he was delivered.

"Oh, God!" Anne cried, reaching for the baby, but Dr. Butts had already snatched him, rubbing him furiously, muttering wild prayers under his breath. Anne couldn't hear the words—was he praying for the child or his own life?

He stopped and his shoulders dropped. "What have you done?" he whispered.

Anne's heart contracted sharply, fear shooting through her body. Dr. Butts turned to her, slowly, holding out the infant, its face shrouded with linen wrappings.

"Catherine died a few hours ago." He said it as an accusation.

Anne held her hands out for the baby. *Its face should not be shrouded,* she thought. *It won't breathe well.*

"Thou art surely a witch!" Dr. Butts said. "I will not die for your sin."

He laid the baby on the bed and ran from the room. Anne thought she was going to faint, but no one was offering her water or wet rags to wipe her face with. Her vision sharpened, and she saw there were servants in the room, pressed against the walls. No one was moving.

She would not faint. She took a deeper breath, dragging the baby closer up the bed. It was not moving.

"No, no," she whispered, peeling back the linen, piece by piece.

It was a boy. But he was not as a child should be; his arms were shriveled and his head was bulging in one area. She could not bear to see him and threw a linen over his still face before she screamed.

The servants moved with a collective will, moving towards the door, keeping themselves as far from her as possible. No one met her eyes. Anne began to sob. She looked with clouded, stinging eyes, and pain was everywhere. Nothing was the same. The turtledoves calling from the courtyard pained her ears; the gold of the room stung her eyes. She was too far from home.

"I want my brother!" she wept.

The last of the servants leaving heard this, his face changing when she said it.

She was taken by barge to the Tower, through the Traitor's Gate. People were running to the water's edge to see her, screaming obscenities ... some in Catherine's name, others in God's.

As she was led along the stone path, she heard unimaginable screams.

The guard smiled. "Seems your brother is already here."

"My brother? Why? What has he done?"

The guard laughed, his grip on her arm bruising her. "They'll work him hard through the night, and take confession tomorrow."

"This is madness!" Anne began struggling, trying to break free and run towards the screams. "George!"

The guard knocked her off her feet and spat on her.

She looked up at the guard's face twisted in hate. Her Yeoman cast a sidelong glance, and Anne saw no one else near them. He elbowed the guard so hard that the man went down on his knees. Turning his back so that Anne could not see his face, he faced the guard and raised his arms.

The guard screamed in terror, scrambling away on all fours. There was no time for Anne to think, for new guards ran from around the corner. They picked her up and continued her descent into hell.

The room was clean enough, and she was given servants, handpicked by Henry, but she was delirious from fear, fear that would not let her sleep or eat. Some moments she was laughing, which made the other women pale and silent. When she wept, only then did they have the nerve to come near and touch her.

"I want to see Elizabeth," she moaned. "Please tell Henry I want to see our daughter."

Elizabeth was brought to her, and Anne beheld her face, so perfect and plump, God's utter grace out of her imperfect union. Anne inhaled deeply as she cradled her, drinking in the fragrance of roses and sunlight. At last the ladies scooped Elizabeth away from her, cradling her gently and promising her many treats.

Anne saw in her mind the men of the court ... how she had stood before them as queen, receiving all honour, and just yesterday, stood before them accused, dripping with shame. Even her uncle, the Duke of Norfolk, who had served her at her wedding feast, betrayed her.

They pronounced Henry's good pleasure that she die by beheading. Henry was not there. Jane's father was, and Anne saw that he wore scarlet now, the colour of nobility. Jane had done well for herself.

She had begun to chuckle quietly, and the men shifted in their seats.

Henry, no doubt, was already commanding her to produce an heir. He needed an heir for more than just the kingdom; he needed an heir to be justified, to silence the blood that began to stain the ground all around him. His train was of blood, his coat of arms was of blood. Jane was in love, no doubt, and could not taste it.

"Have you a defense?"

Anne shook her head. "Henry knows I did not commit this crime. It is not in my heart. Nor is it in my brother's. Henry knows this full well."

She lay awake through the night, her body straining to hear if her brother screamed. He would not confess before death, she knew this. He would not tell them his secret.

But he did.

She rose at 2 a.m. to begin saying her prayers. Every time she drifted to sleep, she was awakened by her own cries. Begging God to speak. Begging for mercy in her hour of need. She checked her clock often, her little Nuremburg Egg that Henry had given her to mark the hours until

they could be together again. It had been a love gift from
long ago.

The night watchmen were agitated, peering in at
her with deep scowls. Her maids said it was because
she was a witch; they were terrified she might escape.
Messages came throughout the night, causing them to
become more animated. The maids heard only pieces of
the conversations.

Signs and wonders were rocking the city. A nobleman of Henry's court had awakened at midnight from
a nightmare, a premonition of Anne's death that caused
him much suffering. The candles all around Catherine's
tomb, tucked quietly away at an abbey, flamed to life
by themselves, and when the priest cried out, they
extinguished. Henry had sent men to the tomb, fear-
ful perhaps that Catherine might rise and decry his
justice. Anne's uncle, the Duke of Norfolk, dreamed
that he would be condemned in the next life, consumed
by flame and sentenced to ride for one thousand years
with four headless horses. He sent word to the Tower
to watch Anne, to prevent her from casting such spells
with the devil.

Anne paid them no mind. What business of this was
hers, how the spirits tormented those who betrayed her?
Their names were safe. It was what they wanted.

The sun had risen about an hour before, when her
cell door opened. Her maids had just finished dressing
her in a black robe, with a white ermine draped across
her shoulders. She stroked the soft fur, a new pelt that
still had the stench of the tannery.

Her Yeoman stood behind the constable of the
Tower. She saw him as if in a dream, a beautiful dream.

She drank in the flecked colour of the stone walls, and the morning air that has just been touched by the sun. It had been a beautiful world. She did not know what the next would be like.

"It is ecstasy," her Yeoman said, his face still straight ahead, holding her arm as she was led down the winding stone steps, the little crooked staircases with steps so narrow that it took great concentration to make her way down. Her billowing skirt meant she couldn't see her feet; she was relying totally on him.

She knew that voice.

She stopped cold on the stairs, and he turned to her. She saw his eyes were enormous gold orbs with pinpoint black irises. He had eyes like the lion she had seen in the royal menagerie. She had stared at the beast when he was brought forth; she had been sad to see such majesty paraded for amusement and doomed to die alone, far from the plains that birthed him.

She realized her Yeoman's steps made no noise, though hers went clack-clack against the stones.

"No one dies alone, Anne," he said. "How I have loved you and walked with you through all your days." His face shimmered, little muscles in his face rippling. She saw tears spilling out of the corners of his eyes. "Do you remember when you were born, and they were rubbing you down with wine, how your eyes met mine for the first time and you grew so still, so serious, that it made me laugh?"

"I am sorry. I do not remember this day."

"These first years, they are God's gift to us. We do not have to shadow ourselves near our children. We take such delight in those days. But you do not remember."

He stopped, his face composing itself into a serene expression, the tears evaporating from his cheeks. She watched him as he turned to shadow at the edges. He leaned down and kissed her on her forehead, inhaling her perfume with a heavy sigh.

"My time of service to you has ended. One greater than I has come to walk with you."

They exited the stairwell into the Tower Green. The block was in sight, a platform raised by only four wide steps. That comforted her somehow; she would not be raised so high as to be an even greater spectacle. Her executioner was there—a thin, stringy man, undeniably French, with a waxen face and obvious impatience to collect his fee. He had been hired, she knew, as a sign of Henry's gracious nature, for his aim was said to be perfect. Few of his victims had needed more than one stroke.

"Why did George confess?" She blurted, afraid her Yeoman would leave, wanting the answer, wanting to keep him here. "I would have protected him to the end."

The Yeoman did not reply, and Anne was terrified of the silence.

"I knew he desired men more than women," she said. "But I kept this shame between us, for the sake of our name. Now we both die in dishonour."

"Shh. He thought it would prove your innocence. He did not see they were infected with the madness of the age. No truth could be spoken to them."

Anne began to cry, and he reached out and caught the tears. "This is the end of sorrow, Anne."

"This is not what I wanted. Known as a whore and

a witch … endless amusement for idle women. I sought to serve God."

"You did. And your name has always been secure in His presence. He has given you a new name, sacred to Him. You are His beloved daughter."

"I am afraid," she whispered.

"When you lay your head on the block, you will feel someone lay across you, His arms over yours, His neck across your own. The blade will pass through Him first, and you will be free. Do you understand?"

"Will I see you again?" she asked.

"I must walk many days upon this earth before we are together again. Elizabeth will be loved. I will never leave her side."

He bowed as the sheriff took hold of her.

Henry betrothed himself to Jane the next day.

The gardens at Hampton Court, indeed, the flowers of all of England, were blooming, new life springing up, the dead blossoms trampled underfoot making the soil rich and fertile. Henry entered into this new union full of hope and eagerness. The people of the realm had no idea that he had unleashed a thousand stinging serpents among them. Suffering was his lasting heir; it claimed his crown and carried his name into all future generations.

Thousands would die under his reign. Jane would die giving him the heir he so longed for. The child, Edward, was not long lived.

Soon England would send her exiles to a new land called America, and King James would authorize a Bible that pleased the crown and could be presented to the people. He would borrow heavily from the Bible first translated by William Hutchins, also known as William Tyndale. It was this book, the infamous Hutchins Bible, which set all of Europe on fire.

Elizabeth would eventually take the throne and become of the most beloved monarchs in the world.

She was never alone.

Chapter Thirty

"But what about Rose?" I asked.

The Scribe ran his hands over the words, each glowing like a red coal upon the paper. "It is too much for you," he replied.

"What? Tell me!"

"And if I do, if it breaks your heart, what will you do? You're going to die in a few minutes."

"Tell me."

He waved his hand over the words, and I saw again, but this time, there was much mist between the vision and my sight.

"Tell me what you see," he said.

"I see an old woman. I think she's blind—her eyes are milky white. She has a book, and it's open in her lap. It's the Hutchins book. Her fingers are running down the page, and her lips are moving, as if she was reading."

"You see her."

"There is someone else there, a younger woman. She is afraid."

"Yes."

"There is water near them—I hear it. And I taste salt … it's the ocean. It's all around them. I think they're on a boat. There's a storm. The younger woman is crying. She is afraid of this journey."

He smiled at me; I could feel it.

"Look closer," he commanded.

I closed my eyes and strained to see. Suddenly I saw the women again, but they were surrounded by lights. My vision carried me above them, above the ship, breaking through the whipping winds and lightning, seeing lights all around it, lights leading in a straight path across the ocean. I saw arms outstretched each to the other, the current turning and obeying their path.

I began to cry, which surprised me.

"They're angels," I whispered. "They're guiding the ship. To America. They want to get the Hutchins book there. It wants to go. It's alive."

I sat back, sensing the book breathing, looking at me.

The vision ended.

I sat, letting the tears cool on my cheek. The only noise in the room was from my breath, but it became small shallow gasps, each breath a jerk in my chest, each breath less than before.

A noise was at the door, like a thousand claws drumming on a table.

He rose and held out his hand for the computer. "It is time. They're waiting."

"Oh, please, God." I fought for a breath and the

words to pray. "I don't want to die! I shouldn't die—I had another chance!"

"But your work is finished. You are not mine," the Scribe answered.

"Rose, she had a daughter, didn't she? And that daughter was in my line—that's why you showed me the vision. That's why you chose me. But I don't know what you wanted from me. There was more than just the story, wasn't there? I sat through all these pages, but there is something more, isn't there?"

I flopped back against the pillow, choking from the exertion, struggling to pull a free breath in.

He said nothing, but his arm moved to take the computer from me.

I shook my head, closing the laptop and hugging it to myself. "Let me at least get this to someone."

He shook his head. "She'll find it."

I knew who he meant: Mariskka.

"This is my story!" I said. "She won't know what to do with it. She doesn't deserve it."

That made him smile. "Oh, but she does. She deserves it more than anyone."

He put his glasses back on and turned to his open book lying on the table next to him. He reached to shut it, and the words grew faint, my life slipping away with them. The words swirled, like a whirlpool, growing dim as they were pulled back into the book. My spirit was leaving with them. The claws grew louder. I could hear wet smacking.

A sword rammed from the air, pinning the pages open. The Scribe jumped back, scowling, as another thing became visible to me. It was unlike anything I had seen, perhaps something I remembered from a childhood tale, when I was not afraid to believe. He was formed in the image of a man, but much larger, with wild yellow hair that parted around the wings of an eagle, muscles pumping and twitching in them, making him shimmer so brightly that I winced. The fluorescent bulbs overhead burst with a pop, flakes of milky glass showering us all as the Scribe and the being stared at each other without blinking.

"You will not shut the book," the gold-haired man said. His had the same gold eyes, with tiny black irises, and when his mouth moved, I could see canine teeth, huge incisors the size of my thumb.

"Aryeh," I whispered.

"It is her time," the Scribe said.

Aryeh held the sword on the book, and the words swarmed all around it like ants. He flexed his arm and drove it in deeper.

"One question and then she dies," Aryeh said.

The Scribe nodded an agreement.

"What is the truth?" Aryeh asked me.

The visions poured out from the book, from all around the sword, the voices and cries and stories. Some were weeping, and some were singing, but all repeated only one Name, as if it was the only language of this next world. My flesh recoiled. I did not want this; I did not want to be one of the voices singing. I had never wanted to be one of them.

I heard the nails again, and something wet dripped on my shoulder. Only these things did not chant the Name.

I drew my last breath, heard it wheezing into my

tattered lungs, and with these last words, my spirit pushing its way out with them. "Those words are the truth. Hutchins was trying to save us all. I have betrayed my mothers. Oh, Jesus, forgive me!"

Aryeh lifted his sword as he swung a hand to me, screaming, "Take my hand!"

It is hard to describe what happened next, as time both stopped forever—and began again for me.

The door burst open, and I heard the nails moving across the floor, devouring whatever was left in my body, screaming in fury that the spirit-marrow was stolen from them. They could still taste it. I pressed my face into Aryeh's chest, breathing in the warm fragrance of peace.

I saw the book close.

My story was ended.

Scion Publishing
New York, New York

"Amazing, really."

He poured a brandy from a crystal decanter. Mariskka loved that; she had only seen it in the movies. He was a classy man, she could tell.

The woman at his right nodded vigorously. She did that a lot.

"My imagination could run away with me on those night shifts." Mariskka giggled.

"We've already had one preempt for the movie rights. This is going to do very well," the woman said.

"Yes, Mariskka," he said, cradling the glass as he walked it to her. He handed it to her and she took a little sip, careful not to breathe in the fumes. She usually drank beer.

"I've never met a first-time novelist who created such a rich, fascinating story. You're going to be very famous, and very rich. How does that feel?"

She smiled and shrugged, remembering how she used to charm her teachers in school, remembering how none of them ever caught on. "I can't take credit for the book. It's a gift from God."

She set the glass down on the table between them, the table littered with papers she had signed. The early reviews of the book had been raving and plentiful. Marisska saw how the Rolex sparkled on her tanned wrist.

When the woman stared at it, Mariskka realized she was lusting for it. She had never caused envy before. It felt wonderful.

"A little something to celebrate your first book?" the woman asked.

"Oh." Mariskka smiled. "Let's just say … I couldn't resist."

Epilogue

William Hutchins was a pseudonym used by William Tyndale, the man who translated the New Testament for the first time into English from the original texts. He used the name William Hutchins to prevent authorities from tracing the book back to him and his printer.

The furor this book caused, the outrage over giving sacred Scriptures to common men and women, launched the Reformation and birthed modern women's literacy. For his work, William Tyndale was strangled and then burned at the stake.

Today the average American family owns four Bibles and has read none of them.

after
words

... a little more ...

When a delightful concert comes to an end,
the orchestra might offer an encore.
When a fine meal comes to an end,
it's always nice to savor a bit of dessert.
When a great story comes to an end,
we think you may want to linger.
And so, we offer ...

AfterWords—just a little something more after you
have finished a David C. Cook novel.
We invite you to stay awhile in the story.
Thanks for reading!

Turn the page for ...

• An excerpt from *In the Arms of Immortals,*
book two in the Chronicles of the Scribe series.

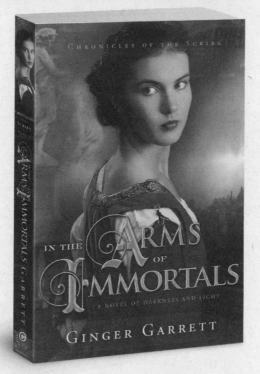

Chapter Two
(text not final)

Mariskka missed a step as she slid down the stairs, feet first. A dry scream lodged in her throat. A man with skin as dark as all-nighter coffee sat at her kitchen table. A book with massive iron hinges lay open in front of him. Words swirled around the page with a hum. Mariskka had the terrible feeling she should know him.

Another man stood by him. His back was turned to her, but she recognized the yellow dreadlocks flowing down his back. He spoke in coarse whispers that sounded like a lion's huff at twilight.

She landed at the bottom of the stairs, her head hitting an iron baluster with a crack, making the men turn.

"Get her up, Mbube," the dark one said. Mariskka noticed his head was clean-shaven, and he wore sunglasses even though the sun was just rising.

The man with the dreadlocks walked toward her. His head cocked to one side to consider her—the look people give animals at the zoo.

She began kicking, scrambling to stand and run back up the stairs. He extended a clawed hand, catching her by the back of the neck. Lifting her gently, he brought her to the kitchen table and deposited her in a chair. The creatures stared at her. If they were going to hurt her, they didn't seem in a hurry.

"Would you like coffee?" the dark one asked.

"I don't drink coffee," she replied.

They looked at each other.

The dark one got up and poured coffee into her favorite mug—the one she stole from the doctor's lounge at the hospice—pressing the button on her Capresso machine for frothed milk. He was making it just the way she liked it. Handing it to her, he turned and opened the pantry, retrieving a vegan protein bar. She had bought it when she first believed money changed people, but it had languished there for months. Money was no match for empty calories.

"Skip the bagels today," he said. "You'll need your energy."

Gulping her coffee, she made it scald her tongue, looking for some way to wake up from this second dream.

"What's going on here?" she asked the clean-shaven one.

"As a woman sows, she reaps," he replied.

"Is this about the furs I bought? Are you guys from PETA?"

Mbube huffed. He sniffed the air and glared at her.

"Get out of my house." Mariskka stood. The clean-shaven one pressed a giant hand on her shoulder, pushing her back into the chair. Both watched her with that intense stare patients gave her when time was getting close to their next dose of morphine.

"You stole my book," the clean-shaven one said.

"Who are you?" Mariskka asked. She had a very bad feeling she already knew.

"I am the Scribe," he replied.

"And him?" Mariskka asked.

"I Mbube," her dread-locked savior said. "I yours."

"You're my what?" she asked. She was flipping through the stolen manuscript in her mind, trying to remember what the whole point of that story had been. If it even had one. She had never really made it past the fourth chapter. She had gotten a headache from all the storylines.

"Wait!" she said. "You're my guardian angel!"

"Your name is not written in the Book of Life. You are under no one's protection," the Scribe replied.

"Everyone has guardian angels," she said.

The Scribe leaned over her, blocking all the light behind him. "Did you read the manuscript you stole?"

"It had a lot of pages."

The Scribe wiped his palm across his forehead and exhaled "And the Bible?" he asked.

"I know what it says," Mariskka replied.

Black words swarmed up from the open pages of the strange book, and he waved them toward her. They flew to her, biting, raising flaming red welts all over her arms. She yelped and swatted at them, but they only bit harder.

He called them back before they reached her mouth. After the words had flowed back into the book, it snapped shut with a grunt.

The Scribe was unmoved by her pain. He had the emotional range of granite.

"Tell me, Mariskka: Do you think that ordinary books, the books you find at yard sales and in dusty bathroom baskets, that these books are just ink and paper? That the tears and passion the author poured into them leaves no lingering emotion behind?"

Mariskka glanced at the book on the table before she answered.

"I guess I never thought about it," she said, tucking her arms in at her sides.

"Yet no book has ever been authored by God, save one. And it lives, breathes, it has even walked among you. He wrote the story. He is the story."

She was sick again, her brain hurting from processing too much, too fast. She held up her hands to stop him. It was like a brain freeze from eating ice cream.

"Believers have angels, Mariskka, children have angels—but you are adrift. A passerby may help you, but no one walks with you."

"Look, don't judge me!" she said, looking between them both. "You've never walked a mile in my shoes!"

"My dear," the Scribe said, his voice turning soft and kind, "we would have carried you if only you believed."

She wanted them gone.

They smelled of her past, of the baking hot cement at Disneyland, the stale hospice gelatin and turpentine odor of capsules and medicine bottles, the damp odor of her childhood bedroom with its enormous fish tank. She had lost so many fish that first year, until she read every book the library had on fish keeping. She had learned how to test the pH, to neutralize ammonia and chloramines, to add bacteria when needed. She had learned how to keep them alive, and they thrived. They nibbled at her fingers when she brushed them along the water at night just before feeding time. They were so glad to see her, so frantic to eat and live.

She ran home from school every day, anxious to

feed her fish, anxious to see them dart between their swaying plants, rushing to the water's surface. One afternoon, after feeding her fish, she watched them gobble the food, spit it out, then go at it again. She giggled when they chased each other for the larger bites. Closing the lid on the food, she walked down the dark hall to her mother's room and heard her snoring. Mariskka understood then. Fish wanted to live. They would fight for it. They had no drugs to mediate between life and death. But her mother didn't fight. It was enough for her that she didn't feel pain.

Mariskka remembered throwing open the bedroom door and shaking her mother by the shoulders, trying to force her to sit up. "Wake up!" Mariskka had screamed. "You don't get to sleep through this!"

Her mother swatted her away, missing Mariskka by a yard. She looked like a windmill, cranking her arms in circles. Mariskka had let her fall back into bed and return to her snoring.

Something had been wooing her mother, and it was too big for Mariskka to fight alone. *Whatever is out there,* Mariskka thought, *whatever you are, I'm no match for you.*

So she had crawled in, under the covers. Wrapping her arms around her mother, she tried not to cry as she fell asleep, too.

That was how she became a nurse.

Now all she wanted was for these creatures in her kitchen to be gone. She was too old to hurt over the past. Even if she had stolen a manuscript and passed it off as her own, so what? A tearful public apology on *Oprah* might even boost her sales.

"Sequels are real killers, aren't they?" The Scribe grinned at her.

Jumping up, she ran to the closet to get her fire safety box, a relic from her mother's estate that didn't lock. *I'm a penthouse packrat,* she thought as she dragged the box out from under coats and scarves and blankets. *That's the curse of stolen money; nothing feels like mine. And I lay awake nights, dreading that I'll lose all this stuff that isn't mine.*

As she heaved the box from the closet, papers spilled across the floor. Some were typed and printed cleanly on white paper; other pages were hand scrawled on pillowcases and sheets. She kept them altogether in a plastic garbage bag, and it was thinned and ripping out, papers peeping and escaping. Dragging the disintegrating bag to the fireplace, she started the gas flames.

Flames were soon eating the plastic garbage bag at the ends first, working their way over the back, the plastic melting in noxious, warping shreds. The paper caught next. The sheets and pillowcases burned steadily, calmly, the words disappearing into black, burning patches that glowed red at the edges.

"It's gone," she said. "Get out."

She didn't know what else to say. *How had she ever survived all those media interviews?* she wondered. Good grief, the media would excuse anything in an author, even illiteracy. Or uneloquence … whatever the word was.

"What is done cannot be undone," the Scribe replied.

"I keep you safe," Mbube said.

"Safe? From what?" Mariskka asked.

"You say yes now. Believe," Mbube said. He moved close, too close. She did not like his breath at all.

"Believe in what?" Mariskka said. "What are you saying?"

"She must learn, Mbube," the Scribe commanded.

Reaching for the book, the Scribe stroked its spine. The book growled, its covers bristling. He whispered something to it, and one iron clasp released. He patted it and the other released, the book opening and the pages turning front to back, back to front, fast and repeating, the sound like cards being shuffled.

"I am the Scribe, the first writer. My books lie open before the throne of God and someday will be the only witness of your people and their time in this world. I will tell you a story of your own," he said.

"I'm going to watch and write it down, right?" Mariskka asked, looking for a pen. If this was how she would get rid of them, she would do it. There wasn't much paper left to write on, though, only a few usable scraps that had blown back into the room from the fireplace.

"You not write this one. You live it," Mbube said.

Sounds began rising from the pages, filling the kitchen, with shadows floating in the air. She heard horses on cobbled streets and women's voices. Men were laughing as if they shared a secret and somewhere, far down another land, a child was calling for its mother.

"No, no," Mariskka yelled. "No, I burned the book! You can't do this!"

The Scribe spoke the words that formed in the air around her face, spinning, forcing her down a dark well. "You now enter our story as a wandering, lost woman, dirty and unpleasant to be near. If you try to speak, they will not comprehend you. They will think you mad. The kindest among them will pity you. The rest of them, well, how little work there is for the devil when men walk the earth!"

Chapter Three

Blood Month had begun. Panthea Campaigna watched the sunburned peasants driving the lean cattle up the cobbled streets, as horses with braided manes and genteel riders picked their way through the hungry, tired masses. Roasted chestnuts were for sale on every corner of the piazza, the carts surrounded by begging children and lazy old men who eyed her boldly and gave her harmless, toothless grins.

The shops surrounding the piazza, with its church tucked neatly in the center, were swarming with nobles and commoners alike, though the peasants knew better than to look upon what their labor had bought the ruling classes. She would have to shop later, much later perhaps. She had to reach the church and return home before it was too late. She would not spend her lifetime regretting how a wasted moment at market had cost her everything. Not that she wholly believed it would work, although she had brought plenty of money. She had generally avoided God when she could. Kneeling in church ruined her fine skirts and humiliated her. The common people looked at her, which she hated.

Lazarro, the village priest, had once said churches were quiet because God was always listening. Everything depended on it now. The negotiation would be straightforward.

Winter was not yet in the air; it was still perfumed by roasting meats, drying herbs, and stalks of dried flax bundled and laid in carts. A few ambitious boys ran from cart to cart, asking for a bronze token to separate the pith from the fiber. The sun was the only true monarch here in Sicily, and even in October it reigned in splendor, sending warmth to the stones and cheer for the final harvest festival. Free wine would be flowing tonight, the vineyards celebrating the last grape harvest of the year. She wanted so badly to stop; this was the last of the good milk, too, before cows were fed fermented grain, not fresh, and threw off tainted-tasting milk. October was the end of every good thing, she groaned to herself.

This was her city: the sound of carts meant she would have bread for the winter, the scent of herbs meant her foods would be seasoned. Everything seemed well enough, she thought. It was a good omen of God's mood.

The number of cows in the square surprised her, though. The peasants only brought the cattle to slaughter that they had not the grain to feed over the winter. This year, there were more cattle than she had seen in previous times, the caked mud around their hooves telling of their long journey. Sicily had colors of soil that surprised the traders from Europe: yellows, greens, reds. The cows, each hoof banded in mud, like the rings of a magical colored tree, lumbered on. The mud fell as they walked, ruining the stone streets swept clean for tonight, distressing the shopkeepers. Mud would be tracked in everywhere. But all the merchants held their tongues. Cows for slaughter meant peasants who would soon be the best kind of customers: drunk and unaccustomed to heavy pockets. They would spend wildly, buying in a frenzy, shoveling the money at the shopkeepers for a taste of another life.

This would be a good week for the shopkeepers, Panthea saw. There would be much blood running from the butcher's shop by morning.

She would not think of another's misfortunes. She would think of the vegetables and fruits that would store well for the cold, calm months ahead, when no man would break ground and four hours of Sicilian sun would not grow gardens. Blood Month was the final month of the harvest year, when workers assessed their state and claimed their wages, when all reaped what they had sown, and the butcher Del Grasso worked late into the night at his killing.

It was a bittersweet time, for she loved the festivals, the bargains, the stories spilled over ale in her father's manor, the commotion that kept her mind from feeling the emptiness at her hearth. Her mother had loved these festivals, too. They would have shared a pie and paid a minstrel for a song. Her mother had always demanded the fee back at the end of the song, claiming the minstrel had no right to charge for such a poor voice. The minstrels would laugh and play her a new song, one the others would not think to ask for. These second songs were always best. It had given Panthea a taste for secrets.

A pregnant dog darted in between the cattle moving up the main path. She could see its ribs, every one of them, though its belly was full almost to the ground. The cattle stopped moving, their heads pulling back when they felt something at their feet. They blocked her entrance to the church, unsure what was underfoot.

Panthea called to the peasant to move his animals. He faced her with a sneer, then, seeing her finery with the blue crest, pasted a smile on his face and bowed his head. She made a clucking sound, and the dog worked its way back to her hand.

"Come on, girl," she crooned. The brown fur across the dog's head was so soft, sweeter than any of her own furs. It was a shame such an animal had no home, no one to stroke this sweet fur and feed it.

She would have saved them all if her father had allowed her. "If I allowed you one," he had said, "I'd have to allow them all, wouldn't I? Yes! Well, no, I can't, even if you have your mother's charms."

Pulling a bronze token from her skirt, she bought a cold meat pie. Rosetta, the baker's wife, was pushing a heavy rolling stand of pies through the crowds, though Rosetta was great with child too, Panthea realized. Rosetta had a strained bodice and a jealous eye as the street dog was given a rich pie. The dog ate with wolfish big bites, then licked the ground and sniffed round for more.

Panthea was about to buy another pie for it when a procession pressed through the crowd, peasants and cattle pushing to either side. Women sang and played tambourine, dancing in slow circles underneath flowing black veils. They looked like the whirlpools Panthea sometimes saw in the inky blue sea that was only a moment's walk from here. Men carrying a wooden pallet came next; a body was shrouded with linen, overlaid with flowers, and bundled with herbs.

The children in the piazza ran to the men, calling down blessings on the fallen soul, and offering prayers for which they were paid by coins tossed in the air. The family of the dead one came last, a woman with tears in her eyes, surrounded by many friends and family who bore her gently behind the procession. Sicilians believed in God and honor, and believed no man could die well without both. This coffin was exquisite; Marzcana had spent many hours in the carvings. It was an honor for the dead man to rest in this piece; the family had done well by him. God and memories were honored.

To Sicilians, the manner of burial was as important as first baptism; indeed, Lazarro taught, was not a body welcomed to earth with cleansing waters and prayers, in the best fashion a family could afford? In the same way, each must be offered back to God, washed by women's hands, blessed by a priest.

The volcano above them rumbled, lightning striking down from a cloud to its steaming core. Peasants crossed themselves and struck the cows, driving them faster. Panthea pushed a token to the pie maker Rosetta, asking her to feed the dog another cold pie. Rosetta's fingers grabbed it too quickly.

"Take care of this dog," Panthea said. "If you need more money, I will be in the church."

Panthea ran for the church, pushing with both hands against the heavy doors weighted with iron handles.

Inside, candles flickered at the altar, reflecting off the gold painted on the columns and the stained glass images surrounding her. She was alone in this swirling sea of illumined faces and fiery streaks of color. The Virgin sat enthroned above her, cradling the infant Jesus on her lap. The archangels Gabriel and Michael flanked her, their stone eyes moving in the shifting light.

She worshipped here, of course, part of the daily

crowd that attended and understood nothing of the Latin service (it was enough that God understood, Lazarro promised), but she had never been alone before God. She did not know what to say to Him. She felt she was a child again, meeting knights of great legend returning from Jerusalem. They had all towered above her, with stories of marvels seen in distant lands, and red valleys of scars that fascinated her. She longed to push her fingers in to discover their depth and ask their meaning. They had praised her for her beauty and sent her away. She was only a girl.

Kneeling, her eyes darting to either side, Panthea wondered how this was all done. With a deep breath to shake off the embarrassment, she stretched out her arms above her. She had seen a saint doing that in a painting.

"I am afraid!" she called. "Will you delay it?"

She peeked up.

No one answered.

Panthea emptied her pockets into the collection box, pausing between each coin to let the sound fully carry.

Michael and Gabriel stared from the cold stone, unmoved.

She dropped her face in her hands. "I am not what this man thinks," she whispered, surprised to feel her palms wet from tears.

Something rustled in the shadows beyond the altar. She wiped her face, holding her breath. It was wrong of her to be here without Lazarro to speak on her behalf. God might get angry at her impropriety. She remembered what Lazarro had said about the prideful.

God brought disaster on them.

Slipping from between the thick doors, Panthea ran down the lane towards the sea. A fog was coming in as the sun was setting.

It would be a dark night, without stars.

Turning the corner to fetch her waiting horse, Fidato, she was run over by a pile of children, pulling a stick behind them, the end of which was being clung to tightly by a woman. The woman looked delirious with fear, and when she tried to speak, such horrible sounds came out that the children scolded her to be silent. It didn't appear she understood them, which only made them shout louder. Panthea hoped they were leading her to Lazarro. Only a priest would touch this wretch. If she was still on the streets by nightfall, she would be sore abused. She wore such odd clothes, and her hair was curled in fat waves. She could not have been a woman from this city.

The outcast stopped in front of a shop that sold paper goods from the city of Almafi. Tears streamed down her face and grated sobs shook her shoulders, making strangers stop and point. The children shouted at her to keep moving, that Romano the shopkeeper would beat any beggar standing too long in the doorway, but the woman could not be moved. Like the others around her, Panthea craned her neck to see what was causing such a reaction from the strange woman.

Seeing no one was observing her, Panthea reached for something set too close to the crowd, unattended among the bottles and jars.

When she saw what the woman looked upon,

Panthea grinned with the others and made her way to her horse. The woman had only been staring at a calendar, which proclaimed it to be the year 1347 Anno Domini.

The woman was surely mad.